Excerpt from WE ... 2021
Excerpt from DA ... 2019
Excerpt from THE ... ight ©

All rights re
associated l...   f

Lone Ghost Publishing

The moral right of the author has been asserted (vigorously).

No part or parts of this publication may be reproduced in whole or in part, stored in a retrieval systems, or transmitted in any form or by means, electronic, mechanical, photocopying, recording, or otherwise (including via carrier pigeon), without written permission of the author and publisher.

Author: **Boulder**, M.M.
Title: MY BETTER HALF.
ISBN: 9798650060758
Target Audience: Adult

Subjects:
Psychological Thriller/Domestic Thriller/ Serial Killer Thriller/ Axe Murderer

This is a work of fiction, which means it's made up. Names, characters, peoples, locales, and incidents (stuff that happens in the story) are either gifts of the ether, products of the author's resplendent imagination or are used fictitiously, and any resemblance to actual persons, living or dead or dying, businesses or companies in operation or defunct, events, or locales is entirely coincidental.

LONE GHOST
Publishing
Never Give Up The Ghost

Also by **M.M. Boulder**
Psychological Thrillers

THE LAST DOOR
MY BETTER HALF
THE HOUSE THAT JACK BUILT
MY ONE AND ONLY
WE ALL FALL DOWN

Writing as **M.M. Crumley**
Urban Fantasy

THE IMMORTAL DOC HOLLIDAY SERIES
BOOK 1: HIDDEN
BOOK 2: COUP D'ÉTAT
BOOK 3: RUTHLESS
BOOK 4: INSTINCT

THE LEGEND OF ANDREW RUFUS SERIES
BOOK 1: DARK AWAKENING
BOOK 2: BONE DEEP
BOOK 3: BLOOD STAINED
BOOK 4: BURIAL GROUND
BOOK 5: DEATH SONG
BOOK 6: FUNERAL MARCH
BOOK 7: WARPATH

www.mmboulder.com

M.M. Boulder

MY BETTER HALF

This one's for my mom...
Lucille knows just how you felt.
It's probably best you never killed anyone...
(That I know of...)

And I'd like to thank Fiona for being all-around amazing!

LONE GHOST
Publishing

Never Give Up The Ghost

1

It was so satisfying. Wrapping the hose around his neck, squeezing, pulling it tight, watching his face turn white, purple, red, blue, whatever color faces turned when they couldn't breathe.

She yanked him towards the ground, ignoring his grasping hands, and shoved his cheek against the wet dirt. "My tulips don't like so much water!" she snarled.

He bubbled something, but she couldn't hear; she was so mad, so mad her tulips were drowning, and she wanted him to drown too.

"Damn it, Mom!"

Nate's voice broke Lucille Stevenson's terrible daydream. She hadn't meant to kill her neighbor in her mind, but how dare he leave his sprinklers running all night. How dare he drown her tulip bed!

"You know I hate plain cream," Nate grumbled. "I told you to get the caramel macchiato kind."

She focused on his words, resisting the uncommonly strong urge to smash the coffee pot she was holding over his head. He was full grown. He had his own home, his own wife. Why was he still coming here for breakfast?

"Mom!"

"Sorry, Nate; the store was out."

"Did you try Safeway?"

Her grip tightened on the plastic handle. If she just... No! What was she thinking? She couldn't hurt her little boy. She couldn't hurt anyone. That wasn't her. She didn't know why she'd even thought it.

"I didn't have time," she mumbled, hating the feeling that she'd done something wrong, even though she knew she hadn't. He didn't actually NEED creamer. Why couldn't he just drink his coffee black?

"You'll go today, won't you, Lucille?" Her husband Richard didn't even look at her when he said it. He just kept drinking his coffee and tucking away at the pancakes Lucille had gotten up at five AM to make.

Glass suddenly shattered, sprinkling the pancakes with deadly shards. Hot coffee spewed over Richard's head, burning him, and he dropped screaming into his plate of pancakes.

"Did you hear me?" Richard demanded, breaking her imagining.

"Yes dear," Lucy agreed. "I'll go today." Never mind she had a million other things to do. She had to clean every inch of their gigantic two-story house, she had to get their taxes ready to take to the accountant, she had to work an eight hour shift, ignoring any sideways comments her boss made, and then she had to make supper, pay the bills, and order the household supplies. But never mind all that. She'd make time to drive to the store she'd just been to so she could pick up creamer for her adult son. Sure. No problem.

She poured her own cup of coffee. Plain. No creamer. She hated creamer. It was disgusting. She'd never understood how Nate could drink it. But it wasn't her job to understand. It was her job to make breakfast.

She ate in silence, listening to Nate gripe about work.

"He's a total ass!" Nate said vehemently.

Lucille flinched. They'd never allowed cussing when their kids were home. But now that the boys were grown, it seemed they could do whatever they wanted. Years ago Lucille had asked Nate to watch his mouth, and Richard had yelled at her for over an hour. He'd said it was his house, his rules. It had always been that way. Always.

Nate finally left, without so much as a thank you or goodbye, and Lucille started cleaning. She had an hour and a half to clean up breakfast and as much of the house as she could before she went to work. She'd take the taxes with her and work on them during her lunch break.

She wasn't sure how she'd ended up here, in this endless loop of chores and servitude. But that really wasn't the worst of it. The worst was how old she felt doing it all. She was only fifty-one. She was still on this side of young, wasn't she? So why did she feel so tired and old?

"I'll be late tonight," Richard said as he left. "Don't wait up."

She watched him leave, wondering what would happen if she cut his brake lines. She thought that was a thing, but she'd have to look it up first to see what a brake line was.

She shook her head, trying to clear it. She didn't know what was wrong with her. Smashing the coffee pot over Richard's head, cutting his brake lines, murdering the neighbor with his own hose. That kind of thinking was insane.

She ran a trembling hand through her hair. She didn't want to kill anyone. She couldn't begin to understand why she was even thinking about it.

She just felt... hot. Hot and angry. Filled to the brim with hot anger. And she didn't know what to do with it. She'd never been angry before. She didn't yell. She didn't argue. She just nodded and did what she was told. Always had. Her father wouldn't have had it any other way.

She put away Richard's robe and slippers, she wiped his whiskers out of the sink, and she dropped his discarded shirt into the laundry basket. She wanted to throw his shirt in the trash, but she didn't.

It annoyed her that Richard thought she was stupid. Like she didn't have any brain. But she wasn't stupid. She knew he didn't have to work late. He worked in an office that closed at five for crying out loud. And she washed his laundry!

Richard was having an affair. He had been, for months, years actually. She'd never cared. In fact, she preferred it.

He and she hadn't had relations in over a year now. He used to call her cold. But he didn't bother anymore. He still called her boring and uptight. But not cold. And if only he knew. She wasn't cold now. She was furious. She wanted to wrap her hands around his fat neck and squeeze and squeeze and squeeze.

But why? Why did she care now? Why was she angry now? It's not like she actually wanted to have sex with him. She hated having sex. It was painful.

The last time they'd done it she'd even bled. In fact, if she had a choice, she'd rather get a tooth pulled than have sex. She'd rather ride a horse naked. Or skinny dip with piranhas. She really didn't like sex, but it wasn't her job to like sex. It was her job to have sex with Richard when he wanted it.

She cringed, imagining his greasy hands on her naked skin. A vase suddenly appeared in her hands, and she broke it over his head.

She flinched, breaking her imagining, and raised a shaking hand to her face. She had to get it under control. Anger was an emotion, and emotions were a sign of weakness. Weren't they?

She finished her cleaning, grabbed the taxes, and headed to work. She parked and walked into the office.

Dr. Banks was waiting for her. She wished he would trip and fall down the stairs. If he didn't die on impact, she could pick up his head and bang it into the floor a few more times. Just until she heard a satisfying crack.

Too messy, she thought, feeling the imaginary blood splatter hotly across her face. She would hold her hand over his mouth instead. He'd struggle, but it would only take a minute.

"You're late," he snapped.

"I'm not," she replied softly, checking her watch just in case she was.

"We've got a full load today."

"We always do," she muttered.

"Try not to screw anything up."

She blushed, grabbing a folder and opening the waiting room door. She'd been a nurse for almost thirty years, and she had never screwed anything up. But she couldn't tell him that. He was her boss.

"Mrs. Feldman," she said with a genuine smile. "Come on back." Mrs. Feldman tottered slowly to her feet and followed Lucille down the hallway.

"How are you today, Mrs. Feldman?" Lucille asked cheerfully, just a tad louder than she normally would.

"Oh doing fine, dear. Just a checkup."

"How's that new medication working for you?"

"I haven't noticed any side effects, so I guess it's okay."

Lucille smiled and carefully fit the blood pressure cuff on Mrs. Feldman's arm. She counted, then took off the cuff, making a note on her chart.

"How are the grandkids?" Lucille asked while she wrote down Mrs. Feldman's weight.

"Wonderful. Jennie's pregnant again. Her third."

"That's great. How many will that be now?"

"Six grandkids and fifteen greats."

Mrs. Feldman grinned happily as she talked about each of them, and Lucille felt an odd pang of jealousy. She wasn't sure she'd ever be a grandma.

Nate and his wife didn't seem overly interested in children. Which was probably good since they were so self-involved. Her other son Teddy was too busy creating video games to date or marry or be a dad. And her daughter Addie traveled all the time for the magazine she worked for. Anytime Lucille brought up marriage Addie just laughed and said, "Not yet, Mom."

Lucy tried not to be disappointed. But there was a part of her that worried. Someday she would retire, and what would she have if she didn't have grandkids? She was a wife, a mom, and a nurse. That was it. She honestly didn't have a single other thing.

"If only these old people would just stop hanging on," Dr. Banks remarked between patients. "I mean, quality of life goes down enough, at some point, you just gotta let go."

Lucille took a deep breath and tried counting to ten. She'd read about counting to ten once in a magazine; at the time she'd thought it was stupid. She'd never been so angry that she needed to worry about saying or doing something she shouldn't. Usually when Dr. Banks went off on his rants she always nodded meekly and walked away.

But the truth was Dr. Banks was a jerk, and Lucille wanted to tell him so. Mrs. Feldman had quality of life. She may toddle when she walked and take six different prescription drugs to keep herself upright, but she was living and laughing and watching her grandbabies.

"It's like putting new parts in an old jalopy," Dr. Banks huffed.

Lucille jumped forward, grabbing the ends of his stethoscope and tightening it around his neck. His eyes bulged, and he ripped at the tube, but it was sunk deep into the flesh of his neck. She squeezed tighter, wondering how long it would take for him to die.

"Lucille? Pay attention!" Dr. Banks snapped. "You're on the clock you know. Drift off on your own time!"

"What?"

He was staring at her with an annoyed look. So she hadn't strangled him. Even though it had felt very much like she had. She could still feel the anger boiling inside her, like lava, searching for a vent hole.

"Sorry."

"Are you sick or something?"

"No; I'm fine." She wasn't fine. Not really. She was hot and irritated and angry. But she wouldn't be asking him for advice. No, no, no. Not when she so very much wanted to stab him in the eye with a hemostat.

2

Lucille managed to get through all eight hours without killing Dr. Banks or anyone else. Then she dropped off her taxes, ran by Safeway to get Nate's special creamer, and drove home.

She ate a cold bowl of soggy soup and stared at the house finches on her feeder. She wished she had a friend to talk to. Just one. Someone she could call and tell everything. They would laugh, and her friend would say everything was all right. It would be a lie, but Lucille would feel better.

If only she knew what was wrong with her. If only she knew why she was so angry. It had started small. She'd been annoyed by Richards's shoes in the hallway and Nate tracking mud onto her clean floors. She'd started grinding her teeth when patients repeated themselves incessantly.

She'd stuffed it all down and ignored it, but it had continued to grow. Today she'd actually considered running over a pedestrian who had flipped her off on her way home. She felt like she was losing her mind. She needed to get rid of the anger before she accidentally did something she couldn't undo.

She thought about calling her daughter to see what she thought, but Addie would probably have some issues with the fact that her mom imagined killing her dad. Five times. Just today.

Richard was glad tonight was the night. The weekends always felt so endless, but then Monday would finally come. He whistled cheerfully as he drove across town to Emily's house.

Sometimes he regretted marrying Lucille, but he hadn't had a choice. His father had insisted Richard marry if he wanted to take control of the inheritance his grandfather had left him.

Richard had never understood exactly what his father expected from him, but he hadn't bothered to try to find out. He'd married the most biddable girl he could find, knocked her up, and played whatever games he wanted with his cash.

He'd been a big disappointment to his father. Fortunately he'd never given a rat's ass what the old man thought.

He shrugged, forgetting about his father and Lucille, and fantasized about Emily. He wondered what game she had devised for tonight. His palms started to sweat in anticipation. He could hardly wait, but he'd have to. She would punish him if he started without her.

Lucille shook her head with irritation as she cleaned up her dirty supper dishes. She didn't have time to deal with emotions and anger right now. She needed to balance the check book and pay the bills. Or pay the bills and balance the check book. She rolled her eyes and sat down at her desk, opening her laptop and pulling out all her statements.

It took her an hour to pay all the bills. Then she started balancing the checkbook. She'd always felt like balancing the checkbook was a waste of time. It's not like the bank was going to get it wrong. But she did it because her mom had taught her to.

She scanned up and down the register, looking for a withdraw posted on the statement. "Wait," she muttered. "That can't be right." She looked at the statement again. "Ten thousand dollars?"

Maybe the bank had made a mistake. She couldn't think of any reason why Richard would withdraw ten thousand dollars. She'd have to ask him in the morning. She circled the amount and finished the rest of the statement. By the time she was done her head was throbbing.

A hot bath and a glass of wine. That would be just the thing. Lucille started the bath, undressed, put on her robe, and went to the kitchen for some wine.

Just as she was opening the cabinet someone grabbed her roughly from behind.

"Where's your cash, lady?"

Lucille froze, and her mind blanked. The man's voice was gravely in her ear, and she could feel his breath on her neck. How? How had he gotten in? Oh god! She was going to die!

"Come on!" he growled. "Where is it?"

She wanted to tell him, she wanted to tell him everything, but she couldn't. She was too scared, too frightened. The fear was too thick in her throat.

"Don't make this difficult," he said, tightening his arm around her throat and ignoring her frantic gasp for air. "Just tell me where it is. I want your jewelry, your silver, anything valuable."

He paused and used his free hand to pull open her robe. Cold air rushed across her breasts, and fear coiled in her stomach. "A quick shag," he whispered, running his tongue along her ear. "And then I'll be on my way."

His hot breath brushed across her cheek, smelling like mushrooms and making her want to vomit. He was going to rape her. She wanted to scream; she wanted to claw at his arm around her throat. She wanted to push his other hand away. The one grasping her naked breast. But she couldn't. She didn't know how.

"Answer me, bitch! You dumb or something?"

A wave of heat rushed through her, melting her fear. How dare he come into her house, grab her boob, and call her a bitch! No one called her bitch! Especially not in her own damn house. Suddenly she wasn't scared anymore. She was angry, furious, enraged; and the anger wanted out.

She was going to kill him. She didn't know how, but she was. He'd pay for touching her. He'd pay for everything.

"Come on, bitch," he snarled, jerking her backwards. "Let's get this over with."

Yes, let's, Lucille thought as the anger suddenly spilled over the top, like a volcano erupting, filling her with righteous fury. She jumped forward, grabbed the wine bottle from the cabinet, spun, breaking his hold, and slammed the bottle into his head.

The bottle hit with a clunk, jarring it out of Lucille's hand, and knocking the robber backwards.

"What the hell?" he snapped, stumbling slightly, but stepping towards her.

Lucille grabbed her wine glass and threw it at his face. The glass broke on contact, cutting his face and tinkling to the floor.

His face turned red with rage, and he roared, "You'll pay for that bitch!!"

Lucille felt a hint of fear. She didn't know how to stop him. He was so much bigger than her, so much stronger. She glanced at the counter and grabbed the only thing there, a fork. She rushed forward, dodging his arms, and stabbed him in his eye before he could stop her.

He screamed in pain, grabbing at her wrist, but she was too enraged to notice.

"Nobody calls me BITCH!" she yelled, fury pouring off her in waves. "Nobody!"

She yanked the fork out and stabbed his other eye, pushing the fork as deep as she could. He shoved at her with one hand and clawed at the fork with the other, screaming like a wounded dog on the highway.

"Shut up, you whiny cretin!" she growled.

Her whole body was on fire. Her skin was so hot it felt like she was standing in a furnace. Her brain was seething. All she could think was she had to hurt him, had to punish him, had to make him pay.

He stumbled into the stove, smearing blood all over the shiny steel. She watched him for a moment, growing angrier with every second. He wouldn't stop screaming, and he was making a complete mess of her kitchen.

She ripped a filet knife from the knife block and sliced it across his grasping hands. "I SAID SHUT UP!!" she yelled.

But he didn't. He kept shrieking and calling her terrible names. If he called her bitch one more time... He did.

Overcome with fury, Lucille jumped on him, stabbing him in the throat. He gurgled frantically but the words become lost in the blood gushing out the hole. His fist struck her wildly in the head, but she didn't even feel it.

She stabbed him again and again and again, dropping to the floor with him, stabbing him until his mouth stopped moving and his throat stopped bubbling pale, red bubbles.

She stabbed him once more, then sat on top of him, panting in exhaustion, trying to understand what had just happened. Her body slowly cooled, and with it came the cold, hard reality of what she'd done.

She scrambled off his body, gasping as pain shot up her feet. She glanced at the floor and realized it was covered in broken glass. Now that she wasn't angry, she could feel the cuts on her feet, and they hurt. A lot.

She limped a few steps away and stopped to stare at him. He was dead, whoever he was. He was lying on her kitchen floor in a puddle of blood, totally and completely dead, and she had killed him.

"Oh my god," she whispered. "What have I done?"

She needed to call the police. She started to go for her phone but froze, staring in wide-eyed horror at his disfigured face.

She couldn't call the police. It would have been one thing to just kill him. He'd called her a bitch. No, that wasn't the reason. He'd broken into her house and threatened to rape her. She was justified in defending herself. She was sure that she was.

But this... This wasn't defending. This was slaughter. The fork was still hanging from his mangled eye, and his neck was just a mass of bloody flesh. His palms were flayed open, and his entire body was covered in blood. He had bled so much. How could he have bled so much?

She would definitely end up in prison if she called the police. They would lock her away for such a long time she would never see her grandbabies.

My Better Half

"What am I going to do?" she whispered, rocking back and forth on her injured feet.

Her hands were coated in blood just like Lady Macbeth. Her white robe was ruined, stained with his blood. Her kitchen floor was a bloody, glassy mess. What had she done? What was she going to do?

"The bath!" she suddenly yelped, running awkwardly towards the bathroom. Water was running over the top of the tub onto the tile and out into the hallway. She slid across the floor and slapped the faucet lever down. She reached her arm into the tub and pulled the drain, then sat on the rim of the tub and stared at her soaking floor.

Just another mess she'd have to clean up. Surely this was a dream. Surely she'd fallen asleep and just had another imagining. She couldn't possibly have killed him. She couldn't have. Not like that. She was too... too unimaginative, boring, scared.

She stared at the blood on her hands. It was tacky and smelled like metal. She had killed a man. She had brutally and definitely killed a man. She stood shakily and washed the blood from her hands, half expecting it to have stained them permanently, but it hadn't.

She mopped the wet floor with towels, washed and bandaged her feet, put on some old work clothes, and walked slowly back into the kitchen.

He was still there, sprawled across the creamy brown floor, face a mask of blood and terror. The blood splattered around him was bright, standing out starkly, almost cheerfully, against the earth tones of her kitchen. There was no doubt about it. He was dead. Totally and completely dead.

Lucille swallowed a sob. "What have I done?" she whispered. "What have I done?"

Her heart pounded fiercely. Richard was going to be home sooner or later. She had no idea when, and there was such a mess. She couldn't even begin to fathom how to clean it all up before he returned.

She thought again of calling the police, but she knew she couldn't. The rage she'd been in when she'd killed him had left a mark. It may have started out as self-defense, but it hadn't stayed that way. She'd been enraged, and she had slaughtered him.

She tiptoed carefully around the blood and retrieved her dust pan. Glass first. She stepped into her Crocs and started sweeping. Glass tinkled, and blood and wine smeared across the floor. After she dropped the glass in the trash, she stared at the bloody tile. Now what?

Realistically she had to move the body, had to get it out of here before Richard came home. She pulled on her rubber cleaning gloves, then plucked the fork from his eye, grabbed the knife from the floor, dropped them both into the dishwasher, and turned the dishwasher on.

She filled a glass with wine and downed it. Her heart hadn't slowed down, and she felt sick. She just wanted to crawl into her bed and hide.

She glanced at the clock, wishing she knew when Richard would be home. She dropped her robe and the soaked towels into the washer and filled it with cold water to soak.

Then she grabbed the dead man's arms and tried to pull him to the door. He didn't budge. She pulled again. He slid an inch, then stopped. "Damn it!" she hissed, panic making her want to vomit.

She stared at him for a moment. He was a human being. Or had been twenty minutes ago. She wondered if he had a wife waiting for him. If he did, Lucille had done her a favor.

Who wanted to be married to man who robbed and raped women? Lucille shuddered. At least all Richard did was cheat on her.

A car drove up, and she froze, listening intently. The garage door didn't open, so she ran to the window and peaked outside, heaving a sigh of relief when she saw it was the neighbor and not Richard.

She had to get the dead body out of here. She opened the dishwasher, jumping as steam poured out into her face. She waved it away and pulled the filet knife back out. Since she couldn't move him like he was, she'd have to make it so she could.

He wasn't a person anymore. He was a lifeless hunk of meat, just like a roast or a chicken, and she needed to cut him up so he'd fit in the pan. Or the trunk.

She laid the knife on his shoulder and sliced. It tore through his shirt and into his flesh. Blood seeped out rather slowly, but she tried to ignore it and kept cutting. Roast for dinner, she thought. That's all.

She gasped when the knife stopped suddenly. His flesh was hanging open like a fileted steak, but she had hit his bone. She sawed at it for several minutes, but with all the gore oozing around the blade she couldn't tell if she was getting anywhere.

She glanced at the clock. It was almost ten. She was running out of time. Richard never stayed out all night. What would he do if he came home and found her with a body? She couldn't even begin to guess, but she knew he certainly wouldn't help her bury it.

There had to be a way to get it into manageable pieces. There just had to be. She tried all the knives in the knife block, but none of them could saw through the bone. She finally ran into the garage, searching desperately for a tool that might work. Richard had gone through a brief home improvement stage, and she was certain he had a saw or something somewhere.

She opened box after box. Her stomach rolled, and her heart hammered wildly. She had to hurry. Finally, she found a red box that said "Sawzall" on it. It looked like a shotgun with a saw blade attached to the front. She lugged it into the kitchen and plugged it in. It didn't quite reach.

"For crying out loud!" Lucille screamed. "What else can go wrong?!"

She ran back into the garage, looking for an extension cord. She grabbed one off the wall and sprinted back to the kitchen, breathing heavily. Any minute. Any minute Richard could pull in.

She plugged the saw in and pulled the trigger. It jerked angrily, and the blade lurched back and forth. When she touched it to the shoulder the blade caught a chunk of flesh and tore it off, spurting blood in her face. She dropped the saw with a gag and rubbed at her face with the back of her glove.

"Keep it together, Lucille," she whispered. "You can do this." She almost laughed. There was absolutely no reason to believe she could do this. She had never done this. She couldn't possibly do this.

She blinked back tears, trying to think, but she couldn't. All she could think was her life was over. She'd killed a man; she was going to be arrested; she was going to prison. Forever.

She looked at the clock again. Richard was going to come home soon, and he was going to be greeted by an absolute mess. She frowned. Lucille Stevenson had never met a mess she couldn't clean up. Never. She could do this.

She picked up the saw with trembling hands and pulled the trigger again. She touched it to the shoulder, and it tore through the already mangled flesh and jerked slowly through the bone.

Finally, after pushing for what seemed like hours, his arm popped off and landed on the floor with a plop. She lifted it, trying to remind herself it was just a piece of meat, and stuffed it into a heavy-duty, black trash bag.

She started the saw again, arms shaking with effort, and went to work on the other arm. When both arms were bagged, she started on the first leg. Sweat poured down her forehead as she held the saw in place, pushing on it with all her might.

Damn, I'm out of shape, she thought, wishing she could take a break. Not that I've ever cut up a dead body before, but really. The saw finally snapped through the bone, and she fell forward. She dropped the saw and caught herself, but her chest landed on the squishy, bloody stub of his leg.

She swallowed a gag, pushed herself up, and shoved the loose leg into a bag. Then she started sawing again. After she finished with the other leg, she stared at his torso. His chest was long, and she wasn't sure it would fit in a bag if his head was still attached. It would certainly make sense to saw his head off. She'd come this far.

She set the saw at the base of his already disfigured neck and pressed the power button. She shuddered as his head wiggled back and forth, gasping when it popped off with a snap.

Her stomach rebelled. She swallowed the bile that climbed up her throat and forced herself to breathe. She didn't have time to panic. It was already eleven o'clock.

She shoved the head into a bag. Then she wiggled a bag up and over the torso. Once the torso was completely covered, she tied the red plastic strips as tightly as possible and sat back on her feet.

"God!" she exclaimed. "What a mess!"

The bags were covered in blood. There was blood all over the floor. There was blood and strips of mangled flesh hanging from the saw blade. Eleven bloody knives lay spread out on the floor. Her clothes were stained red, and she looked as if she was wearing gloves made of blood.

She glanced at the clock with a frown. Richard should have been home by now. It didn't take him that long to climax. Ten minutes at most, but he'd been gone for hours. She had to hurry.

She washed her gloved hands, opened the dishwasher, and shoved the knives in. She stared at the saw for a moment, then threw it in the dishwasher too. It would surely ruin it, but it would be clean. She'd put it back in the box, and Richard would be none the wiser. She rolled up the extension cord, and, after a moment's thought, tossed it in the dishwasher as well.

She poured in more soap and started the dishwasher again. She got out six clean trash bags and carefully put the bags containing the arms, legs, and head in new, clean bags, stacking them in the only blood-free corner of the kitchen. She couldn't easily lift the torso, so she'd have to deal with it once the floor was clean.

She tried not to think about Richard. She tried not to wonder when he'd be home.

She got out the mop and started mopping. There was so much blood she had to keep changing the water. Who knew one person could spew so much blood?

She mopped and mopped, breathing heavily, wishing she'd just given him the damn money and let him have his way with her. It might not have even been that bad. If only he hadn't called her "bitch".

Richard used to call her a bitch. After the "honeymoon" stage, once he'd realized she was cold, he called her a bitch all the time. She hated it. But she put up with it. What else could she do? He was her husband. She had married him, hadn't she? Done deal.

When she finished the floor, she grabbed a rag and started wiping down the counters and cabinet doors. Finally the entire kitchen was clean except the floor under the torso.

She pushed and shoved until the torso was in a clean bag and dragged it across the room to the others. Then she mopped the floor again, rinsed the mop head with bleach, put it away, stripped off her clothes, shoved them in the washer, and ran upstairs to put fresh clothes on. Almost done.

She heard Richard's car just as she was pulling a clean shirt over her head. "No," she moaned. She was so close. She ran down the stairs, reaching the kitchen just as he did.

"Lucille," he said, voice a bit surprised and eyes a little glazed with alcohol. "I thought I told you not to wait up."

Her heart was pounding so hard she wondered he couldn't hear it. "I got caught up cleaning," she murmured.

"Oh." He glanced around the kitchen. "Good. It has been looking a bit shabby lately."

Lucille bit her lip. It hadn't been. She cleaned all the time. And it's not like he ever helped her clean. He didn't help her do anything. He didn't even mow the lawn in the summer. She paid the neighbor's son to do it. She did everything, took care of everything.

But right now she just needed him to go away. "I still have a little bit to finish up," she said with a smile. "See you in the morning, dear," she added, hoping he would go straight up.

He shrugged and said, "Just don't wake me when you come in." She caught a whiff of acrid perfume as he waddled past her towards the stairs.

She frowned at his back. She couldn't believe how old he looked. His belly had gone to fat, his hair was receding, and he walked like he needed a cane. Who would willingly have sex with him?

She shook her head. This was not the time. She had a body to get rid of. She opened the door leading into the garage and lugged each bag over to her car, dragging the bag with the torso. She popped open her trunk and stared at it in relief. She'd always said it was big enough to carry a body in.

She shoved the bags into the trunk and climbed behind the wheel. What now? What did one do with bags full of body parts?

3

Lucille tried to remember all the movies she'd watched with people needing to dispose of bodies, but she didn't watch movies like that. She preferred... She didn't actually know what she preferred. Richard always picked.

She shook her head. "Focus!" she snapped. "Body in the trunk!"

If she dropped the bags in the reservoir would they come to the surface? She felt like they would. If she dumped them in the prairie, coyotes would probably find them and drag body parts all over the place. She shuddered at the idea of some kid going out to play and finding an arm in his favorite hiding place.

She laid her head on the steering wheel in exhaustion. It was way past her bedtime. She was tired; she was scared; she was too old for this.

Her grandpa used to say "the simple solution is usually best". He wouldn't approve of what she'd done, but his advice was still sound. She was taking out the trash. So she'd take out the trash.

She drove across town until she reached her regular grocery store. It was closed for the night. The lights were on, and deep inside night stockers were hard at work filling shelves with cans and boxes, but nobody was out back by the dumpsters.

She drove down the alley and parked by a dumpster. She'd never been in an alley before. She didn't even know how she'd known the dumpster would be here, but it was. Along with a lot of other filth.

She didn't want to step out of the car. She didn't want to breathe alley air. She didn't want to walk on alley dirt. She cringed, imagining all the junk and disgusting stuff that would stick to her shoes and follow her home.

"Get over it," she muttered, popping the trunk and stepping from the car. She ignored the something that squished under her shoe and walked to her trunk, breathing as shallowly as possible.

She chucked one bag at a time into the dumpster, flinching with every bang and glancing around to make sure no one was there. Soon only the torso was left, and she stared at it in dismay.

Her arms felt like overcooked noodles. She needed to work out more, join a gym, lift some weights. How could she possibly heave the torso over the side of the dumpster? She was exhausted, and she hadn't been able to lift it in the first place. She closed her eyes and breathed deeply. I am Lucille Stevenson, she thought. I am strong. She snorted. Maybe fifteen years ago.

But she didn't have a choice. She had to get the damn torso into the dumpster or she was screwed. She grabbed the bag and pulled it slowly out of the trunk, being careful not to let it drop to the ground. Once it was on the bumper, she knelt down and tried to leverage it onto her shoulders.

She wished she'd just given him the money. She could have endured a few minutes of nasty business. It wouldn't have been any different than her couplings with Richard. Afterwards, she would have called the police, they'd have written a report, and she'd be in bed already. Asleep.

Her muscles wouldn't be screaming in agony. She wouldn't be so tired she felt like she might actually die. And she wouldn't be here. In this nasty alley, by this nasty dumpster, with this nasty bag of trash on her shoulders.

She grunted and heaved the bag up, stumbled to the dumpster, and dropped it over the side. It tumbled to the bottom with a bang. If she was lucky no one would ever even know the body was there.

She got back in her car and turned the key. Her hands were shaking so much she wasn't sure she'd be able to drive. But she needed to get out of here before someone came along and found her. She needed to go home.

Richard peeked through the blind again. Lucille was still gone. What the hell could she possibly be doing? They'd been married for thirty years, and the only time he could ever remember her staying up past midnight was when one of the kids was sick.

It sometimes annoyed him that he'd picked such a colossally uninteresting woman to marry. But other times he thanked his lucky stars she was as thickheaded as she was. She'd never once asked him to account for his whereabouts. She never asked what he'd been doing, who he'd been doing, how or why.

But she'd been acting strange lately, and he didn't like it. It was almost as if she knew. He shook his head. This was Lucille he was talking about. There was no way she knew. She was simply too dumb and unimaginative.

He turned from the window and got into bed, rubbing the sore spot on his upper thigh. She'd probably just forgotten Nate's creamer and run out to get it.

Lucille drove slowly, breathing, reliving the last several hours. She felt like she was stuck in a nightmare. Why had she killed him? Why? But she knew. She just hadn't been able to stop. She was so angry. So full of hot, liquid anger. It was as if the anger had taken over her body and made her do it.

She tried to find comfort in that. Like it hadn't been her fault. It hadn't been her, Lucille, that had actually killed that man. It had been the anger.

But the anger hadn't not called the police. The anger hadn't chopped him into six pieces, bagged him, and dumped him in a dumpster. That was all her.

"In for a penny, in for a pound," she repeated to herself as she drove. She'd never really understood that expression until today. She was all in, and there was no going back.

When she got home she took her remarkably clean clothes out of the washer and threw them in the dryer, knowing she would throw them away. They may be clean, but she'd always see the blood when she looked at them. She shuddered at the mere thought of those clothes ever touching her skin again.

She took the saw and extension cord out of the dishwasher and put the saw back in its box in the garage and hung up the cord. She glanced around the kitchen one final time, looking for any telltale signs of murder, but didn't see anything. So she went upstairs, took a shower, and fell into bed.

Her alarm woke her at five. For a second she glanced frantically around the room. Her last thought had been of the dead man lying in the dumpster, black bags sticking to his flesh, waiting to be found, but then she had fallen asleep. And slept. Like she hadn't slept in years.

She yawned and stretched, getting slowly out of bed. She was sore in places she had never been sore, but, honestly, she felt great. And that freaked her out. How could she feel great? She'd killed a man, sawed him into pieces, and disposed of his body. She should be weeping, torn up inside, wracked with guilt. But she wasn't. She was... She was... satisfied.

She shook her head and headed downstairs to make breakfast. Satisfied? Was she sick? Deranged? Out of her mind? But no. He had been going to hurt her. Maybe he would have even killed her. She was allowed to protect herself. And it didn't matter how she'd done it. It didn't make her a monster. She was strong. She was brave. She was hungry.

She giggled at herself and grabbed a banana from the counter, eating it while she made French toast with walnuts and cream cheese. She made French toast every Wednesday. Richard insisted on it. She hummed as she whipped the eggs and poured the cream in.

By the time Nate showed up for breakfast, coffee was made, the table was set, and each place had a plate of steaming French toast. Nate's special creamer was even sitting next to his coffee cup.

Lucille smiled at him automatically, wondering where her cute little boy had gone, and filled his cup with steaming hot coffee.

"Did you see the front page yesterday?" Nate asked Richard, ignoring both Lucille and the fact that his creamer was waiting for him.

She shrugged and sat, smiling slightly as she watched Richard eat his French toast with the fork she'd used to stab the robber in his eyes. It was clean, but Lucille still felt just a little thrill of pleasure with every bite he took.

Richard and Nate talked back and forth like they always did, but Lucille didn't listen. She was drinking her coffee, savoring it. If she had died last night, she would have never had coffee again. Ever. She would have never eaten chocolate again or drank wine. White wine, red wine, rose wine, sparkling wine. She hadn't drunk enough wine.

But more than just that, this was a day she might not have had. A gift. A pleasure. And today she was going to do something new. She was going to make a change. Because it seemed like such a waste not to.

"Lucille!" Richard snapped.

"What?"

"Are you listening?"

"No."

"What?" he sputtered, like she'd never not listened to him before, and maybe she hadn't.

"What did you need, dear?" Lucille asked, smiling and batting her eyelashes.

"I said I need you to take my good suit to the drycleaners. I have a meeting next week."

"Isn't the drycleaners on your way to work?"

"How the hell should I know?!"

Lucille fought the urge to yell back at him. She always took his dry-cleaning; what did she care? But she did. The angry part of her cared very much. It was out of her way and only a block from his office. She snapped her mouth shut. She was his wife. She was supposed to take care of his laundry. That was a woman's job.

She swallowed and said meekly, "Yes, dear," even though what she really wanted to do was stab that stupid fork into his hand and watch him bleed.

She left for work early so she could swing by the drycleaners. "Extra starch," she told the man behind the counter. He gave her a strange look, but nodded.

She'd been bringing Richard's dry-cleaning here for twenty years now and she'd never asked for extra starch. Richard hated extra starch. Oops.

She drove to work, slipped past Dr. Banks without talking to him, and brought back the first patient. Most of Dr. Banks's patients were elderly, and he hated that. He went on and on about quality of life. He tried to cut back on medications; he explained to them that they were reaching the end. It drove Lucille nuts.

But she was too old to switch jobs now. Not to mention she'd been working for him for fifteen years. She should be used to his crap. But she wasn't. Just like she'd been married to Richard for thirty years, and she still wondered what she'd seen in him all those years ago.

Her father said you picked a horse and stuck with it. No matter what. Your husband, your job, your car. You bought it, you bought it. Lucille wished that wasn't true. She wished she could trade her job in, her husband in, her car in. She wished she could trade them all in and get new.

"Lucille!" Dr. Banks barked. "Let's hurry things up a bit!"

"Sorry, Dr. Banks. I was making a list of Mr. Gerry's complaints."

"Two complaints at a time, Lucille. You know that!"

Lucille nodded. She did. It was Dr. Banks's rule, but it was a stupid rule. Why should Mr. Gerry have to come back again and again and again?

"Lucille!"

"Yes, Dr. Banks."

She wished she could smash the clipboard over his head. Or pop a syringe into his ear.

By five she was exhausted and just wanted to go home, but she had promised herself that today would be different. Today would be better. Today she would take just a bit of the day for her.

She drove to a strip mall near the grocery store and slowly walked into Health Club, a small, trendy looking gym.

A woman behind the counter smiled and said pleasantly, "How can I help you?"

"Um..." Lucille felt shaky all over. She felt like a fool. What was she doing here? She started to leave, but she stopped herself. Something new.

"I've never done this before, gone to a gym I mean. I wonder... Um... Is there someone..."

"Would you like to speak to a trainer?" the lady asked kindly.

"What's a trainer?"

"A personal trainer. A trainer helps you set goals, works with you as many times a week as you think you need it, and holds you accountable for your progress."

"Um... yeah. That sounds good." Better than trying to figure out weights on her own.

"Let's see," the woman said, glancing down at her desktop. "It looks like there's only one trainer free right now, Angela. Would you like to see her?"

Lucille heaved a sigh of relief. She was glad it was a

female trainer. She wasn't sure if she could work with a male trainer. She'd be too embarrassed.

"Yes, thank you," she said. "That would be nice."

"Wait here; I'll be right back."

As soon as the receptionist was gone, Lucille thought about walking out. It felt wrong to be here. She had so much work to do. She needed to dust, clean out the drawers in the kitchen, clean the bathrooms, mend Richard's golf pants, and make supper.

Her stomach plummeted. She'd forgotten about supper. Richard would be home in twenty minutes, and he would expect supper ready and waiting on the table. In thirty years of marriage she'd never not had supper waiting for him when he got home.

God, he'll be so pissed, she thought worriedly. *So what?* a voice inside her head demanded, making Lucille jerk in surprise. It still startled her when her inner critic spoke up. She'd named it "angry me" because everything it said was furious. It had advised her to kill Richard, to kill Dr. Banks, to kill the mailman when he didn't put the flag down, to kill Nate when he didn't wipe his shoes off. She usually ignored it.

She didn't think it was healthy to talk to herself. Especially when herself didn't have anything good to say. But she was a little sick of getting pushed around so she snapped back. So what?! He'll yell at me and tell me I'm a bad wife. That's what!

Who gives a shit? angry her snapped. I feel like I do. *He's a dick,* angry her growled. *Let him make his own supper. We nearly died last night. We're doing this!*

Lucille stared at the door. She desperately wanted to leave so she could whip together a supper for Richard before he noticed she was gone. She didn't want to get yelled at. She hated being yelled at. In fact she went out of her way not to get yelled at, but angry her was right. It was time to do something for Lucille.

"Ma'am," a cheerful voice said from behind her. "My name is Angela. Would you like to tour the gym?"

Lucille turned and smiled widely. "Nice to meet you Angela. I'm Lucille, and I'd love to."

Angela was taller than Lucille, maybe five foot ten, and she was much younger and much fitter. She made Lucille feel a little dumpy, but her smile was kind, and Lucille liked her immediately.

"We have a free weight room, a weight machine room, and a cardio machine room," Angela explained as they walked. "There's a sauna and two rooms for classes like Yoga and Tae Kwon Do."

"Wow," Lucille breathed, trying to take it all in. "That's a lot." There were people everywhere, most of them wearing skimpy, tight-fitting clothes and looking very fit in them. Lucille couldn't wear clothes like that. Richard would have an apoplexy.

Someone behind her grunted, and Lucille looked over her shoulder to see a tall, fit, muscular man heave a bar of weights over his head. He was sweaty. Very sweaty and very big. All over.

Lucille accidently glanced down and saw that his pants left very little to the imagination. She squeaked in surprise, feeling a wave of heat wash over her, and looked back up. He winked at her.

Her mouth dropped open in disbelief, and she quickly looked the other way. She was sure her face was as red as her kitchen floor had been last night. She felt just as hot as she had then too. Just not angry hot. A different type of hot. A type she'd never felt.

"So Lucille, what're your workout goals?"

Lucille looked at Angela, trying to remember what they'd been talking about, but she couldn't. All she could remember was the mischievous grin on the muscled man's face and the twinkle in his bright, blue eyes.

"Goals?"

"Do you want to build muscle, lose weight, build cardio, flexibility?"

"Um... yes."

"Yes what?"

"All of those."

Angela laughed. "Alright; we can do that. Let's go to the office and build a plan."

Richard's supper is going to be very late, Lucille thought as she followed Angela.

"So let's make a list," Angela said. "We'll start with muscle. Are you interested in toning or building?"

Lucille could still feel the helplessness that had swamped her when she'd tried to move the dead man on her own and realized she couldn't. She remembered how exhausted she'd felt when it was all said and done.

"Both," she said earnestly. "I feel old, and I'm not! I don't think. Am I?"

Angela laughed. "You're not old. You're what forty-three or so? Prime of your life!"

Lucille snorted. "Fifty-one. I'll be fifty-two pretty soon."

"Well you look absolutely great for your age," Angela said seriously. "And you're NOT old."

"Well, I feel old, and I know I'm weak, and I'm much fatter than I used to be. I want to fix it all!"

"Health is about more than exercise," Angela said. "Do you want to look at your diet and lifestyle as well?"

"Yes!" She really did. She wanted to change everything. She hated cooking French toast every Wednesday. She hated chili every Friday night. She hated it all. She hated cleaning the house. Why didn't she just hire a damn maid? Then she would have so much free time. Or convince Richard to buy a smaller house. She chuckled silently. He would never downsize. He was too busy overcompensating.

"So let's do this," Angela said. "Let's set a time that works for you. We'll work out for forty-five minutes, then talk about diet and lifestyle for fifteen. In the meantime, think about how much weight you want to lose and what your overall goals are. Think about if there's something specific you want to train for, a specific weight, event, things like that. Does that sound good?"

Lucille nodded. It was a change, a healthy change, and that's what she wanted. "So what about prices?" she asked, hoping it wasn't too much. Richard only allowed her a two hundred dollar allowance for things like clothes and "frivolities", and she was certain he'd consider the gym a frivolity.

Angela handed her a paper. "These are the rates for the gym. My time is in addition to your membership fee. There's a fifteen percent discount if we met three times a week for a month, otherwise it's sixty dollars an hour."

Lucille looked at the sheet and did some quick math in her head. In just one week her allowance would be shot. *Allowance! You work hard for your money; you should use it on whatever you want!* That's not fair, Lucille thought, feeling awkward talking to angry her while Angela was watching her.

All of our extra money goes into savings. *You know that's not true!* Lucille felt a sudden burst of rage. Angry her was right. It wasn't true. All of HER extra money went into savings, but she didn't have a clue where Richard's extra money went.

For thirty damn years she'd followed his rules and made his breakfasts and watched his TV shows. Today she was going to the gym because it's what she wanted to do. She wanted to feel strong again, fit, healthy, beautiful.

"Let's do it," she said, signing the contract before she could talk herself out of it.

4

Lucille climbed into her car feeling more optimistic than she had in years. If she ever had felt optimistic. Which she wasn't sure she had.

She couldn't ever remember doing something just for herself. First it was always what she needed to do to please her father, then what she needed to do to please Richard, their children, and Dr. Banks. Never once had she thought about what would please her.

She felt a little guilty about the money. She felt really guilty about Richard's supper. But deep down she knew she needed this.

Her optimism quickly faded when she saw it was already six thirty. Richard would be irate. She glanced at her phone. He'd called sixteen times. Now she wished she hadn't gone by at all. She should have waited.

No, you shouldn't have! angry her snapped. *It was important.* Not as important as Richard's dinner. *Bullshit. He could stand to lose a few pounds.*

Lucille shook her head, ignoring angry hers voice. Angry her was wrong. Lucille had been told over and over and over by her father, by her mom, by Richard. Her most important job in life was to care for her husband. And today she had failed.

Her heart stuttered as she drove past the grocery store. She searched the parking lot for police cars, wondering if anyone had found the body. If they did, what would they think? Deep down she knew she'd never be a suspect. Not Lucille Stevenson. Boring, cold, dependable housewife. Not her.

She parked her car in the garage, sitting in it for a minute, trying to shield herself for what she knew was coming. She had to go inside eventually. Maybe he'd already eaten. Maybe he wouldn't be that mad.

But he was. He was absolutely livid. "WHERE WERE YOU?!" he yelled as soon as she walked inside. "You didn't answer my calls! And where the hell's my dinner?!"

Lucille fought the urge to cringe. "I just... I had... an errand to run."

"An errand?! Damn it, Lucille. What the hell's wrong with you? You know I expect my dinner when I get home!"

"I know, dear, I just..."

"I don't care! From now on when I get home, dinner better be here!"

"I'm sorry," Lucille stuttered. "I'll make dinner right now."

"Don't bother! I'm going out!" Richard slammed the door behind him, and Lucille heaved a sigh of relief.

She'd honestly expected worse. He probably thought he was punishing her by leaving, but he wasn't. She was glad he was gone. Let him get his food and sex elsewhere. She preferred it that way.

Damn that woman! Richard thought as he backed his car down the driveway. Making him wait for dinner! "An errand to run," he sneered as he slammed his car in drive and took off down the street.

He was so sick of her. He'd thought about punishing her with sex, but he just wasn't interested. She was cold, always had been. It was like having sex with an iceberg. The last time he'd tried it she'd actually bled. How could a woman be that damn rigid?

He stopped at a stop sign and texted Emily. "I'm free. Can I come over?"

He hated asking, but Emily didn't care for it when he just showed up. The last time he'd done it she'd left him tied up for four hours. Just once he'd like to tie her up, be the one in control. But he couldn't really complain. She always made it good for him.

Lucille made herself a salad, poured a glass of wine, and sat at the table with a notebook and pen. What were her workout goals? She wanted to be able to lift a man's torso without struggling so much. But she wasn't going to write that down. How about she wanted to be able to easily lift a hundred pounds? That seemed reasonable. She hoped.

What about running? Did she want to be able to run? An image popped into her head of her running away from the man, leaving him far behind. But she just had to keep running and running because there was nowhere to go. No; she didn't care about running.

Flexibility sounded good though. She felt like flexibility might have come in handy. She just wasn't sure how. Maybe if she was more flexible she wouldn't be so sore right now. It hurt her arms just to lift her wine glass.

She took a sip of wine, wondering at how calm she was. She felt like she should be sobbing in the bathroom, lights off, bottle of wine clutched in her hand. But she wasn't.

She felt fine. She wasn't worried they'd find the body. And if they did there was really no way they could trace it back to her. Even if she'd left behind hair or fibers or something she didn't know him. He was just some random robber guy, and there was nothing to connect them. The police wouldn't know to look for her.

It just seemed like killing someone should be a big deal. Like she should be struggling with it, questioning herself, picking up the phone and turning herself in. But she didn't feel any of that. Maybe she was in shock. Maybe it would hit later on, and she'd collapse. But until then, she'd lift weights.

She looked at her list. "Easily lift a hundred pounds" and "more flexible" didn't seem like enough. She wanted to lose weight, but she hadn't weighed herself since right after Addie's birth. She'd never forgotten the look of absolute disgust on Richard's face when he'd seen how much she weighed. She added "lose two pants sizes" to her list, but she couldn't think of anything else.

She just didn't want to be Lucille anymore. Not this version of her she'd turned into, maybe not any version of her. She wanted to be different.

Detective Sanders watched as they searched the dumpster for the rest of the body. She'd already interviewed the dumpster diver. She didn't think he'd be dumpster diving again any time soon. His face had been a terrible shade of green, and his lips had trembled the entire time they'd spoken. Honestly some people just couldn't handle the darker side of life.

She didn't have that problem. Seeing the victim's face, gouged, ripped, and torn, bloated from stewing in a hot dumpster for a day or two didn't bother her at all. She laughed suddenly, imagining the dumpster diver's face when he'd ripped open the bag. She bet he screamed like a girl.

"Got it, Detective!"

"All of it?"

"Think so."

"Crack 'em open; let's take a look."

"You sure, Detective? The ME isn't here yet."

She shrugged. "Do it anyway." Denton would yell at her, but she needed to see everything without him getting in her way. She'd taken a good look at the head and figured out a few things already. Or assumed some things. Denton would say it wasn't a fact until he proved it, but Sanders believed in observation, and she was damn good at it.

The killer had been enraged. You didn't kill someone the way this man had been killed if you were just trying to get rid of them. Both eyeballs had been punctured with something, leaving behind four, odd shaped holes. Sanders would bet her paycheck the killer had used a table fork. Which meant the murder had most likely occurred inside someone's home. Or possibly a closed restaurant. Somewhere a fork might be handy.

There had been a blunt trauma to the side of the victim's head, but Sanders didn't figure it had been enough to kill him or knock him out. She couldn't be sure though; she'd leave that to Denton to figure out.

"Here you go, Detective."

Sanders stared at the bags. The lighting in this back alley was crap, but she could see enough to tell that the killer had been extremely efficient. The victim had been cut into six pieces, and each piece had been bagged, double bagged actually, and the bags were tied quite neatly at the top.

Sanders thought it was a little strange the killer had put each part in its own bag. Two arms would have easily fit together. And why remove the head? It didn't weigh that much on its own.

She quickly looked over each body part. He had cuts on his hands, but there was no other damage she could see except to the victim's face. She frowned and stepped closer to the torso, bending down to get a good look.

His neck had been torn to shreds. And not just from the blade used to chop him up. She'd bet that was the wound that had killed him.

She used her pen to open the bag around the right shoulder. The cut marks looked a little different than all the other cut marks. She'd guess the killer started there, and it had taken them a minute to figure out how to cut through the bone. Maybe it was their first time.

"SANDERS!"

Sanders stood and turned with a grin. "Sorry Denton, I thought you were right behind me."

"If you've contaminated my goddamn evidence I'll have your badge!"

"You always say that," Sanders replied. "Maybe one of these days you'll follow through."

"Get out of my way!" Denton snapped.

She grinned and moved. She was done anyway.

Denton hated working with Sanders. She was a good damn detective, but she had no respect for protocol and she was always making wild leaps and accusations. Then she'd come to him and want him to find the evidence to support her claims.

It didn't matter how many times he explained to her that that's not how the hell things worked, she still insisted on doing it.

Evidence first. Facts first. Then fit the theories into the facts, not the other damn way around. How hard was that?

Denton stared at the six open black bags, wishing he'd gotten here sooner. She'd probably already jumped to a hundred conclusions and not one of them would be based on actual evidence.

"You shouldn't have opened the bags!" he snapped at the uniformed officer standing by the dumpster.

"Sorry; Detective Sanders said..."

"I don't give a shit what Detective Sanders said! Go get me some coffee and find out when the dumpster was last picked up!"

"Yes, sir!"

The uniform scurried away, but Denton didn't pay him any attention. He had work to do.

5

Lucille reviewed her list one more time, but she couldn't think of anything else to add. She'd agreed to meet Angela five times a week to begin with, but that meant she wouldn't be home when Richard got home.

He was already going to blow a gasket about the cost, and she didn't want to add to it, like she had tonight, by not making his supper. She'd have to make his suppers ahead of time. She didn't imagine it would bother him if she wasn't around as long as he got fed.

She finished her wine and went into the kitchen. She still couldn't believe how clean the floor looked. She couldn't believe yesterday night it had been covered with body parts and blood.

She opened the refrigerator and started cooking. Two hours later she had a couple weeks' worth of meals for Richard labeled and in the freezer.

Before going upstairs to bed she checked the front door to make sure it was locked. It wasn't. Maybe that was how the robber had gotten in. She'd need to be more careful. Nate was the only one who used the front door; she'd have to remember to check it after he left.

She scanned the lower rooms just to make sure everything was good. Nothing looked out of place, and there were no robbers skulking in the corners. It occurred to her that the safety of her home had been violated. She thought about being upset about it, but she couldn't quite summon it. He was dead. Problem solved.

She went upstairs to get ready for bed, took off her clothes, and looked at herself in the mirror. She never looked at herself naked in the mirror. It was too depressing. She couldn't even remember what she'd looked like before she'd had kids, she just knew it wasn't like this.

Her breasts were saggy, her tummy paunchy, her thighs and butt bulbous. She looked... pathetic. No wonder Richard didn't bother anymore.

Well he looks like a bloated fish! angry her snapped. *All pale with those dead fish eyes and all that gut.* Lucille swallowed a giggle. She shouldn't think of Richard like that. He deserved her respect. *For crap's sake! What has he done to deserve your respect?*

It took Lucille a minute to think of a response. He's a good provider, she finally said. *That's all you got? You work just as hard as he does, and when you worked for the hospital you actually made more money than him.*

That was true. But still. She'd been raised to respect her husband no matter what. And anyway, she had picked him.

She climbed into bed feeling better all-around than she had in years. It was late, and she was tired but not exhausted. She felt lighter. Like not all her energy and life had been used up on meaningless chores.

She fell asleep thinking that the robber, whoever he was, had changed her life, and maybe she should have thanked him before she killed him.

She woke at four fifty-nine AM and stared at the darkened ceiling. Today was Thursday. Thursday was pancake day. She hated pancakes. Today she was going to make something different. Something healthy.

She hummed to herself as she pulled out rarely used boxes and started making oatmeal. Oatmeal with fresh fruit and yogurt would be a refreshing change.

"What the hell is this?!" Richard barked when he sat down.

"Breakfast," Lucille said softly.

"It looks like vomit," Nate said.

"It's oatmeal," Lucille whispered, feeling the now familiar rush of hot anger pour over her.

"Why the hell're we eating oatmeal?!" Richard demanded. "It's Thursday. Thursday's pancake day."

"I don't like pancakes," Lucille replied, voice a little stronger, anger pumping through her veins, making her feel braver than she usually did.

"Well I don't like oatmeal," Nate said, voice a little whiney.

"Eat at your own house then!" Lucille snapped. She was so angry. So very, very angry. And she was sick of catering to all their wants and needs and not taking care of her own. She was sick of not standing up for herself. She was sick of them.

"If you want to eat here, you'll eat what I put on the table, and today that's oatmeal!"

"What the hell's wrong with you?!" Richard demanded. "Last night you didn't have dinner ready when I got home and today you're acting all crazy about oatmeal. Is it your time? You know I don't like it when you give into emotional mood swings. It's a choice. You can't let your emotions lead you around like a damn dog!"

She growled angrily, standing as she did. She was too full of anger to think about what she was doing or saying or thinking. She wasn't thinking. She was feeling. And she was feeling MAD.

"You will both eat what I put in front of you without complaint, or you will find someplace else to eat! Is that understood?"

"Geez, Lucille," Richard said scornfully. "It's just oatmeal. Stop making a big deal out of it. Why don't you go take some lady pills to calm yourself down?"

Lucille wanted to grab all the forks off the table and stab Richard in his snarky mouth. She wanted to break the plates over his head. She wanted to smash his ugly face into the table. She was so angry.

She opened her mouth to speak, but nothing came out. They were both looking at her with identical looks. Like she was a silly female, giving into her emotions like some crazy lady. But she wasn't.

She didn't need "lady pills". She didn't even know what "lady pills" were. It was not her time of the month. She was angry because they were jerks.

Kill them, angry her hissed. No! Are you insane? I can't kill them! *Why not?* Because... Because that's murder! *So?*

Lucille shook her head, turning away from them and walking upstairs. She had wanted to say something else, wanted to throw the oatmeal in Richard's face, but then that voice, that other her, that angry her had said "Kill them" and it was like ice to her soul.

She'd killed that one man because he had been going to hurt her. Maybe even kill her. That was it. It was done. She was never going to kill anyone ever again. She wasn't a killer or a murderer. She was Lucille.

So this anger, whatever it was, needed to go. It was bad. It was evil. It wasn't her, and it scared her. Made her feel out of control, and she couldn't have that. She needed to be in control.

Her entire life had been built on controlling what she could. Because, frankly, there was so much she couldn't control that if she didn't control something... she wouldn't have anything.

It was all right to make oatmeal. Her job was to cook, and she'd done that. And it was all right to ask them not to complain. But she could not break plates over their heads or stab them with forks. That was a line she would not cross. She had killed that man because he had attacked her, but she wouldn't kill Richard or Nate or anyone else. From here on out, she would control the anger.

She looked through her closet for something loose she could work out in. She wouldn't be caught dead wearing those skintight pants most of the other women wore. She'd look like too much sausage squeezed into a wrapper, and she felt awkward enough as it was. She picked something out, shoved it in a bag, got dressed for work, and went back downstairs.

Richard and Nate were both gone. Their empty bowls were still on the table. Even her bowl was empty.

"I guess they didn't mind the oatmeal after all," she muttered to herself as she cleaned up.

She left a note for Richard explaining how to heat up his food and went to work. She ignored Dr. Banks as much as she could, and after work she drove slowly towards the gym. She was already regretting the contract she'd signed. Now if she didn't go she'd still have to pay.

We need this. You shut up. I don't like you. You're insane. *I'm not insane. I'm you.* Like hell you are!

Lucille gasped. She never cussed. Not even in her head. Women didn't cuss. It wasn't ladylike.

Just shut up, she snapped. I don't want you here. *No,* angry her whispered. *You need me.*

Lucille shook her head. She didn't know why angry her had a voice now. She never had before. Of course, Lucille had never been overly angry before. She'd been meek, quiet, dutiful.

She frowned as she stepped out of her car. She was sick of dutiful. Let Richard learn to use the microwave.

She opened the doors, searching for Angela's tall frame but not seeing her. A wave of panic caught her, and she stepped backward, towards the exit.

"Excuse me, miss," a deep voice said behind her.

She startled, turning quickly and blushing a deep red when she saw the fit man with the blue eyes standing behind her. She hastily stepped to the side so he could move past.

"Sorry," she mumbled.

"No problem at all," he said cheerfully. "You working with Angela today?"

"Um... Yes, I mean I think so. I don't see her."

She felt so awkward. She didn't normally talk to men. Not outside of work. She really didn't go out much. Except to work. Had she always been so reclusive? She didn't know.

"Would you like me to take you back?" he asked, smile open and friendly.

"Um... I don't know. Maybe I should wait here."

His grin widened. "I'll take you on back. I see your feet edging for the door."

Lucille's face turned bright. "They're not," she mumbled.

"Are a bit. Come on. My name's Henry," he added as he started forward into the gym.

"Um... Lucille."

"You seem more like a Lucy to me," he said with a wink.

Her eyes widened. He'd winked at her again. When was the last time someone had winked at her? Maybe never! And Lucy? No one had ever called her Lucy. Why had no one ever called her Lucy? It was so much quicker, so much easier to say.

"Angela," Henry called out. "I'm delivering Lucy. She was trying to sneak out the front door."

"I wasn't!" Lucille exclaimed.

He winked at her again, nodded at Angela, and walked away.

"I wasn't!" Lucille said again.

"He was just teasing you," Angela said. "And I wouldn't blame you if you were. It's scary trying something for the first time."

Lucille opened her mouth to argue, but she couldn't. It was scary. She was terrified. What if she was too weak to even lift a weight? What if she couldn't hold a single Yoga pose? What if she fell and broke her face?

"It's okay," Angela said. "We'll take it slow. Are you ready to get started?"

Lucille nodded shakily. She'd changed before she'd left work, much to the amusement of Dr. Banks who thought she was wasting her time.

"So did you think about your goals?" Angela asked.

Lucille nodded and handed Angela the paper she'd written

last night. Angela read it and smiled. "This looks reasonable. Let's get started with some light free weights."

Lucille didn't know what that meant, but she followed Angela into the weight room and listened while she explained what they were going to do.

For the next forty-five minutes Angela helped Lucille through several exercises, explaining the focus of each one as they went. It wasn't nearly as hard as Lucille had been expecting. It wasn't easy either, but it was doable.

When they were done, they talked about eating healthy and good lifestyle choices. "Stress will hold you back more than anything," Angela said. "If there are things in your life that are stressing you out, you either need to get rid of them or find a way to deal with them healthily."

Lucille lost herself momentarily as she imagined Richard in the black plastic bags instead of some guy whose name she didn't know. She tried to imagine what her life would be like without Richard. All she could see was a balloon floating free into the sky. But she couldn't kill Richard. So she'd have to learn to deal with him in a healthy way.

"I'll see you tomorrow?" Angela asked, interrupting Lucille's train of thought.

"Yes," Lucille said. She felt tired but also more invigorated than she had in forever. She felt like she might actually be able to change. Like she might actually be able to be more.

She left the gym, walking rather faster than normal. When she got to her car, she took a minute to look around. It wasn't quite sunset, but the sky was beautiful. The trees everywhere were just thinking about turning green. It was a beautiful day for change.

She jumped into her car, ignoring her phone's incessant

ringing, and drove towards the river walk. She hadn't made time to walk on the river walk in years.

She parked, left her phone in the car, and started walking. There were lots of people out. People with dogs, people on bikes, people jogging, people just walking and talking, people running behind little kids. Lucille smiled as she watched them and thought about her day.

Something was changing. Something deep inside her. More than just the anger. More than angry her. She didn't actually like angry her, but she liked the change. She was finally starting to see herself as Lucille. Not Mrs. Stevenson, not Richard's wife, not Nate's mom, or Dr. Banks's nurse, but Lucille. Lucy.

She had never been called Lucy before, and she liked that it had been Henry to do it. When he smiled it was genuine and actually reached his eyes. Richard's smile had always been smarmy and insincere.

"Lucy. Lucy Stevenson." She grinned. It rolled right off the tongue, and she liked it so much better than Lucille. She'd always hated Lucille when she was growing up, but it was her name. You couldn't change your name. But it turned out you could.

A red-winged blackbird flew overhead, making its trilling call. Lucy watched it for a minute, envying its freedom.

You can be free too, angry her whispered. Shut up.

She breathed deeply and sighed. It was time to go home. She couldn't avoid Richard forever. He may be a lousy husband, but that didn't give her the right to be a lousy wife.

Sure it does. I said SHUT UP!

She wished angry her would go away. She was pretty sure it was a bad sign. But without angry her she would be dead.

She could still feel her fear when the man had grabbed her. She remembered thinking "I'm going to die".

But then the fear had just evaporated when he'd called her "bitch". The fear had left, and the anger, the boiling hot anger, had taken over. If it hadn't have been for the anger, she'd be dead. Or at least robbed and raped.

Several months ago when she'd first started experiencing the anger she had asked her doctor about it. Not the voice, she hadn't mentioned that, just the hot rush of rage. He'd shrugged and said, "I wouldn't worry about it. If it becomes too much I can refer you to a counselor."

Lucy didn't want to go to a counselor. There was nothing wrong with her. She just got a little angry sometimes, that was all.

"I won't let you!" someone shouted, pulling Lucy out of her thoughts. Up ahead a young couple was arguing fiercely.

"This is a once in a lifetime chance, Jay. My grandma offered to pay for everything."

"No! I don't want you gallivanting around Europe without me. You can't go!"

"But Jay, I won't be gallivanting. I'll be with my grandma. She's seventy-five for Pete's sake!"

"I don't care, Julie. I won't stand for it."

Lucy rolled her eyes. What a dick. Just as she was walking past them her mouth opened. She hadn't meant to say anything; it wasn't her problem, and she had no right to interfere.

"Take it from me, Julie," she said catching the girl's eye. "Go to Europe. Men are a dime a dozen and easily replaceable. If you're not already married to Jay here, run like hell. He's not worth it."

"Watch your mouth, old lady; this ain't none of your business!" Jay shouted, face turning bright red.

There was a large stick just two feet away. If Lucy grabbed it, she could smack dumb Jay over the head. Just a few times. Three at the most, ten on the outside. Just enough to teach him a lesson.

Lucy breathed deeply, forcing the anger back down, trying to reign it in. "Julie, your grandma wants to take you on an amazing, once-in-a-lifetime trip. Think of all the memories you'll make with her. Don't let Jay ruin it."

Jay stepped toward her, but Lucy raised one eyebrow, flexing her legs, getting ready to grab the stick. Julie grabbed his arm. "Let's go, Jay. Please."

Lucy smiled widely, turned her back on them, and kept walking. She hoped Julie didn't make the biggest mistake of her life. Men like Jay were poison. He would never encourage Julie to be the woman she could be or the woman she wanted to be.

Just like Richard. Just like Nate. Just like Lucy's father and Dr. Banks. She was surrounded by toxic men. It astounded her she'd never seen it before, never realized. It seemed totally obvious now, but knowing didn't change anything. She was stuck with them now.

Detective Sanders looked over Denton's report. It didn't tell her anything she didn't already know. First time or not, the killer had been good. They hadn't left behind a single trace of evidence. No loose hairs, no fingerprints, no incriminating photographs.

She smiled, thinking of her own incriminating photographs. It was always important to keep incriminating photographs. Just in case. But that didn't have anything to do with the murder at hand.

It annoyed her that unless something else came to light

whoever this killer was would go free because she didn't have a single lead.

The victim, one Charlie Wood, had been a criminal with a fairly long rap sheet. Anyone could have wanted him dead. Or he simply could have messed with the wrong person. There were no links, no ties, no connections to anything or anybody specific, but that didn't mean she'd stop looking. She never stopped looking.

6

Richard wasn't home. Which didn't surprise Lucy. He often spent his evenings out. Doing whatever it was he did with whoever he did it with.

There was a note on the uneaten dish of food. "What the hell is this shit?"

Lucy dumped it in the trash, anger pumping through her like mad. She'd worked hard to make meals for him. And he had just left it out on the counter to rot! Who the hell did he think he was?

Her shoulders slumped. He was her husband. That's who. She hadn't told him where she was going, what she was doing, or anything. Her father probably would have hunted her mom down and dragged her home if she'd dared do something like that.

Fortunately Richard wasn't her father. The only thing Richard would do was yell at her and complain. She could probably handle that. He yelled at her all the time anyway. At least now she'd done something to deserve it.

She cleaned up the kitchen, did a load of laundry, prepped for breakfast, ate a light supper, and thought about going to bed, but she just wasn't tired yet.

Which was strange because she was usually exhausted. But tonight she was pumped up from her day. She had stood up for herself. She had lifted weights. She had even changed her name.

She'd done something. She had made a change. So instead of going to bed she drank a glass of wine and read part of a trashy romance novel on her phone. She'd never read a trashy romance before. Her mom had always told her that kind of trash led to unrealistic expectations, and Lucy could see why.

She'd never felt anything close to what the book described. She'd never felt tingles or crashing waves of sensation or heat between her thighs. She wondered if anyone did. She wouldn't mind, but she didn't see it happening. She was too old now, and anyway, she'd already bought her horse. Never mind he had turned out to be a dud.

She felt another rush of anger. She worked so hard to please him, and he had never done anything, not ever, to please her. He didn't buy her presents or give her cards; he didn't say thank you for her hard work; he didn't compliment her.

Just kill him. No, damn it! I'm not killing anyone! *It'll make you feel better.* What? *Remember how good you felt? It was a release, a wonderful release; all that anger finally had a place to go.*

Angry her was right. Lucy had been so angry when she'd killed that man. So angry she wasn't sure she could have stopped herself. Afterwards, she had felt drained but in a good way. In a way that had made her sleep deeply and peacefully. In a way that had relaxed her.

"Oh my god," she whispered. "I'm insane."

You're not. Just repressed. What the hell does that mean? *Like a steaming pot with a screwed on lid.* Just go away, Lucy begged. I just want you to go away.

Lucy stared at her empty wine glass, terrified that the voice was right. For a minute there after killing that man, her anger had been less, more manageable; but it was already building back up, getting harder and harder to control.

At one point today she'd actually picked up a tongue depressor and started towards Dr. Banks. She'd stopped herself from shoving it in his ear just in time.

Maybe she did need to see someone. Maybe she did need help. But it was too late. She'd already killed that man. She couldn't get help now. Not if she wanted to stay out of prison.

She fell asleep wondering what to do.

Her alarm went off, and she rolled out of bed. She hated alarms. Just once she'd like to sleep in until nine or even noon. She'd heard of people doing that.

She cast a glare at Richard. He was snoring, mouth hanging open, drool rolling out onto the pillowcase. She shuddered. She hated that he was her husband. She'd rather be married to an ape. A big, hairy ape.

She walked downstairs. It was Friday. Friday was blueberry muffin day. Forget blueberry muffins. She'd make toast. And they better damn well be happy about it.

When Nate showed up the table was set. But the napkins weren't square, the forks weren't on the napkins, and the toast was burned.

Nate glanced over everything, looked at her, and opened his mouth to speak. Lucy glared at him. He closed his mouth and sat down.

"God, Lucille!" Richard snapped. "You burned the damn toast!"

She hated hearing that name. She hated being called Lucille. She wished she could shove the toast down Richard's throat.

She spilled coffee on his hand when she poured it, trying not to smile when he shrieked in pain. "Damn it, woman! Get yourself under control!"

She frowned. She should do that. Not because Richard told her to. But because she wasn't crazy. And she was acting a little crazy.

"Burnt toast is good for you," she said as she sat. "Helps clean out your insides."

Nate was watching her with wide eyes. She grinned at him. "Don't you think, Nate?"

"Whatever you say, Mom," he said, voice devoid of any sarcasm. She smiled even wider at him, pleased he'd sided with her for once, even if it was out of fear.

Richard was ignoring her now, face buried in his paper, but he suddenly made a snort of disgust and threw the paper on the table.

"Something wrong?" Nate asked.

"Just some stupid city junk," Richard said dismissively.

Lucy poured her coffee and opened the discarded newspaper. She didn't normally read the newspaper, but she didn't want to sit and listen to them today.

She read the first headline and swallowed her coffee with a gasp. They had found him. They had actually found him. "Dismembered Body Discovered in Local Grocery Store Dumpster."

She should have used the reservoir. She should have buried him somewhere. She should have blended him up and dumped him down the drain.

She read the entire article, heart hammering like a horse's

hooves. They don't have anything, she repeated over and over to herself. They don't have anything. And they didn't. They had no suspects, no witnesses. They'd identified his body, he was a known criminal, and that's all they had.

Lucy put the paper down with shaking hands. She honestly hadn't expected them to find him. Who looked through the garbage? It's okay, she assured herself. There's nothing. She had gotten away with it. Because there was no possible way for them to link her to him.

She set the paper to the side without looking at anything else and ate her toast silently, vaguely hearing Nate mention something about money.

Which reminded her that she'd forgotten to ask Richard about the ten thousand dollar withdraw. "Sorry for interrupting," she said softly, "But I was balancing the check book and saw a withdraw for ten thousand dollars. Did you make it, Richard?"

"So what if I did?!" Richard snapped, tone so hostile it made Lucy jump.

"I... I..." Lucy stammered. Why did she suddenly feel like she'd done something wrong?

"Damn, Dad," Nate said. "She's just asking you a question."

"Mind your own goddamn business!" Richard growled.

Lucy stared at them both in surprise. Nate defending her? Richard acting like a crazy person? Her world was turning upside down.

"So did you?" Lucy asked hesitantly. "'Cause if you didn't I need to contact the bank."

"Yes! I said I did, didn't I?!"

"Okay," Lucy whispered, fighting between the urge to retreat in fear and the urge to scream at the top of her lungs. It was both of their money. He didn't have any right to use an amount that large without consulting her. Not that he ever consulted her.

She opened her mouth to say something, but Richard beat her to it. "You're coming straight home tonight!" he demanded.

The urge to retreat vanished. "No."

"What do you mean 'no'?!"

"No."

"What the hell's going on with you?!"

"Nothing. I joined a gym, and I'm working out after work."

He looked her up and down with a sneer. "Well you could stand to lose fifty pounds or so, but you'll have to do it at a different time. You're putting me out."

"I made you food. All you have to do is put it in the microwave."

"Damn it, Lucille! What kind of wife doesn't make her husband a proper supper after he's been at work all day?"

Lucy's resolve started to fade. He was right. She wasn't making him a proper supper. That was her job. That was why he had married her. For food and sex.

But what about her? What about how hard she worked? What about what she wanted? What about a husband who cared about her? Who knew her?

"I made you food!" she snapped. "Deal with it."

He stared at her in surprise. She never defied him, never argued, never put up a fight. "We're not done with this conversation," he growled. "I expect you here when I get home." Then he was gone; Nate following sheepishly behind him.

Lucy stared at the door, resentment and anger crashing

through her. She wouldn't be here when he got home. She would be at the gym. He could eat his supper, or he couldn't. She didn't give a damn. She'd been a faithful, devoted, obedient wife for thirty years. She deserved a break.

Denton made sure his office door was closed, then pulled out the file. The file on his wife. It had been four years since Eddie Harris had gunned her down in broad daylight.

None of the witnesses would testify. They were all too scared, but it hadn't mattered. The police had all the evidence they needed. Gun powder residue on his hands. A ballistics match to Eddie's gun. And a tape recording of the threatening phone call he'd made earlier that day.

It should have been an open and shut case. But Eddie's employers had long arms. And somehow all that evidence became contaminated and was suppressed during the trial. So Eddie had walked free.

It made Denton question why they tried so hard to gather evidence, especially when detectives like Sanders paid no attention whatsoever to protocol. If anyone found out she'd opened the trash bags with the body parts in them before he'd gotten there, all the evidence he'd gathered could be suppressed. He didn't know what the damn point was.

He stared at his photos of the dumpster victim. He wasn't that much different than Eddie. He was a strong arm for hire. Sometimes he got caught, but he didn't ever stay behind bars for long. Maybe it was all right somebody had chopped him into pieces and thrown him out. It was the only way he'd ever get off the streets.

He rubbed his eyes and fought back a wave of exhaustion. He was so sick of this. The constant fighting to keep bad guys locked away. There had to be a better way.

He jumped when his phone rang and shoved Silvia's file back in its hiding place. "Denton."

All day long Lucy fought insane urges to push Dr. Banks into the wall, stab him with a scalpel, claw his eyes out, or conk him over the head with a chair. The anger was there, just under her skin; and he kept pushing at it.

He made snide comments about the old people. He made snide comments about Lucy's weight and how slow and useless she was. He expounded on how survival of the fittest needed to extend to the elderly as well.

She wished she could show him survival of the fittest with the business end of a golf club. But she didn't. She couldn't. She was his nurse. He was her boss. He was an ass, but he was still doing his job. And she was doing hers.

By the time she pulled up outside the gym, the anger had morphed into a hulking pile of rage. She was angry about everything. She was angry at her mom for telling her to be a good wife. She was angry at her father for being such an ass. She was angry at herself for marrying Richard. She was angry at daylight savings time, bank drive-thrus, and freaking water parks. She was angry at everything. Even cute little kittens. Because they didn't stay cute!

For a second she thought about calling her doctor and asking for an immediate referral to a counselor. But what could she say? I'm angry. I killed a man, and it made the anger less. But it's getting worse again. What should I do?

Lucy breathed deeply, forcing everything away. She wanted to go to the gym. She liked working out. She could do this. She could do this without getting angry.

Someone rapped lightly on her window, and Lucy jumped.

"You coming in?" Henry asked, white teeth flashing behind his big grin.

The heat that was covering her melted suddenly, pooling in her thighs. Her eyes widened. So that's what it felt like. She blushed, feeling more embarrassed than she ever had.

"Um..."

"I'll walk with you," he said.

She shrugged and slowly got out of her car. He was so big and muscly. She was so short and frumpy. They must look ridiculous even standing together. She and Richard fit in an odd way. He was old and ugly, and so was she.

"What do you think?" he asked.

"About what?" Lucy stammered.

"Angela."

"Oh. She's wonderful!" Lucy exclaimed with a grin. "She's patient, and she explains everything so well. I'm glad she's the trainer I got. I don't think I would have... Anyway... I like her."

"Good." He'd started walking towards the gym, and she reluctantly followed him, watching his leg muscles as she did. What did a man do with so much muscle?

"You're awful big," she blurted out. Oh god, that sounded wrong. "I mean, muscly. You're muscly!" That wasn't much better. He was grinning at her, but he didn't say anything, so she kept talking, trying to explain herself. "I mean, why? Oh never mind."

She was acting like a child. Richard would be mortified.

Henry chuckled, and Lucy's stomach tingled in response. "I like to work out," he said. "Also I'm a lineman, and it helps with the job to stay fit."

"Oh." Lucy didn't know what else to say. She didn't even know what a lineman was. "Um..."

"Yes?" He grinned at her.

"What's a lineman?"

He laughed, and Lucy turned red. She honestly wished the ground would just swallow her up. Or the anger would come back so she didn't feel so stupid. She could tell his laugh was good-natured and he wasn't laughing at her, but she still felt stupid.

"I work on the power lines," he finally said, eyes twinkling.

"Oh."

"Let's get you in to Angela. She probably thinks you've flown the coop."

Lucy blushed again. She wasn't good at conversation. She was with patients but not with handsome strangers. She wasn't good at that.

He opened the door and gestured for her to go ahead. She frowned and stepped past him. It had been a long time since anyone had held the door open for her. "Thanks," she whispered.

She saw Angela waiting for her, glanced at Henry, tried to smile, then walked quickly off.

"I think he likes you," Angela said.

"Huh?"

"Henry. I think he likes you."

"That's ridiculous!" Lucy snorted. "I'm old and fat. And he's... he's... not!"

"You're not old and fat," Angela said with a laugh.

"I am. I haven't been checked out in thirty years." She wasn't sure she'd ever been checked out, but she wasn't going to say that.

Angela smiled. "That's not because you're old or fat, Lucy. You're a beautiful woman. Still in the prime of your life. If only you could believe that, you'd see how much living you have left to do."

Lucy stared at her in shock. No one had ever called her beautiful. It almost hurt hearing it, and she was afraid to believe it. She didn't see beauty when she looked in the mirror. She saw downtrodden and worn.

"Now, let's go tone you up," Angela said cheerfully.

Lucy didn't get to think any more about Henry or what Angela had said because Angela kept her working hard for forty-five minutes, pushing and encouraging her at every turn. Afterwards they talked more about healthy lifestyles and food choices.

When Lucy headed home she felt more relaxed than she had all day. She just hoped it lasted. She heaved a sigh of relief when she pulled into the garage and saw Richard was gone.

She walked into the kitchen, hissing in irritation when she saw he hadn't eaten his meal but left it out on the counter again with a note that read "This is unacceptable."

"Screw you," she muttered, dumping the food into the trash.

She ate a piece of cheese toast then started going through her cabinets. Angela had encouraged her to take a look at her food and see how much of it had chemical additives.

"Chemical additives are hard for our bodies to process," Angela had said. "There have been a number of studies that suggest chemical additives can actually contribute to body fat."

Lucy had nodded, listening intently, but not really believing Angela. If additives were bad for people why would they allow them?

Lucy pulled out a box of crackers and read the ingredient

list. "Oh my god!" she exclaimed. There were over thirty ingredients, and she couldn't pronounce at least ten of them. She threw the box of crackers in the trash and picked up another box.

"Seriously?! This is ridiculous." She threw that box in the trash too. By the time she was finished her cabinets and refrigerator looked just like Mother Hubbard's. She wasn't sure how she was going to cook, but she wasn't using that junk.

Just then the door opened, and Richard walked in. "Damn it, Lucille! What the hell're you doing now?"

"Cleaning the fridge."

"It's almost twelve o'clock! You should be in bed by now."

Lucy stared at him. "Why? Am I a pumpkin?"

"What? No, goddamn it! You're old."

"I'm younger than you," Lucy hissed. "Why aren't you in bed?"

He stared at her like he'd never seen her before. "So is it your time? Did you stop taking your pills or something? I've never seen you like this."

"Like what?" Lucy snarled. It always came back to that. She was a woman. And women were emotionally unbalanced. She couldn't even count the number of times she'd heard it.

"You're unhinged," Richard said, tone softening, like he was concerned for her health. "Acting crazy. I'm worried about you."

For a second she almost believed him. And she might have, if it hadn't been for his eyes. He'd managed to soften his face, but his eyes were hard, and they were snapping angrily. He wasn't concerned about her. He was worried about his supper. His breakfast. His laundry.

Oh hell. She'd forgotten to pick up his dry-cleaning. She hoped his meeting wasn't on Monday.

"I'm fine," she said, trying to grin. The anger was making it hard. She wanted to yell at him, pelt his head with cans of food, and watch him scream like a girl. But he was standing in front of the window, and she didn't want to break it. Furthermore, she just wanted him to go away.

"You didn't make my dinner," he grunted.

"I did. You didn't heat it up."

"That's not my job."

The anger rose, filling her so much she had to force her hands closed. She wanted to beat on him until he disappeared.

"It is now," she ground out. "I won't be here for supper from now on. I'll be at the gym."

"That's bullshit, Lucille! You're my wife. You belong here."

"Cooking for you, cleaning up after you?" Lucy took a step towards him, trying to drop the can she had unintentionally picked up.

"Well, that's your job. You're the woman. You cook and clean."

"Really? And what do you do?" Lucy whispered, stepping nearer.

"I go to work."

"So do I."

"Well, I..." He didn't seem to know what to say.

She stepped closer, almost close enough to bash his head in.

He stepped back, suddenly seeming to realize her intent. "I'm going up to bed," he snapped, leaving before she could throw the can at him.

She glared after him. She was so sick of him. She'd wanted to... bash his head in. She dropped the can that was clutched in her hand. She hadn't meant to pick it up. She wished she hadn't. She was just so damn angry. And the anger wanted out. She wanted to follow him and push him down the stairs.

Do it. No! *It'll feel so good.* It would. She knew it would. She knew with a strange certainty that there would be nothing more satisfying than bashing his head in with a can of tomatoes.

"What's wrong with me?" she whispered. She needed to cool down before she did something stupid. She walked to the freezer and grabbed an ice cube, running it over her face.

It was so cold on her skin it burned, but the heat and anger faded a bit. She grabbed another cube and held one in both hands, watching as the ice melted and dripped onto the floor. It was like she had a raging fever. Only her fever was full of anger instead of sickness.

You should've killed him, angry her said. Nobody asked you! *One good knock over the head. Leave the body, "find" him in the morning, play the grieving wife.* SHUT THE HELL UP!

Richard slammed their bedroom door and tossed his shoes at the mirror. He wanted to toss Lucille at the mirror, but he knew he couldn't do that.

He had no idea what was going on with her, but it was damned inconvenient timing. He frowned, remembering the defiant look in her eyes. She'd argued with him, stood up to him, yelled at him! Who did she think she was?

Thirty years of marriage and she'd never, not once, argued with him. He'd made sure of it. He paced the room for a second, but he just couldn't think tonight. He was too frustrated and angry.

Between Emily not answering his calls and Lucille deciding she needed to have a spine, he was at the end of his rope. He needed a release, badly. But he'd just have to wait. Cinnamon would do in a pinch, but for some ridiculous reason it just wasn't the same if Emily wasn't forcing it out of him.

He sighed and climbed into bed. He just had to make it a little longer. And then he would be free.

7

That night Lucy did something she had never done, even though she had wanted to a few times. A few million times. She slept in the guest room.

At five AM she woke feeling happy and refreshed. She rolled out of bed and stretched. Then she went downstairs to make breakfast. Saturday was breakfast burrito day.

Not gonna happen, she thought as she opened the refrigerator and looked inside. She was going to need to go shopping. She'd thrown nearly everything out.

She hadn't gotten a chance to eat her oatmeal, and she still had some, so she pulled it out and started a pan of it cooking. She hummed as she got out the yogurt and strawberries.

She brewed coffee, ate by herself, cleaned up her dishes, left Richard a note, and drove to the grocery store. For two hours she picked up cans and boxes and read labels.

Then she walked out to her car, got inside, and sat there in a silent state of shock. Almost everything had something in it. It was like they were trying to kill her. Or at least make her fat.

I bet our fat butt is from chemicals, angry her said. You can't prove it. *Can. Stop eating chemicals.* How?! Lucy felt a whisper of despair. Everything had so much junk in it. How could she ever change the way she was eating? She didn't know how to cook any differently. She cooked the way her mom had taught her to.

She Googled "healthy eating" on her phone. Tons of websites came up, and it was completely overwhelming. She didn't know what to look at first, so she Googled "healthy food" instead. Still more websites. But on the side was a picture of a grocery store she recognized. It said local health food store, and that's what she wanted, healthy food. She'd never been there because Richard didn't have a high opinion of health food nuts. She just wouldn't tell him.

She drove across town and walked in, feeling a little exposed and silly. She grabbed a cart, walked down a random aisle, and started reading the ingredients on cans.

"Better," she muttered to herself. Maybe not perfect, but better. It would take her some time to figure out what she was doing, but she'd start here and work her way forward.

She made a slow circuit around the store, being very careful what she put in her cart. She bought enough stuff for a week and loaded it into her car. Change is hard, she thought. What if I'm still fat and old in a week, three weeks, a year? What then?

We're not fat and old! Lucy ignored the voice. Maybe if she stopped talking to it, it would go away. *I'm not going anywhere,* angry her said with a snort.

Lucy drove home, frowning when she saw Richard's car was still there. She had hoped he'd be gone. She glanced at the clock. It was already one o'clock, so he was probably awake.

He was. He was sitting at the table, reading the paper, and eating his oatmeal. She hoped it was cold.

"There you are!" he snapped.

She put her bags on the counter. "I left you a note."

"My breakfast is cold!"

Good. "Use the microwave."

"I shouldn't have to!" he barked.

Lucy felt the anger growing, so she walked back out and got the rest of her groceries. He followed her. Not to help though, to berate.

"I don't understand what's going on with you!" he shouted. "The last couple days you've been acting crazy, not like yourself at all. You need professional help, Lucille! Call your doctor and make an appointment."

She shouldered past him, dropped the grocery bags on the floor, and turned with a snarl. "There's nothing wrong with me!"

"There is! You haven't been cooking or cleaning. You didn't pick up my dry-cleaning. You haven't been you!"

Heat poured over her, filling every facet of her mind. "I HAVE been cooking!" she screamed. "I HAVE been cleaning; I HAVE been picking up after your lazy ass!" She stepped toward him, raising her finger to point. "Just like I have been for the last thirty years! What have you done for ME?!"

Richard's eyes were wide as he stumbled backwards. "What do you mean? I go to work!"

"SO! I go to work too! AND do all that other stuff! It's time you started taking care of yourself!"

"What?"

"You're not a child, and I'm not your mommy! You're a grown man. Fix your own damn food!" she screamed, poking him in the chest.

He blinked at her, as if her words made no sense whatsoever. "What?"

"FIX YOUR OWN DAMN FOOD!" Lucy screamed, fighting the urge to punch him in the face. "Damn I wished I'd picked a different horse!"

"What the hell are you talking about?" Richard's face was a pale purple, and Lucy knew if she stayed here he'd start yelling at her. She had to get away from him before she did something she'd regret. She was so angry; she was livid; she felt like she might explode.

She grabbed her keys off the counter and ran to her car. She wanted to tear his face off. She wanted to beat his head in with his own arms. She wanted to smash his face through the window. She wanted to make him pay for every minute of her life he'd stripped from her. She wanted to kill him. Richard. Her husband. The father of her children.

What was wrong with her? Why was she thinking these thoughts? Richard was the same ass he'd always been. Nothing had changed. Why did she suddenly care?

You should've always cared. He treats you like crap. Yeah but... *But nothing! A husband is meant to love and protect you, not belittle you and make you into a slave.* He didn't... I mean, he doesn't... oh shut up.

Richard watched Lucille drive away with a frown. Damn it! She had actually yelled at him. Yelled! He'd never heard her yell. Not ever. Something was seriously wrong.

He picked up his phone and called Addie. "Hi, Addie, it's Daddy."

"Daddy! How are you?"

"Good, sweetheart, but I'm worried about your mom."

"Mom? Why?"

"Have you talked to her lately?" He had to be careful, just had to gently lead her where he wanted her to go.

"Last week. She seemed fine."

"She didn't seem... different?"

"No. Daddy, what's going on?"

"I'm not sure. I just thought maybe she had confided in you or told you what's going on. She's been different lately." He waited for a second then said softly, "I don't know, I thought maybe she was giving into her time of the month, but it's carried on." He put his feet on the coffee table and smiled as another thought occurred to him. "And I think she's been drinking more lately."

Addie didn't respond for a minute. He knew she liked to think things out, so he waited patiently. "Has she seen her doctor?" she finally asked.

Like a horse to water. "I asked her if she might consider talking to her doctor, and she refused."

"That's not like her."

"I know."

"I'll try to feel her out, Daddy. I'm sorry I'm not there to be more helpful. Just, I don't know, maybe just be sweet with her, try to help her get through this."

"I'm doing my best, Addie; she just keeps pushing me away." He paused, then whispered. "I love her so much."

"I know you do. I'll keep in touch, okay?"

"Okay. Thank you. Love you. Talk to you soon."

Richard chuckled softly as he disconnected. Females were so easy. He glanced at the clock. Emily wouldn't be free for another couple hours, but there were other ways to get what he needed.

Lucy drove to the river walk and parked on the backside.

The backside was usually deserted because it was kind of creepy, and most people preferred to walk along the river than through the woods.

But today she just wanted some quiet time and some space to think. Maybe if she walked fast enough she could burn away all that hideous anger.

It's not hideous. It's healthy. Healthy?! Anger is NOT healthy! It's like acid. It's eating away at me! *Sure, but in a good way.* What? What could possibly be good about acid? *It's eating away at Lucille. So you can be Lucy.*

Lucy felt all the color drain from her face. Was that really what it was doing? But really who was Lucille? What did she like? What was she interested in?

Lucy walked forward blindly, trying to think. She loved her kids, but they were grown and gone, except for Nate and breakfast. She didn't have any hobbies or interests. She didn't mind being a nurse, but she was a nurse because that was the career she'd picked when she was ten years old and they had handed out assignments in class. It was the horse she'd picked.

She tried to think of anything she actually cared about or liked. She cooked because she had to, cleaned because she had to.

"Oh my god," she whispered, sitting on a bench. "I'm nothing."

The voice didn't argue with her, didn't say anything. For once Lucy wished it would. She wanted to be wrong, but she wasn't. Lucy didn't exist. Lucy was an empty shell. But an empty shell could be filled. She'd start with the gym because she wanted to be fit. What else? What else was Lucy in to?

"Hey you!" a voice yelled, breaking her thoughts.

She glanced up, startled to see the young man from the other day, Jay, striding towards her, face a nasty shade of red.

"You meddlesome old bat! You should've minded your own damn business! Julie broke up with me because of you!"

Lucy stared at him in shock for a moment. The closer he got, the more intimidated she felt, until she almost apologized for her behavior. But then the anger rolled in. Jay was a jerk. Julie was better off without him.

"I just told her what she wanted to hear," she said with a shrug.

"Who the hell do you think you are?" he screamed at her, standing just in front of her.

Lucy's nostrils flared. He was invading her space. Yelling at her and invading her space. She didn't like it. Not one bit. She stood slowly and said, "Back off!"

But he didn't back off. He raised his hand and turned it into a fist. Lucy didn't know if he was really planning to hit her, but she wasn't going to wait to find out.

She jumped at him, surprised to find that her key ring was already clutched in her hand, keys facing outward towards his face. She jabbed him hard in the cheek, jerking when blood burst across her face.

He yelled in pain but grabbed her arm, jerking her in tight. "I'll get you for that you crazy bitch!"

That was exactly the wrong thing to say. "Nobody calls me bitch!" she snarled, smashing the keys into his face again and again as quickly as possible and forcing him to drop her arm and defend himself.

She felt his cheek give under the force of her keys. Blood splattered, hitting her mouth, but she was too angry to care.

She pushed forward angrily, punching him in the eyes. They fell to the ground together, and even though he was bigger than her and younger, she landed on top, taking him by surprise.

"Get the fuck off me!" he screamed as he hit the ground, but she didn't care. She was too angry to care. He'd raised his hand to attack her. He'd threatened her. He'd called her bitch. She wanted him to pay.

She punched his face again and again and again. Blood spurted wildly, and he clawed at her hands, trying to stop her. He was still yelling, but his words had become garbled and incoherent.

Anger poured through her. She hated him. She hated how he'd talked to his girlfriend. She hated the look in his eyes and the words that spouted from his mouth. She wanted him to die.

His face was gooshy under her hand, like punching a bundle of wet socks. Suddenly he stopped fighting her and started grabbing at his throat. His eyes bulged, and his face turned blue under the blood.

Lucy ignored his gasps, drawing her hand back and hitting him again and again. His hands ripped at hers one last time, then his eyes rolled up in his head, and his body shuddered and went still.

Her keys slammed into his face once more, but then she stopped herself. He was dead. She could see he was dead. How could he be dead? His face was cut and mashed to hell, but she was certain that wouldn't have killed him.

The anger was fading, leaving her cold, and she suddenly realized he'd choked. Probably on his own teeth given the condition of his mouth. She fought not to gag. She hadn't really meant to kill him. Not at first.

He'd threatened her, and she'd been sure he was about to hit her. She'd known if she didn't beat him to it, she was screwed. So she'd jumped at him and started hammering her keys into his face.

Once she'd gotten started she'd definitely WANTED to kill him. She'd wanted to make him pay for everything bad he'd ever done. But she hadn't really meant to kill him, not really.

She heard a dog bark and glanced around in horror. She was on a public walking trail in the middle of the day. It wouldn't be long until someone came along. She needed to get out of here now. She scrambled off his body, gasping when she realized her shirt was covered in blood.

She quickly wiped her hands and keys on the back of her shirt, glancing around frantically to make sure no one was in sight. She pulled her shirt over her head, wiped off her face with the outside, turned the shirt inside out, and slipped it back on.

She briefly considered moving his body, but she already knew she wasn't strong enough. Her only chance was to get out of here. She searched the ground to make sure she hadn't left anything behind and started walking back towards her car as fast as she could.

She fought the urge to run. She couldn't run now. She had to keep walking. She needed to act normal. Not like she'd just beaten a man to death.

She just hoped she didn't run into anyone. And she hoped she made it to her car and out onto the road before anyone found the body.

Her hands trembled as she opened her car door and slipped inside. I can't believe I just did that, she thought anxiously. *Felt good, didn't it?* No! Damn it! It didn't! I'm covered in a man's blood. He's dead because I killed him. One time I can excuse. But twice? No!

He was gonna hurt you. Maybe. *Could you risk it?* I don't know, damn it. Leave me alone!

Lucy buried her face in her hands. What was happening to her? And why? She swallowed a sob. She needed to get home. She needed to drive home and clean up. Her breathing came faster and faster. What if Richard was there? She had no place else to go; she'd have to risk it.

She started her car and reached for the shifter to put it in drive. Pain shot through her hand. She closed it, then opened it slowly. One of the keys must have been facing in because she had deep, bloody gouges in her palm. She turned her hand over, looking at it. Her knuckles were scraped and raw. And her wrist was beginning to ache fiercely.

You should add punching to your gym list. Just shut up!

Lucy carefully shifted and drove slowly home, keeping a wide eye out for police cars. She pulled into the garage, heaving a sigh of relief when she saw that Richard was gone.

She walked in, quickly started a load of laundry, adding the bloody clothes she was wearing. She washed her keys with soap and boiling hot water, hoping it didn't ruin the fob. Then she went upstairs and climbed into a hot shower. Her hand burned like hell.

She would add punching to her list. But not because the voice said so. Because she wanted to know how.

She scrubbed her face and hair furiously. She didn't want any of Jay's blood on her. She couldn't believe she'd killed him. She couldn't believe she'd killed two men in under a week. That was insane. She was insane. She needed help. But how could she get help without turning herself in? She couldn't. And she couldn't turn herself in. Not now. Not when she'd just started feeling.

She scrubbed herself until the water turned cold. After she dried herself off and dressed in cozy clothes, she poured herself a glass of wine and snuggled into her favorite recliner.

Her hands were still shaking. She couldn't get them to stop. She still didn't quite understand what had happened. Jay had verbally attacked her. She'd defended herself. He'd raised his hand; she'd felt threatened. So she'd attacked. She'd wanted to attack. She'd wanted to bash his face in. She'd wanted to when she'd first seen him with Julie.

She rubbed a hand over her face. The anger was changing her. Making her aggressive and violent. She didn't mind standing up for herself. She didn't mind protecting herself. But she did mind the killing. Why had she killed them?

What else would you have done? What do you mean? *How else would you have protected yourself?* By... um... by... *Exactly.*

Lucy opened her mouth to argue, but she couldn't. She didn't know what to say. She was alive, and they weren't. If she hadn't killed them she couldn't be sure that she would be alive. And she wanted to be alive.

You did what you had to do.

Maybe. Just maybe angry her was right.

8

Detective Sanders stared at Jay Johnson's body. He had only just turned twenty-two, but he already had a criminal record. Assault. Assault with a deadly weapon. More assault. Breaking and entering, followed by assault. Jay Johnson had a nasty temper.

"Damn," she said. "I'm not sure his own mother would recognize him."

"Took a beating, didn't he?" Denton said.

For once they'd arrived at the same time. Not that it mattered. Sanders could see well enough over Denton's shoulder.

She'd already talked to the jogger who had found him. Fortunately the man was an ex-marine. He hadn't vomited or gone into shock or broken down into sobs. She hated interviewing sobbers. They were so hard to understand.

The sun beat down on her back as she walked around Denton to get a better view of the rest of the body. The kid's face was trashed. He looked like he'd had a fight with a lawn mower and lost. But there weren't any wounds on his body. Just his face. Just like the dumpster job. And she'd bet her new Salvatore loafers that just like the dumpster job the killer had been irate. Totally irate.

"What killed him you think?"

"Couldn't say yet."

"You could make a guess."

"I don't make guesses," Denton growled.

"But you could."

"No. Why don't you go scare someone straight, play bad cop, torture your boy toy, I don't care. Just get the hell outta my way."

Sanders chuckled softly. "You're so cheerful today."

"Sanders!"

"I'm going. Gotta talk to the victim's family anyway." Denton just grunted, but Sanders knew he'd call when he had something.

Damn she annoyed him! Impatient! It was a damn process. He couldn't just spout off "Well, I think he probably choked on his own damn teeth". What if he was wrong?

Denton took another careful photograph. Not that he was ever wrong but still, it paid to be careful. He never made wild conjectures until he had the evidence to back it up. Never.

Lucy had fallen asleep in her chair, glass of wine in hand. When she woke she was stiff, but she'd slept wonderfully.

She put down her glass and stretched towards the ceiling. Her mind felt clear. In fact she felt good all over. It sickened her just a bit that killing someone could make her feel so good.

She reached towards her toes. She couldn't touch them

yet, but she was closer than she had been the first time she'd tried. She stretched from side to side, then started to tap her sternum like Angela had showed her.

She gasped in pain and slowly opened and closed her hand. It hurt like hell, and the cuts on her knuckles were red and puffy. She stretched it out slowly. She really would have to add punching to her list.

"What the hell're you doing?!" Richard snapped from behind her.

Lucy jerked in surprise. She hadn't heard him coming, and she hadn't expected him to be up so early. It couldn't be much after five.

"Stretching," she replied, voice softer than she would have liked.

"You look like an idiot."

Lucy felt herself deflate a little, but then she remembered she didn't give a crap what Richard thought. She sat down on the floor and reached for her toes.

"Where's my breakfast?" Richard demanded.

"I'll make you something when I make my own, but you'll have to wait."

"I'm hungry now!"

"Then make yourself something."

"That's not my job!"

A rush of anger rolled over her, but Lucy closed her eyes, breathing deeply. She didn't need to be angry. She could calmly and reasonably state what she wanted.

"Then you'll have to wait," she said evenly.

"I'm making you an appointment with your doctor," he threatened.

Lucy stood and faced him. "You can't actually do that," she said with a smile. "I mean, you can call and make an appointment, but you can't make me go. I don't need to see a doctor. I'm fine. Better than fine. You're just pissed 'cause my fine equals you not getting waited on hand and foot. That's over. You'll have to start taking care of yourself some. Get used to it."

Richard's face turned bright red. His hands flexed, and Lucy raised an eyebrow. He didn't actually think he could hit her, did he?

"I'm going out!" he finally growled.

"Okay."

As she dressed she thought things over. The anger was clearly a problem. It needed managed. She had every right to stand up for herself. Verbally and physically, but fantasizing about killing people, especially Richard and Dr. Banks, was not healthy.

Whenever they made her mad, she needed to breathe, count to ten, and respond verbally in whatever way needed. She hadn't even yelled at Richard just now. But she had still won the skirmish.

The truth was she was beginning to like this new her. She liked not getting pushed around. She liked not cooking the same damn meal every Tuesday. She liked working out and talking to Henry and taking time for herself. It was nice.

All she needed to do was to ignore the voice and control the anger. If she did those two things she was going to be just fine.

She felt much better having a plan. She was good at plans and lists and cleaning up messes. Her life was made up of doing those things. Which wasn't a bad thing. She just wanted to expand her horizons a bit, develop a personality, figure out who Lucy was.

While she ate her breakfast she flipped through the paper

looking for the crime reports. There it was. Jay Johnson. Found murdered on the river walk. The police were asking anyone with information or who might have seen anything to call in.

Lucy reread the article several times. They didn't have anything. And as far as she knew the only one with any information was her. And she wouldn't be calling in.

She couldn't believe she'd killed two men. She couldn't believe she'd gotten away with it. At least she was pretty sure she'd gotten away with it.

She kept thinking the guilt would kick in and eat at her, making her feel terrible. And eventually, if it went on long enough she would be forced to turn herself in.

But she didn't feel guilty. And she had no intention of turning herself in. In fact, she refused to feel bad. They had attacked her. They had tried to hurt her. She hadn't done anything wrong.

For a second she allowed herself to remember killing them, to remember the rush of anger and the relief afterwards. She remembered tearing at their faces; she remembered the warm blood, the terror in their eyes, in their voices. But she didn't really care about all that.

What she cared about was the moment afterward. When it was done, and they were dead, and she'd used all her angry energy killing them. That's the moment she liked. The moment that made her feel... good.

She pushed the paper to the side and stood. She couldn't just sit around all day reliving those moments of relaxation. She had work to do.

Her phone rang, and she swallowed a yelp. She could tell from the ringer it was Addie. She thought about not answering, but she hadn't talked to Addie in a few days so she answered with a cheery, "Morning, baby, you're up early."

"Just wanted to make sure I caught you before you got busy. What're you doing today?"

Lucy shrugged, then remembered Addie couldn't see her. "I don't know. Probably do some cleaning."

Addie didn't respond right away. Finally she asked, "How're things going?"

"Good."

"Oh."

"Addie, what's going on?"

"Nothing, I just wanted to check up on you. Are you feeling okay?"

"Yes! Why wouldn't I be?"

"I don't know. Dad just mentioned that you hadn't seemed quite yourself lately. He's worried about you."

Lucy sighed. She hadn't thought he'd stoop so low, but she should have known. He'd use any tactic to get her back in line.

"I'm fine, Addie. I've started going to the gym after work, and your dad doesn't care for that. He's opposed to using the microwave to heat up his supper." She laughed lightly like it was a silly thing when it really wasn't.

"Oh. Is that really all? A gym?"

"Yeah, I've been feeling my age, and I just want to feel... better about myself."

"Okay. Well, if you need to talk or something, you know I'm always here," Addie said, sounding a little unconvinced.

"I know, baby. Honestly, everything's fine. I think your father just overreacted is all."

"Alright. Talk later?"

"Yep. Love you."

Lucy hung up the phone with a roll of her eyes. It always seemed like the kids took Richard's side. Like she was the bad guy or the stupid one or the failure. But she wasn't, and she was getting a little sick of him using them against her.

Kill him. Problem solved. Shut up. If I want your opinion, I'll ask for it.

She cleared the table and started her chores. She cleaned the house because she liked having a clean house. She watered her tulips. She rearranged her kitchen cabinets. She went for a walk around the block, stopping and visiting with a few neighbors along the way. The day sped by, and before she knew it, it was Monday again.

When she woke up, she reminded herself of her plan. Breathe. Count to ten. Respond verbally. And it seemed to work. She easily ignored Richard's criticisms during breakfast, and she didn't imagine killing him. In fact, she hadn't imagined killing him in over twenty-four hours, so she felt she was making progress already.

She picked up his dry-cleaning on her way to work because she knew he would never do it, but she did it cheerfully. She didn't mind running errands.

She ignored everything stupid Dr. Banks said, breathing and counting every time she felt the anger rise. It worked. She only slipped once. When he said Mrs. Feldman was old enough that she should just pack it in. She hadn't been able to ignore that, but she had forced herself to put down the pair of scissors she'd picked up before she could do anything bad with them.

After work she drove to the gym. She was excited about going inside. She already felt stronger and more energetic, and it had only been a handful of days. She couldn't wait to see how she would feel in a week or two.

She moved to get out of her car, but her heart jumped and her mouth went dry. A police car had just pulled into the lot and was cruising towards her. She held her breath, eyes widening as it drove closer and closer. It parked right beside her, and she felt her whole body break out in nervous sweat.

Was he there for her? How could he know? How had he found her? She watched him tensely, but he didn't pay any attention to her. Instead he made a phone call.

Relief was slow when she realized he wasn't there for her. She was fine. There was no way anyone could connect her with those men. No way.

She walked into the gym on shaky legs, ignoring the desire to glance behind her, to make sure he wasn't watching her. She knew he wasn't. She opened the door and slipped inside.

Already she'd grown to like the sounds of the gym. They were comforting, relaxing, invigorating. Angela greeted her, and they got to work.

"Lucy!" Angela exclaimed after a few minutes had passed. "What happened to your hand?"

"Huh?" Lucy glanced at her hand. It didn't hurt too much anymore, so she'd mostly forgotten about it. But the backs of her knuckles were still puffy and red. "Um... I hit something?"

"What a board?"

"Um..." Lucy didn't know what to say. She hadn't concocted a story for her hand. She'd forgotten about it. "My, um... tulip bed wasn't cooperating."

"Damn! You go hard core."

Lucy shrugged. "That reminds me, I'd like to learn how to punch."

Angela laughed. "You may wanna wait a week, but Henry could probably help you with that."

Lucy blushed. She wasn't sure she could ask Henry to help her. Every time she was near him her brain went all wiggly. "Maybe," she murmured.

She left the gym feeling good. If only she'd known how invigorating working out was thirty years ago.

In the spirit of change, she went home, pulled out her computer and signed up for Facebook. Richard thought Facebook was a waste of time, but Lucy didn't have any friends. She used to have friends, but year by year things had come up and people had faded away. Her last good friend had been Addie's best friend's mom. When Addie was five.

It took her a good hour to find all her old friends, but she did, and she friended all of them. Then she looked at several community pages and signed up for a bunch of events. Wine and paint. Intro to photography. She even joined a romance book club.

It was a good day. The best she'd had in a long time. She felt relaxed, in control, and happy. She couldn't remember the last time she'd felt happy.

Richard lay on his back, staring at the ceiling. He was hot and sweaty; maybe he'd take a shower before he went home. Cinnamon had already left, but he only had the room for another hour, so he didn't want to drift off to sleep.

He didn't want to go home to Lucille. He hated going home to Lucille. Her face, her voice, everything about her just pissed him off. How he'd managed to make three kids with her was beyond him.

He took a swig of whiskey from his flask, then cut the tape off his other wrist. If only he didn't have such shitty luck. He kept thinking it would change one of these days, but it hadn't yet.

He'd just have to make his own luck.

For days everything went as planned. Lucy still cleaned and cooked and worked. She did all those things, and she didn't even mind doing them. She made sure to keep Nate's creamer on hand, and she actually laughed when she saw ruby red lipstick on Richard's collar as she started the laundry one day.

But she cooked what she wanted to cook, and she went to the gym every evening after work. She went for walks, she tried jogging, and she even chatted with Henry a few times, but not without her tongue tying into knots.

She stopped jumping every time she saw a police car drive by. They had nothing, and she knew it. She was home free.

She went to her wine and paint class. She liked the wine, but she wasn't a painter. Too much mess. She went to the photography class and learned she liked taking photographs of people in moments. And she learned she could make new friends. She immediately hit it off with a woman her own age named Stacy.

Stacy was sweet, but she also knew who she was and what she wanted. She'd been married as long as Lucy, but she actually liked her husband. She had two grandbabies and three dogs, and she was nice.

For the first time in over thirty years, Lucy felt like she was a person. Like she had her own thoughts and likes and dislikes. She felt free, new, happy. It was wonderful.

The only problem was the anger. At first counting to ten had helped. Then she'd had to start counting to fifteen, then twenty. Two weeks after she'd started, she stopped. Counting didn't help. Breathing didn't help. Nothing helped. She was still angry, and she didn't know what to do about it.

The fantasies returned in full force. She killed Richard with his silk neck tie, his golf clubs, her hair dryer, the cheese grater. It was morbid. It was terrifying. She wanted it to stop. She told it to stop.

But the angrier she got, the more vocal angry her became. Urging her to kill Richard, to kill the hobo who had flipped her off for not giving him any money, to kill the checker at the liquor store who hadn't carded her when she bought her wine. Angry her wanted to kill everyone.

Well, not EVERYONE. Not Angela or Henry or Mrs. Feldman or Stacy. Not even Nate. Nate hadn't complained once. And he'd stopped cussing so much in front of her. In fact, the other day he'd even said "Thank you for breakfast," when he left. Maybe there was hope for him after all.

But those were the few exceptions. Even Addie was starting to annoy her. Lucy didn't know what Richard had said to Addie, but she called every couple days asking how Lucy was. And she used that tone Lucy sometimes used on patients who were in denial about their health conditions.

"So have you been to the doctor recently?" Addie asked one day.

"Yes, Addie. I went a couple months ago."

"What did he say?"

"He said everything was fine."

"How're you feeling?"

"Fine. Better than ever."

"Are you sure?"

"Yes, Addie. I'm sure. Will you please stop worrying? There's nothing to worry about."

Lucy had only briefly wanted to punch Addie in the face. Not enough to really hurt her just enough to make her shut up. And that worried her. Addie had always been her sweet one, the one she enjoyed spending time with the most, but now she was avoiding her, ignoring her phone calls and texts.

Lucy didn't know what to do. She didn't know how to handle the anger or the voice. But she knew she'd have to do something and soon.

Detective Sanders stared in irritation at the two unsolved case files on her desk. Somehow she knew they were connected, but she didn't have any evidence, any eyewitnesses, any leads. She was dead in the water.

She always closed her cases, always. These would be no exception. She'd just have to look harder. There had to be a connection somewhere. She'd interview Johnson's family again. She'd look harder at Wood's connections. She'd find something.

Richard tossed his shirt on the floor with an irritated grunt. Ever since Lucille had moved into the guest room his room looked like a pig sty. Apparently, in addition to not cooking and having sex, she didn't think it was her job to pick up after him anymore.

The last couple weeks had been annoying as hell. He'd yelled at her, tried to guilt her, tried to manipulate her, tried to intimidate her, and berate her, but none of his usual tricks were working. She'd smile at him benignly then walk off and do whatever the hell she wanted.

It absolutely baffled him. For thirty years she'd been nothing but a rug to walk on and now she suddenly had a spine.

It was time to change tactics. Perhaps it was time to give Lucille's boss a call. And if that didn't work... Well, he'd think of something.

My Better Half

It was five. Her alarm hadn't gone off, but Lucy was already awake. She'd been awake for hours, dreading Monday. She didn't want to go to work. Friday had been a very bad day. She'd killed Dr. Banks in her mind no less than fifteen times, and she honestly wasn't sure she could be in the same room as him without actually trying to kill him.

She sighed but pulled herself out of bed. She was glad she had moved into the guestroom. It was wonderful finally having her own space. She still felt a little guilty for not cleaning Richard's room, but she figured he was a big boy and he could handle it.

It had taken Richard five days to notice she was gone. When he finally had he'd cornered her in the kitchen and snapped, "Why the hell did you move out of our room?"

"Because I don't want to have sex with you and you snore."

He had stared at her in confusion for a moment, face turning white, then red, then a sick shade of purple. "It's just as well. Having sex with you is like trying to have sex with a frozen corpse," he'd sneered.

That had been a week ago, so counting to seventeen and breathing deeply several times had prevented her from using her coffee cup as a club on his tiny dick.

She'd felt such a sense of relief telling him that she wasn't going to have sex with him ever again. He didn't try very often, but when he did Lucy never said no. Her mom had told her time and again it was her duty to have sex with her husband. It didn't matter whether or not she liked it; it was her duty, and Lucy was very good at doing her duty.

But she'd had thirty years to think it over, and she'd decided she didn't give a whit if it was her duty. She would never let Richard lay his fat, ugly hands on her ever again. She'd beat him to death first.

He didn't do a thing for her sexually. He never had. She'd married him because she'd wanted to get away from her father, he'd been relatively handsome at the time, and he'd asked. Not because he gave her the shudders. Not like, god help her, Henry did.

A shiver rolled down her spine just thinking of Henry. She enjoyed the sensation for a second then pushed it away. She was still a married woman. She'd still picked her horse.

She stretched and fully touched her toes. She was going to have to go clothes shopping this week because her pants were much too loose. She'd looked in the mirror last night and almost liked what she'd seen.

She sighed. If only being fit was enough. She was making changes, and she wasn't letting Richard walk all over her. She wasn't a doormat or a weakling. She was growing a spine.

It seemed like the anger should go away now, but angry her wasn't satisfied. Angry her had fifty years' worth of built up anger, and she wanted to let it out. Angry her wanted blood.

Lucy made breakfast, cleaned up, and drove as slowly as she could to work, wishing she had called in sick.

The first thing Dr. Banks said when Lucy arrived was, "I don't know why Ms. James keeps coming in. I can't do a thing for her. She's fat. If she lost a hundred pounds, then maybe I could help her."

Lucy bit her lip. She wanted to tell him that maybe it wasn't as easy as all that to lose weight. Maybe Ms. James was affected by some chemical in her food or her food containers. Maybe she literally couldn't lose weight.

"She's as fat as a horse," he said with an agitated snort.

Lucy growled. Her hands clenched. She released them. They clenched again. It wouldn't be hard. All she had to do was push him into the table, shove a scalpel through his eye, scream, and say he tripped. It was a freak accident.

She tried breathing. She tried counting. She tried closing her eyes and blocking his nasal voice, but nothing worked. She was so hot, so angry, she felt like steam should be wafting off her. She needed to kill him.

"No!" she hissed, trying to control herself.

"No what?" he asked.

"Um... no..." He'd broken her thoughts, and suddenly she felt like she could control it. "You should discuss diet with her. Eating foods without additives might help her lose weight."

"What kinda hippie crap have you been reading?"

The anger rolled back in full force, and Lucy couldn't hold it back any longer. She dropped the chart and ran as fast as she could out the back door. She ran up the street until she was far enough away from him that she couldn't accidentally kill him. Why did he have to be such an ass?

There was only one solution. She was going to have to quit. *Or you could kill him.* I CANNOT kill him! *Can.* Damn you! You can't just kill people 'cause they're assholes. You can't! *You can.* Are we arguing semantics? Lucy thought agitatedly. *Um... I dunno. Are we?* I don't know. Yes, you physically can, but morally it's totally unacceptable. *Oh, so we WERE arguing semantics.* Shut up!

She walked up and down the street, fanning her face with her hands. She couldn't go back in that office until she had her anger under control. Finally, after fifteen minutes of walking, she no longer felt consumed with anger. Just fear. Fear that she would do something she couldn't undo. Fear that she would make a mess she couldn't clean up.

9

"Where the hell did you run off to?" Dr. Banks barked as soon as Lucy stepped back into the office.

She shook her head in frustration. He had absolutely no sense of self preservation. The anger boiled up, but instead of bashing him over the head with the computer keyboard, she said, "I quit."

They stared at each other in shock for a minute. Both because they couldn't believe she'd said it.

"You can't just quit!" he finally blurted.

"I can," she said, surprised at herself. "I am."

"With no notice?"

"Nope. Quitting. Right this minute. I simply cannot work for you another second. You're a... a jerk! A total jerk!" *You go girl!*

His mouth opened like a fish, and she almost laughed, but she was working too hard to control herself; the keyboard was still in reach.

"You treat patients like they don't deserve your help, like

they're unworthy. You have no compassion, no empathy." His face turned red, and he started to say something, but she wasn't done. "You're a terrible doctor. You sometimes treat the symptoms, but you care nothing for the human, the person, the soul behind the symptoms. I've put up with your ridiculousness for fifteen years. I'm done!"

She grabbed her purse and left before he recovered enough to argue with her. She knew she was leaving him in a bind. She knew he couldn't operate functionally without a nurse. But she simply couldn't be in the same room with him without wanting to choke him to death. She was saving his life.

That was amazing! Shut up! *You were like in his face!* I said shut up. *But I can't. I'm so impressed with you. I mean, I think I love you.* Will you shut the hell up?! Anyway, you are me. You can't love me! *Oh, but I do.* Lucy shook her head, wishing she could block angry hers voice with earplugs.

She drove in a circle around the city, wondering what to do. She'd never quit a job before. Not like that. It felt... It felt good. She wished she'd done it years ago, but now she felt a bit adrift. She didn't mind being a nurse, but was there something else she'd rather do? She certainly didn't want to sit home and do nothing all day.

She stopped at the corner store, purchased a paper, and drove to a coffee shop. She flipped to the help wanted section and looked over the ads. There were plenty of jobs for nurses and not that much for anyone else. Nothing looked interesting.

She hated to do it, but she pulled out her phone and called Addie.

"Mom? Are you okay?"

"I'm fine. Why?"

"It's the middle of the day."

"So?"

"You never call in the middle of the day."

"Oh. I just quit my job."

The line was silent for a minute. Then, "Seriously?"

"Yes."

"Wow! I mean, that's huge! Are you okay?"

Lucy rolled her eyes. Why wouldn't she be? "I'm fine; I'm just not sure what to do now. There're lots of jobs in the paper for nurses, but I thought I might want to try something new."

"Really?" Addie's voice was full of disbelief.

"Really."

"But why? You're a wonderful nurse!"

She was starting to wish she'd called Nate instead. "Yes, but I thought I'd like to try something different."

"Okay. Well the best jobs usually advertise online through social networking sites like LinkedIn and Indeed."

"What?"

"It's a lot different than the days of filling out a paper application and turning it in."

"Huh."

"If you're sure you want to do this, I'll email you some links later today so you can get started."

"Okay, would you?"

"Yeah. Are you sure you're okay?"

Lucy sighed. "Yes. I'm fine. I just got a little fed up with Dr. Banks's attitude, that's all."

"Oh." Addie was silent for a minute, then she said, "And I'm mad at you!"

"What? Why?"

"You didn't tell me you signed up on Facebook!"

Lucy blushed. It had been fun to reconnect with all her old

friends, but she'd been a little embarrassed, so she hadn't friended anyone in her family yet.

"I just did it the other day." She wasn't lying; it just depended on your definition of "the other day".

"I sent you a friend request."

"Okay."

"Listen, Mom, I gotta go. Talk more tonight?"

"Okay; love you."

"Love you too."

Addie hung up, and Lucy was left alone with her lukewarm coffee and useless paper.

Well this was a fine pickle. She had no job, an anger problem, and two dead bodies lurking in her closet. Not her literal closet, her... She shook her head. She was a mess. Which was stupid because she was doing better than she'd ever done.

"Lucille?"

Lucy glanced up and exclaimed, "Mrs. Feldman! How nice to see you!"

"You too, dear. No work today?"

Lucy grimaced. "I quit."

"Oh dear. Can I sit?"

"Yes! I'm sorry. Please do!"

Mrs. Feldman put her coffee and scone on the table and sat across from Lucy. "Finally got fed up, did you?" she asked in an amused tone.

"Of?" Lucy asked cautiously.

"Dr. Banks! Most obnoxious man I've ever known. If I could find someone else who accepted my Medicare I wouldn't go anywhere near him!"

Lucy laughed with surprise. "I wasn't sure... I mean he does a little better with the patients than... Oh never mind. He's a terrible person."

"So what will you do?" Mrs. Feldman asked, taking a bite of her scone.

"I honestly don't know. There seem to be plenty of jobs for nurses, but I want to try something different. My daughter said I have to use some kind of social networking sites. I'm starting to wish I hadn't quit after all. Things have changed a lot in the last fifteen years."

"Sure have," Mrs. Feldman said softly. "Sure have. Good ol' days of just walking in and saying 'Hey can I have a job' are long gone."

Lucy nodded, feeling a little depressed.

"But fortunately you know someone who knows someone," Mrs. Feldman said with a wink.

"What?"

"My son owns a vineyard, and he's been looking for a new visitor center manager. You'd be perfect."

"Please tell me you're serious right now!" Lucy exclaimed.

"Yes. I'll call him right now. Give me a minute."

Mrs. Feldman stood rather shakily and walked over to a corner to make her phone call. Lucy waited anxiously, feeling a strange sense of excitement. She loved wine. She liked people. The idea that she could actually make money by giving people wine was a crazy idea.

"He said to come by his office tomorrow," Mrs. Feldman said, handing Lucy a business card. "Here's his address."

Lucy stared at it. "Seriously? You're wonderful!"

"You're a fantastic nurse, Lucille, but more than that you understand people, you're patient, you're kind. You'll be wonderful at anything you do." Mrs. Feldman smiled and added, "Enjoy your coffee. I'll see you later."

"Bye," Lucy murmured, feeling a little awed that Mrs.

Feldman thought that of her. Of course Mrs. Feldman didn't know that Lucy had almost driven her car over a pedestrian who'd walked before the walk sign turned on. On purpose. Because it had majorly ticked her off.

But fortunately, Mrs. Feldman would never know Lucy had an anger problem. She'd never know Lucy had killed two men. She'd never know Lucy had quit in order to save Dr. Banks's life.

She looked at the business card in her hand and smiled happily, feeling such a sense of relief. She couldn't believe it could be that easy. Obviously she'd still have to convince Mrs. Feldman's son she was the right person for the job, but she could do that.

"Oh my goodness!" she exclaimed, suddenly realizing she didn't have anything to wear. Her closet was full of scrubs and clothes that no longer fit. She jumped to her feet. She needed to go clothes shopping!

She thought about calling Stacy and seeing if she wanted to go with her, but she felt like this was something she should do on her own. The last time she'd gone shopping Addie had gone with her and picked out all Lucy's clothes for her. Lucy hadn't particularly liked anything Addie had picked, but there hadn't been any point in arguing with her.

Lucy drove to a shopping center on the edge of town, feeling a frisson of excitement and trepidation. She stepped into the first store and wandered around the clothes racks. Most of the clothes were very bold. She'd never worn bold colors before.

She reached for a long flowing shirt with bright flowers. A voice in her head snapped "No!" But it wasn't angry her. It was Richard. She knew he'd hate it. But did she like it? That was the question.

She stood there for a minute, hand halfway to the shirt, trying to decide. She honestly didn't know, but she finally grabbed it. It wouldn't hurt to try it on.

She slowly picked out several shirts, pants, and skirts, ignoring Richard's and her mom's voices, and walked towards the dressing room. After she took her own clothes off she glanced cautiously at herself in the mirror.

Damn. We look good. For once she had to agree with angry her. They did look good. Or SHE did look good. There was no they. Just Lucy.

She buttoned a pair of pants she'd picked. They were two sizes smaller than her old ones, but they were still too loose. All the clothes she'd picked were too loose.

"Can I get anything for you?" an assistant asked from outside Lucy's door.

"Yes," Lucy said, slipping her hand and the clothes through the cracked door. "Would you get these all one size smaller please?"

"Certainly, ma'am. I'll be right back."

Lucy examined herself while she waited. She needed new underwear too. Hers were old and plain and baggy. She tucked her hair behind her ears. Her hair hadn't started greying like Stacy's had. It was still chestnut brown and wavy, but it was a little heavy and it didn't have any style. She needed a haircut too. Clothes, underwear, and a haircut. She grinned at herself in the mirror. She was actually having fun.

She went to the lingerie store next. She'd never been to a lingerie store. Her mom had told her only loose women wore fancy underwear, but Lucy didn't think that was true. She'd caught a glimpse of Stacy's underwear the other day and they were not plain.

Her entire body flushed uncomfortably when she saw the giant sized photographs of nearly naked women plastered all over the walls. She wasn't sure she could do this. A bag of underwear from a department store would do just fine.

"Can I help you, ma'am?" a cute, petite woman asked.

"Um... I don't... I mean..." Lucy blinked rapidly, feeling like a deer in headlights. "I don't..."

The woman smiled and asked, "Are you looking for something particular?"

"I... I..." Lucy blushed even deeper and whispered, "Everything?"

"We can do that! What size are you?"

"Um... I don't know."

"We can figure that out too. Right this way please."

Lucy followed the woman deeper into the store, feeling something close to panic. If Richard knew she'd come here he'd yell for hours, maybe even days.

Who cares? I care! *We need underwear.* But we don't need THIS underwear! *Yes, yes we do. What if Henry saw you in your skivvies? You wouldn't want to be caught wearing what you're wearing now, would you?* Heat rushed through Lucy, making her so hot she wished she had a whole tray of ice cubes. Why would Henry see us, I mean, ME in my skivvies? That's ridiculous. *Is it?* Shut up!

Lucy stood absolutely still as the woman measured her chest and hips. Then she let the woman pick out several things for her to look at. Lucy was still too embarrassed to have an opinion. When she left she had enough new underwear and bras for two weeks, a very skimpy nightgown the woman had insisted she buy, and several cozy pair of pajamas.

It all seemed like too much, but the woman had winked and said, "You'll be glad you have it all, trust me."

Four stores, a smoothie, and one imagined murder later, and Lucy had several bags full of clothes. Workout clothes, interview clothes, working woman clothes, relaxing clothes, pajamas, and the lacy lingerie.

Shopping was exhausting but so much fun, and she couldn't wait to wear her new clothes. She already felt like a new woman; a new wardrobe was only the icing on the cake.

She'd even asked a lady where she got her hair styled, and the lady had given her a number for a chic salon nearby. Lucy had called, and they were able to get her in that afternoon because they'd had a cancellation.

This was turning out to be the best day ever. She'd quit her job, gotten new clothes, and she was going to get a stylish haircut instead of a twelve dollar job at the corner shop.

"Hi, Daddy," Addie said.

He bit back a sigh. Her voice had always kind of annoyed him. It was too pandering. "Addie, how are you?"

"I'm good, but I talked to Mom earlier."

"And?"

"Well, I think you're right. Something is definitely wrong. She quit her job today."

"She what?!" Richard stopped himself from cussing and reminded himself to play the concerned husband. "Did she say why?"

"She said she was sick of dealing with Dr. Banks. She's never mentioned having a problem with Dr. Banks before, and she's always really loved her job. But the worst part is she doesn't even want to be a nurse anymore!"

Richard accidently laughed. "Why's that funny?" Addie snapped.

"Well what else can she do?"

"I don't know, Daddy! Something's wrong though! She keeps saying everything's okay."

"I know, sweetie. I wish I could help her." Richard grinned. The more that he thought about it, the more he realized this was working out perfectly. More than perfect really. Maybe his luck had finally changed. "But she's pushing me away right now," he added in a sad tone.

"Oh, Daddy! I'm so sorry. I wish I was there."

"I wish you were too. Maybe you could talk some sense into her."

"I'll talk to her later tonight, and I'll let you know what she says."

"Thank you."

"Love you, Daddy."

"Love you too."

He hung up and chuckled softly to himself. At first he'd thought Lucille's "midlife crisis" had come at a bad time, but he was beginning to think it couldn't be more perfect.

10

Lucy drove home, started a load of laundry, ate lunch, and typed up her resume. It only took her twenty minutes. And it only took that long because she kept reorganizing it. She'd only had two jobs, so she'd padded a little by including her organization and cleaning skills. She wondered what someone would say if she added "can take care of a dead body".

She started another load of laundry and drove to the salon.

"What were you thinking?" the stylist asked.

"Um... I'm not sure. I was thinking it just needed a little bounce and style. What do you think?"

"Do you want to keep the length?"

Lucy frowned at herself in the mirror. Her hair was longer than most women's her age, but she'd always liked it long, even if Richard did think it made her look immature.

"Yes," she finally said.

"We'll just trim it up and give it some body then."

By five o'clock Lucy was feeling good. She had a fresh new hairstyle, and she was wearing one of her new workout outfits. She'd gotten some of those crazy tight pants, but she was wearing a cute, purple skort over them, which made her feel very feminine but still capable.

Angela whistled when she saw her. "Lucy! You are looking fabulous!"

Lucy grinned widely. "I quit my job today, but I have an interview tomorrow, and I figured I needed some new clothes." She blushed. "All the way around though, 'cause I'm... well, you know, thinner... everywhere."

Angela laughed. "I know! You look amazing!"

"Well, I have been working out," a deep voice said behind Lucy.

Lucy blushed deep red, but Angela just laughed. "You know I was talking to Lucy, Henry; although you look amazing, as always."

He does look amazing, Lucy thought, admiring his tanned biceps. *I wonder what his skivvies look like.* Lucy's eyes widened. Oh god, shut up!

"Would you like a ticket to the gun show?" Henry asked with an exaggerated eyebrow lift.

"What?" Lucy stuttered, feeling both embarrassed and confused.

"Don't encourage him," Angela sighed.

Henry flexed one of his massive arms. "See? Guns, gun show."

Lucy stared at his arm in amazement. She'd never known a man with such a fine form before. His arm was covered in a fine sheen of sweat, and Lucy wanted to run her fingers down it to see how it felt. Would it be hard?

"Lucy?" Henry said with a chuckle.

"What?!" Lucy exclaimed with a jerk, face flushing even a deeper red.

"You okay?"

"Yeah, I was... um... just... thinking?"

"Let's get to work," Angela said, voice thick with amusement.

Lucy couldn't stop herself from glancing at Henry's arm one last time. She wished she could touch it. Just once. Whenever he was close angry her turned into... hot her, brain melted her, jelly her. Her brain turned off and her lady parts turned on. She'd never felt that way before, and it was confusing. She didn't have any more idea what to do with those feelings than she did with the anger.

By the time she got home, Dr. Banks and her anger had been forgotten. She was a new woman, a fit woman, a confident woman. And she liked it.

"WHAT THE HELL?!" Richard yelled as soon as she stepped into the house.

Lucy was dumb with shock for a second. She wasn't sure what had happened or what she'd done wrong.

"Now you're not even making me SUPPER?" he screamed, face a brilliant red.

"What're you talking about?" she stuttered.

"I worked like a dog all day, and when I came home it was to an empty house and no food!"

Lucy grimaced. She'd forgotten to make more meals for him. She automatically apologized. "Sorry; I forgot."

"You forgot! God, Lucille; I had to eat at McDonalds! McDonalds!"

The shock was wearing off, and the anger was taking over. "So?" Lucy snapped.

"So? Are you trying to earn the world's worst wife award?"

My Better Half

Lucy's body went rigid. If he didn't shut up she was going to beat him to death with her purse.

"No sex, no food, half-assed cleaning, and cold as hell!"

She wasn't cold at all. She was so hot she was having trouble seeing straight. She had to get out of here. She had to leave now.

She backed out the door and ran across the garage to her car, trying to ignore the bellow of Richard's words behind her.

"I should've asked Mina Edcott to marry me! At least she put out!"

Lucy jerked her car door open and forced herself to breathe while she waited for the garage door to open, then peeled out of the driveway.

She drove for hours, paying no attention to where she was going. She couldn't see through her anger. She couldn't hear. She wanted to drive back across town, drag Richard across the room by his thinning hair, and shove his hand down the garbage disposal.

She hated him more than she could have thought possible. She hated him so much. He'd overshadowed her for thirty years, influenced every decision, dictated every aspect of her life. He had criticized and ridiculed and attacked her. She had had enough!

Stop! angry her suddenly ordered.

Lucy careened to a stop, then glanced around. She was on a side street somewhere, and it was filthy. The type of mess not even she could clean up.

Get out of the car! Are you insane? I don't even know where I am. *Just do it.* I won't. *Do you want to kill Richard?* No! *Then get out of the damn car.*

Lucy wasn't sure what the two had to do with each other, but she grabbed her purse and stepped from the car.

There's an alley on your right. Go down it. Seriously? I don't think that's a good idea. *DO IT!*

Lucy sighed. She didn't know why she was listening to angry her. It was probably a stupid thing to do. She dropped her keys in her bag and started down the alley. It was already dark, and going into the alley was like walking into pure night. It stank like rotten food and feces. After just two steps she felt like she needed a shower.

Why am I doing this? *Just trust me.* Lucy almost laughed, but she was too busy holding her breath.

A lilting voice suddenly echoed down the alleyway. "Hey pretty lady! You lost?"

Lucy froze. She couldn't see yet, and she had no idea where the voice had come from. A light sparked up ahead, and she saw a silhouette of a man lighting a cigarette.

"Or maybe you came here to have a little slap and tickle with ol' Ralphy."

"Ralphy?" Lucy croaked, straining to see his features. His face was covered in rough whiskers, and the hand holding the cigarette was encased in a rotten looking glove.

"Me!" He giggled. "I'm Ralphy. At least that's what Momma called me. Pa called me Dipshit."

"I'm sorry?" She took a step back. She shouldn't be here. She belonged in her two-story house with a glass of sparkly wine.

"Ha! I pushed him down the stairs one night. Broke his neck on the floor." He laughed loudly, the sound sending chills down Lucy's spine.

"Haven't had me a woman in years. Most of the whores know better than to come down Ralphy's alley. Ever since I stuffed that one's head in a pillowcase. I carried it around with me for weeks. 'Til it got maggots." He giggled again.

Lucy gagged and stepped backward once again, feeling a very real sensation of terror. He was insane. Absolutely insane. She was scared to turn around. He was too close.

"Where you think you're going, pretty lady? We haven't slap and tickled yet."

He moved forward quickly, and Lucy gasped in fear. *Now would be a good time to get the screwdriver out of your purse!* I don't have a screwdriver in my purse! *Sure you do. I put it there this morning.* Oh my god! You planned this! *We need it.*

Lucy didn't have time to argue. Ralphy was so close now she could smell the stench of alcohol on his breath. She tumbled frantically in her purse, feeling for the screwdriver. She wrapped her hand around its cold, hard handle just as Ralphy grabbed her other arm and pulled her towards him.

"The things I'm gonna do to you gonna make your head spin," he chortled. "If you survive."

Lucy's fear vanished, replaced with burning hot anger. Nobody, NOBODY, touched her without her permission. Not anymore.

"Fuck you, asshole," she growled, ripping the screwdriver free of her bag and slamming it into his ear.

Ralphy jerked, and his eyes blinked in surprise. His grip didn't loosen though, and Lucy wasn't sure if she'd gotten it in far enough to kill him. But it didn't matter because she wasn't done with him yet. He was a sick freak, and she was going to make him pay.

She tore the screwdriver loose and jammed it into his eye, pushing it in as far as she could. He screamed in anguish and shoved at her, trying to break free, but Lucy grabbed his filthy coat with her other hand and held it tightly, keeping him close.

"Nobody touches me!" she growled, ripping the

screwdriver from his eye and shoving it into his cheek, feeling it smash through his teeth.

He was screaming for help, wailing at the top of his lungs, but she didn't care. No one was coming to help him. He was going to die. She was going to kill him.

She ripped the screwdriver loose again, feeling his blood splatter on her face. He clawed at her hand, trying to break free. His long, sharp fingernails tore at her skin, but she didn't loosen her grip.

She stabbed him again and again. She stabbed his eyes, his cheeks, his mouth; she stabbed at his head, over and over and over until the bone gave beneath the blunt edge of the screwdriver, and hot blood splashed over her hand.

He'd stopped screaming, but she didn't think he was dead yet. She yanked the screwdriver out of his face and drove it deep into one of his eyes. He stumbled, and she pushed him to the ground, tearing the screwdriver loose and ramming it into his eye socket over and over and over, until he stopped moving and his mouth fell slack.

She stabbed him three more times for good measure, shoving the screwdriver into his mashed socket all the way up to the handle and wiggling it around.

She ripped the screwdriver free and stared at him. His face was so mutilated he looked like a tray of hamburger meat. She couldn't believe she'd done that. *He deserved it.* I really think he did, Lucy thought, pushing herself to her feet.

She wiped the screwdriver off on his shirt and slipped it back into her bag. She wished she had something to clean her face off with. And her hands. She felt disgusting.

She kept looking at him for a moment, his still body and totally disfigured face. She waited to feel sick, but she didn't. She felt better. Much better. And she felt absolutely no regret.

He was as sick as they came. He'd needed put down, and she had done it.

I can't believe you planned this, she snapped at angry her as she headed back towards her car. *I can't believe you said 'fuck'!* Lucy rolled her eyes.

"Who's there?" a scared voice suddenly called out.

Lucy froze, terror filling her. Someone had seen her. Someone had seen her kill him.

"It's okay," another voice responded. "It's an angel."

Lucy looked back and forth, searching for the voices. Who were they? Why hadn't they stopped her? What would they do now? Would they call the police?

"An angel?" the first voice asked.

"An angel. She killed Ralphy."

Oh god. She was going to prison. She shouldn't have killed him. She shouldn't have come here.

"Ralphy's dead?"

"She killed him."

"Thank you, angel," the first voice yelled.

"Yes, thank you, angel!" a chorus of voices said. "Thank you!"

Lucy stumbled backwards, overwhelmed by the echoes of their voices. There were so many. They had seen her, and they didn't care. They were happy. They were happy, and she was an angel.

Richard parked in front of Emily's house and wondered briefly where Lucille had gone when she'd run off. Yelling at her seemed to set her off. Which wasn't necessarily a bad thing.

The more unbalanced she seemed the better off he would look. He breathed deeply, anticipation thrumming through his veins. It wouldn't be long now.

11

It took Lucy a minute to figure out where she was, but as soon as she had her bearings, she drove towards home. She didn't go there though. She pulled off in a church parking lot and just sat.

Her phone rang. She could tell by the ringer it was Addie, but she couldn't talk yet. She breathed deeply, trying to evaluate how she felt. She felt better. Much, much better. *Told you.* Told me what? *That you needed it.* Lucy didn't ask what she'd needed. She knew. She'd needed the kill.

The anger grew and grew and grew. It didn't matter what she did. It didn't matter how much she verbally expressed herself, she was still mad. Fiercely mad. And she couldn't un-mad herself.

Not unless she killed someone. Then the mad seemed to fade into the background for a bit. She had just killed a man, and instead of feeling bad or horrified or scared or shaky, she felt relaxed. Like super relaxed.

This was not good. But on the other hand was it so bad?

The other people hidden in that alley thought she was an angel. They thought she was an angel because she'd killed a bad man. A very bad man.

Surely there was no harm in that? Killing a bad man. In fact, she could almost say it was a good thing. A very good thing.

You could. Yes, I could. *You'd be right.* I would be right. And that robber, he was bad. *Yep.* And Jay... Well, I can't say for sure he was bad, but he was going to hurt me. *Yep.* I could tell. *Yep.*

Stop saying "yep". It's annoying. *Okay.* Lucy rolled her eyes. She couldn't believe she was sitting in a parking lot, a dead man's blood splattered on her shirt, talking to herself. Or angry her. The other her. *Your better half.* Not hardly, Lucy snorted.

We're like superheroes. What? *Superheroes! Meting out justice! Keeping the streets safe!* No. *Yes!* No. We've, I'VE, killed three random guys. We are NOT superheroes. I am not a superhero.

In fact, I'd say I'm a borderline crazy person. Minus the borderline. *That's Richard talking.* It's really not. Sane people don't have entire conversations with themselves. Sane people don't imagine killing everyone who pisses them off. Sane people don't have to kill random bad guys to keep from killing their own husbands.

Lucy frowned. How'd you know anyway? *Know what?* That Ralphy was down that alley? *Didn't.* What do you mean you didn't? You planned the whole thing. You had the screwdriver; you told me to stop; you told me to walk down the alley.

I grabbed the screwdriver this morning because I knew you were close. As for the alley. It was an ALLEY. At night.

Chances were pretty good you'd run into someone bad. Hum. Not much of a plan. *I wanted to kill Richard.* Okay, it was a better plan than that.

Why can't we kill Richard? It's not that I don't want to. I really, really do, but he's not bad. I mean he's a dick, he's demeaning, and he's annoying as hell, but he doesn't beat on me, he doesn't beat up other people, he's never murdered anyone. He's not BAD.

Humph. So you only want to kill BAD people? What?! No! I don't want to kill anyone. We're not killing again. I mean, I'm NOT killing again.

Really? Really! *Have you learned nothing?* What do you mean? *What's gonna happen in another two or three weeks?* Um... Nothing? *Ha! The anger's gonna be all up on you again, and the only way you can control it is if you kill.*

What?! No! I'm not killing again. I'm done. Why would I want to kill? It's... It's... Lucy couldn't go on. The truth was she liked it. A lot. And that, more than anything else, totally freaked her out.

When she was doing it, it felt good. Great! Killing gave all that anger a place to go, a place to strike. It made her feel wonderful, powerful, alive.

But that confused her. How could hurting someone make her feel better? How could stealing another human's life make her feel relaxed and calm? What was the difference between her and Ralphy then? Wasn't she just as bad as him? *It's not really the same.* I don't see how it's not.

Lucy stared at her hands. A spray of Ralphy's blood had dried over her knuckles. He had fought her at the end there, and her left wrist was covered in ugly, jagged scratches. She shuddered at the thought of his filthy nails cutting into her skin.

She needed to get home and cleaned up before a police

officer pulled her over or something. She started her car, jumping when her phone shattered the silence.

Addie. Again. Lucy swiped to answer. "Hey, baby."

"Mom, are you okay? I've called six times."

"Yeah, I've just been out driving."

"Driving? It's after midnight!"

She wasn't a damn pumpkin! "Look your dad made me mad, so I went for a drive."

"Oh." Addie was silent for a moment. Then she said, "I know you said you're doing okay, but I'm worried about you. I talked to Nate yesterday."

Lucy sighed; she didn't need this right now. She honestly wished Addie would just leave her alone.

"He said you've been... different lately."

"Different how?" Lucy rolled her eyes and turned into her driveway.

"I don't know. He said you were, I don't know, more aggressive?"

"Is that bad?" Did they just expect her to stay the same for another thirty years?

"No, I mean, I'm glad you're being more assertive. I just wondered what brought it on. Are you sure you're feeling okay?"

"I'm fine," Lucy said, putting her phone on speaker and taking off her lovely brand-new, totally blood-splattered clothes and tossing them into the washing machine.

Addie didn't respond so Lucy added, "I guess I just woke up one morning and realized I needed a change."

"Okay," Addie said doubtfully. "Dad mentioned you moved into the guest room."

Lucy frowned as she scrubbed the blood off her hands. "I'm not sure I see how that's any of your business, Addie."

"I'm just worried about you, Mom! I've been doing some research, and I've found out that sometimes as women age they go through physical changes that can affect their emotions and thinking."

Lucy breathed deeply and counted to ten. She definitely couldn't kill Addie. Even if she was pissing her off.

"I sent you some websites to look over," Addie went on. "I just think if you read them, you'll see that you need to talk to someone and figure out what's going on."

She made it sound so reasonable. Like Lucy was broken and needed fixed.

"Look, it's late, and I have a job interview tomorrow," Lucy said, covering up her irritation with a cheerful tone. "Can we talk later?"

"You do? How?! That's wonderful."

"Yeah." Lucy faked a yawn. "But I need to get my beauty sleep."

"Oh, sorry, Mom. Please look at the websites. I'll talk to you later. Love you."

"Love you too, baby."

Lucy swiped to hang up. She fought the urge to call Richard and chew him out for trying to use Addie against her. But it was better if he didn't know she knew. He thought she was dumb, and she'd rather he went on thinking that.

She examined her hands. They were clean, but her scratches were already red and puffy. She spread some ointment on them, then she retrieved the screwdriver from her purse and dropped it in the dishwasher's utensil tray. She checked her purse for blood, then ran upstairs, took a shower, put on her new pajamas, and fell into bed. Killing was exhausting.

When she woke up, several minutes before her alarm went

off, she felt fantastic. Which scared the hell out of her. Was she really going to have to kill people just to function? Surely there was another way.

There isn't. I'm not talking to you. *Why not?* You're... naughty. *Oh, I'm so sorry. Would you like me to sit on the naughty step?* Shut up!

Lucy made breakfast and ignored Richard all morning, which was surprisingly easy even though he griped and yelled and generally carried on. After she'd cleaned the kitchen, she took care getting dressed, changing five times and trying to evaluate herself in the mirror.

She looked confident. At least she thought she did. She felt queasy. It was ridiculous to interview for a new job in your fifties. She should be set, done. She shouldn't have quit. No; she should have. She'd done the right thing.

Once she looked as good as she thought she could, she drove outside of town towards the vineyard. When she reached it, she turned, drove between two large, beautiful columns and down a long road towards a neat Italian looking villa.

This was a silly idea. She really didn't know that much about wine, just that she liked to drink it. She shouldn't have let Mrs. Feldman talk her into this, but it was too late now.

She walked slowly into the office and approached the healthy-looking, middle-aged man standing behind a long counter. "Excuse me," Lucy said. "I'm looking for Mr. Feldman."

"Ah, you must be Lucille!" he responded cheerfully, coming around the counter to shake her hand. "You can call me Will."

"Oh..." Lucy returned his vigorous hand shake. "Then call me Lucy."

"Perfect. Let me show you around."

"Um... Did you want to see my resume?"

He shrugged carelessly. "Mom says you'll be a perfect fit. She picked my wife, and that turned out great. So as long as you want it, the job's yours."

"Really?" Lucy stammered. "I don't actually know that much about wine. Except I like to drink it."

"You'll learn."

Lucy blinked in surprise. "But... but... You don't even know me!"

"Mom likes you. She likes about fifteen people outside of family, so I figure you're alright."

Lucy blinked. She couldn't believe it could be that easy. But he was smiling, and she could tell it was genuine. "Okay. Give me the tour," she said excitedly.

Will grinned widely and started walking, talking as he went. "My wife, Ashley, helps me on the weekends, so I'll only need you during the week. This is your office." He pointed to a room with curved windows and bright paintings of Italian landscapes.

"I get an office?"

"Yep, and an employee discount."

She laughed. "That's just evil!"

"I know," he said with a grin. "Anyway, this is the store."

Three hours later, Lucy had seen the entire operation, filled out all the paperwork, bought a bottle of wine, and headed home.

She started on Monday. Her job would be to greet visitors when they stopped by, manage the phone and the shop, and set up tours when appropriate. All in all, she thought it sounded like a lot of fun. Much better than listening to Dr. Banks pontificate.

When she got home Lucy called Stacy. "Hey! I got the job!"

"Whohoo!" Stacy cheered. "I knew you would!"

"I didn't. But I did, and I bought a bottle of wine to celebrate."

"What're you waiting for then?"

"Huh?"

"I'm free," Stacy said with a short laugh. "Come on over, and we'll celebrate."

Detective Sanders walked around the victim's body. She hated alley murders. They always stank like crap and despair.

She'd already interviewed the few homeless people she'd been able to find, and they all said the exact same thing. "An angel killed him." "An angel killed Ralphy." "Ralphy was killed by an angel."

That told Sanders two things. She was leaping to conclusions, but some of her best work came from wild assumptions. One, the killer was a woman. And two, Ralphy was a bad man.

She knelt beside him and looked carefully at his face. One of his eyes was practically gone, a gapping bloody hole left in its place. The other eye had one smooth puncture hole. There were multiple holes in his cheeks, part of his skull was cracked and broken open, and there was a line of dried blood from his ear to his neck. The rest of his body had no wounds that she could see.

She grinned, feeling a pulse of excitement. This was it. Murderers and druggies were exactly the same. Once they got a taste for it they couldn't quit.

She felt Denton pause behind her. "What're the chances they were all three killed by the same person?" she asked.

He snorted. "Different weapons, different locations, nothing to connect them, first body chopped into pieces and dumped, the others left where they were. I don't see it."

"That's 'cause you're always looking at the facts. I look at the people, the emotions."

"What's your point?" he growled.

"The killer was angry."

"Based on?"

"Just look at this man! His face is destroyed! So were the other two. Just totally messed up. Fubar!"

"Go on."

"Different weapons, but all applied the same way. Face. Eyes. Mouth. Same method of attack."

"Maybe."

"And they're all bad guys." She counted them off on her fingers. "Wood, thief and attempted murder. Johnson, multiple counts of assault. And Ralphy here was killed by an angel. Which tells me Ralphy was probably a bad man."

"So what're you thinking?"

"Is it possible we're dealing with a vigilante?"

"I talked to Mom last night," Addie said, voice worried and tense.

Richard grinned, glad Addie wasn't there to see him, and asked with concern, "What did she say?"

"She already has a job interview, but she didn't tell me where. I sent her some websites and asked her to look at them, but she didn't say she would. She's not listening to me."

Richard sighed deeply and tried to infuse his voice with worry and sorrow. "We'll just have to be there for her and hope she comes to her senses before it's too late."

The rest of Lucy's week rushed by. She went to the gym, enjoyed her somewhat awkward conversations with Henry, ignored Richard, and generally enjoyed herself. The anger was there, but it was subtle and easily controlled, and Lucy told herself that since she wouldn't be around Dr. Banks anymore it would continue to be manageable.

But she'd forgotten what complete asses people could be. Her first day of work she dealt with an irate dealer out of Arizona. He was mad because the shipper had dropped his crate of wine off the back of the truck. Lucy carefully explained to him that they would file an insurance claim with the shipper and replace his order. She asked him to take photos of the damage and send them to her and assured him she would send out a replacement as soon as she had the photos of the damaged shipment.

He went ballistic. "I won't do business with a company that won't replace their product!" he yelled.

"Sir, I explained; we will replace your shipment; we just need photos of the damaged shipment first."

"Are you calling me a liar?!"

"Of course not. But I cannot file an insurance claim with the shipper without photos." Lucy struggled to keep her voice even. She could feel the anger clawing at her insides, but he was miles and miles away. And even if he wasn't, she couldn't bludgeon him over the head with her telephone just because he was a royal ass.

"Give me your manager! Right now!" he screamed into the phone.

"Please hold."

Lucy called Will and explained the situation. "Sorry, Lucy," he said. "You did everything right. I'll talk to him, and see if I can't get him to see reason."

She stood and paced her office for a second, breathing deeply. The heat was wafting off her, making her feel sick. Damn she hated stupid people.

You should just kill him. And how the hell would I do that? He's in Arizona. *Okay, that's tough.* Weren't you paying any attention? *I zone out.*

Lucy rolled her eyes. She was getting way too comfortable with angry her, and if she thought about it, it kind of bothered her. But part of her really liked angry her. Angry her didn't have boundaries or limits; she didn't care about rules or thoughts that weren't her own. In short, angry her was free, and Lucy both envied her and liked her because of it.

The rest of Lucy's day went fine. Tuesday would have been fine too, except she went to the store and this little old man cut in front of her at the checkout. It took all her effort not to run him over with her cart. Back and forth, back and forth.

And then the neighbor's dog barked and barked and barked all night long. Lucy couldn't decide which one she wanted to kill more. Her neighbor or the dog.

Wednesday an argumentative man dropped a bottle of wine while he was trying to force Lucy to understand the difference between aroma and bouquet. It took Lucy an hour to get everything clean. She hated cleaning up other people's messes. Angry her suggested pushing his head into a barrel so he could really appreciate the aroma.

By the time she left work, her jaw ached from grinding it. She drove to the gym, fighting the insane urge to ram her car into all the drivers who pissed her off.

She sat in the parking lot for ten minutes, trying to breathe, trying to find a calm place, but she couldn't. So she went inside and worked out with Angela, trying desperately to force all her rage out through her movements, but it didn't work.

When she and Angela were finished, Lucy approached Henry cautiously. She liked talking to him, but she always felt silly because her tongue got tied in knots or she got distracted looking at his arms or legs or butt. *He does have a damn fine butt.* I know.

"Did you want me to do a slow spin?" he asked jokingly.

"What?" Lucy stammered, tearing her eyes off his upper thighs.

"You're staring. I thought maybe if I did a slow spin you could take in your fill."

Lucy giggled accidentally, feeling her face turn red.

"It's okay, you know," Henry added. "I don't mind. I'll spin for you anytime."

Lucy burst out laughing. "You're incorrigible!"

He winked and said, "But isn't it nice?"

"I wanted to ask you..." She turned red again. She wasn't sure she would be comfortable working with him, but she thought punching a bag might help with the anger so she forced herself to ask. "Angela said if I wanted to learn to punch you might be able to help me."

"Maybe," he drawled. "What's in it for me?"

Lucy's mind blanked. She had no idea what he wanted.

"I'm kidding, Lucy," he chuckled. "Of course I will."

"Um... Are you sure?"

"Yes!" He elbowed her slightly. "I'll get to look at you; you'll get to look at me. Win, win."

Lucy blinked. Maybe Angela was right; maybe Henry did like her. But why? She wasn't anything special. *That's crap! How can you say that?* Mom, Father, Richard, they all told me often enough. *Screw them! You are special. Lucy*

Stevenson is special! Lucy frowned; she wasn't convinced angry her was right.

"Come on," Henry said, leading her into the room with the punching bags. He picked up two red, rectangular pads and slipped them onto his hands. "Show me what you got."

"What?" Lucy stared at him.

"Punch my hands."

"Um... I really don't know how to punch."

"Just show me how you'd do it, then I'll know what we need to work on."

Lucy frowned, stepped towards him, and threw a punch towards one of the pads. She missed, slipped a bit, and fell into him. He caught her, holding her for just a second against his warm body, before setting her upright.

"We'll work on everything then," he said softly. She glanced down from his lips and nodded. He was so good looking; it just wasn't fair.

Lucy gasped when he took her hand. "Look," he said. "First we need to work on your fist."

Lucy could barely hear him. Heat ran from her hand down into her nether regions and pooled there. She couldn't believe such a simple touch could have such an effect.

"Keep your thumb on the outside," he instructed. "Right here." He curled her fingers and moved her thumb. Lucy stared at their hands. His hand was big and tanned. She felt so small, so dainty.

He tweaked her fist upward. "And keep your wrist lined up, or straight, with your top two fingers. Like this. Otherwise you'll break your hand."

That jolted her out of her hot daze. "Break my hand? That's a thing?"

He chuckled. "Yes, that's a thing."

He spent an hour showing her how to hold her hand, where to put her feet, and where to punch from. It was exhausting, but in a good way.

"We'll work again tomorrow," he said as they left the gym together.

"Oh, no. I don't want to mess up your workout time. I didn't realize it would be so intense. I just thought you'd show me how to punch the bag."

He shrugged. "There's more to it than that. We'll work for a week or two, then you can work on the bag on your own. Okay?"

"Only if you don't mind," Lucy said worriedly.

"I don't mind at all." He grinned at her, making her melt again. "See you tomorrow."

Lucy watched him drive away. *He is one fine hunk of a man.* Shut up. I'm married. *We can look, can't we?* Oh yeah; we can look.

Denton glared at the blood results. He hated it when Sanders was right. He just didn't understand how she could walk onto a scene and spout off stuff like "they were all killed by the same person" and be right.

He was so focused on the minute details, the weapon, the marks, the cause of death, that he sometimes missed the big picture, the one that pulled everything together into one cohesive image.

But now he was curious. The killer had been so careful. There hadn't been a single speck of evidence, yet somehow they had managed to leave behind a blood sample at each crime scene.

It seemed too easy, too convenient. And he never trusted easy or convenient.

12

Emily slowly closed the leopard print shackles. "Don't struggle," she ordered. "It will only make it worse."

"What're you going to do to me?" Richard whined, sweat rolling down his naked back.

"Whatever I want."

Emily smiled. She liked sex well enough, but she liked sex better when she was one hundred percent in charge. Fortunately some men liked to be dominated, and she was so very good at dominating.

When she was finally done, Emily unlocked the shackles and threw him a wet washcloth. "Clean yourself up," she ordered.

"Emily," he said, wiping the sweat from his brow. "I want to be with you more."

Emily sighed. It could never be easy, could it? All she wanted was easy, uncomplicated sex. She didn't want a husband or even a lover. "Now Richard, you know that was never part of the deal. Four times a week. That's it."

"But Emily," he insisted, "I want to be with you more. I want to spend the night."

"No. You know my rules."

"My wife's a cold bitch, and I want to stay here."

"Rules, Richard. I don't want to hear about your wife."

She hated it when partners became difficult. It always happened. They eventually got more attached than she was and wanted more. But she couldn't give them more. She didn't want to give them more.

If she had to break it off with Richard it would take her months, maybe even a year or more to find another partner who would put up with her domination style. She just didn't have the time.

"Emily..."

"No. It's this or nothing."

His face turned red, and she knew he was angry. But she also knew he was about to cave. He needed her. Much more than she needed him.

His lips twisted, and he opened his mouth. She raised an eyebrow. He closed it, then finally said, "I'll see you in a couple days."

"Good." She rewarded him with a smile, shoved him out the door, and locked it behind him.

Her phone rang, and Emily picked it up. "Sanders," she barked.

"Your instincts were right," Denton said.

She knew it cost him to say it, but she didn't gloat, just waited for Denton to continue.

"I found a second blood on one of the bags, and it matches the blood I found on the Johnson kid. I found the same blood under the alley victim's nails," he said.

"Did you run it?"

"You know damn well I did. It came back unknown, but we've got something. They're connected; just like you thought."

"Yeah, if I can only find a suspect to match it."

"That's your job," Denton said flatly. "I did mine."

Richard drove aimlessly across town. He didn't want to go home yet. His argument with Emily had riled him up, and he needed a release.

Emily was a domineering bitch. He liked it for sex, but it pissed him off that he had no say at all in their relationship. All he'd wanted was to spend the night. He got sick of slinking home after midnight just to make sure he didn't have to deal with Lucille.

Cinnamon didn't care what he did. Not as long as he paid her.

Lucy had high hopes for Thursday. She woke feeling relaxed and cheerful. Richard hadn't been home when she got home from the gym last night, so she'd taken a bath, read more of her romance, and fantasized just a little about Henry. Not much, not enough to make her feel guilty. Just enough to make her feel hot in all the right places.

But all that good stuff, all her relaxation, all her working out still wasn't enough to balance the anger. Richard started complaining the second he sat down at the breakfast table. Nate kept trying to change the subject, but all Richard could focus on was the fact that grapefruit was not a complete meal.

Lucy finally had to leave the table. The urge to attack him with her grapefruit spoon was so strong she actually had to stop herself once. She did Yoga in her bedroom to calm herself down, but the anger was still there. Just underneath the surface.

You're gonna have to do it. I can't. *Why not?* That's murder. Pre-meditated murder. *Someone's been watching legal dramas.* Lucy sighed. It bothered her that angry her didn't seem to have much of a conscience. But knowing that angry her was right made it even worse.

She couldn't control it. It was all wrapped up inside her. Filling her head, making her burn with fierce anger, making her yearn to kill.

It wasn't very plausible that she'd keep walking into situations where she would need to defend herself. If she wanted to kill someone she was going to have to plan it out.

It wasn't that she didn't think she could do it; she was great at planning. The problem was if she did... If she did, the line would be crossed. The fine line between protecting herself and killing others for her own pleasure. The fine line between self-defense and murder. The fine line between killer and serial-killer.

She didn't want to cross that line. She didn't want to be that person: judge, jury, and executioner. She just wanted to be Lucy. Wine lover, gym goer, picture taker, mom of three, hopeful grandma.

She touched her toes and breathed out. Richard's car zoomed out of the driveway, and she growled, the hot anger filling her once more. She bit her lip in frustration. She would control it. She had to. She had no other choice.

There're lots of other choices. Richard. Dr. Banks. That annoying neighbor with the yappy dog. No. *Oh come on. What about Herbie Jones?* From high school? *That's the one!* Damn, you carry a grudge. *He told everyone we were loose. Just because we didn't let him touch our ass.* My ass! And who cares?! *Richard might not have proposed if he'd thought you wouldn't put out.* Lucy almost laughed. Maybe she should kill Herbie Jones.

Her phone beeped, and she glanced at it. It was a text from Addie with another website. The text read, "Please look at this one. Love you, Mom."

It annoyed Lucy that Addie's love apparently didn't include Addie's acceptance. Lucy had never felt so happy, so cheerful, so alive. But Addie didn't care about that. All she cared about was that Lucy wasn't the same as she always had been.

Lucy shoved all her anger into a tight little box and got ready for work. On her way out she checked the front door to make sure it was locked. It was. She'd asked Nate the other day, and he'd said he always locked it when he left, but Lucy kept checking.

A group of adorable couples came in, and Lucy served them wine and cheese. No one was stupid or mean or annoying.

Except Richard. Because somehow he'd found out. And he'd come. He slammed open the door as he walked in and screamed "LUCILLE! Where the hell are you?!"

Lucy jumped in surprise, dropping the plate of cheese she was holding.

"What the hell're you doing?" he snarled over the sound of china shattering. "Working at a glorified liquor store? Are you trying to embarrass me?"

"Be quiet!" Lucy hushed, blushing a deep red. She apologized to the couples and asked them to please step out on the deck to view the vineyards.

"Why are you here?" she snapped after the door closed behind them. Her initial shock had worn off, and she was mad. Really, really mad.

"Addie told me you quit your job."

"So?"

"So?! You're a nurse! What the hell're you doing here? You're no better than a waitress!"

"So?" Lucy snapped. "What's wrong with that?" She bent and picked up a shard of broken plate off the floor. She didn't mean to, but she did, and now she had it in her hand, just waiting, just waiting for Richard to move towards her, to try to hit her. Wanting him to try to hit her.

"What the hell's going on with you? I didn't marry this," he gestured at all of her. "Whatever this is!"

"What's that supposed to mean?" Lucy snapped, stepping towards him, shard clutched tightly in her hand. So what if he hadn't hit her yet. She hated him, and she was going to kill him. Never mind it was broad daylight and she'd never get away with it.

His lips were still moving but she couldn't hear what he was saying. The anger was roaring through her mind, blocking everything out, consuming her. Richard had to die.

"What's going on out here?" Will's calm, but firm voice broke through Lucy's anger, freeing her from her pure rage. She dropped the plate shard, closing her hand around the liquid warmth in her palm. She'd been gripping it so hard she'd cut herself.

"None of your business!" Richard snarled.

"'Fraid you're wrong," Will replied with a wide smile. "This IS my business, Lucy is my manager, and you're on my property."

"Well she's my wife, and this is none of your goddamn business!" Richard yelled.

"If you don't leave now, I'll have to call the police," Will said.

Richard froze, and his eyes turned shifty. "We're not through with this conversation," he ground out, then he turned on his heel and stomped out.

"Are you okay?" Will asked. "Do you want me to call the police?"

"No," Lucy replied, embarrassed that her voice was weak and shaky. She'd never seen Richard like that. The look in his eyes... Almost as if...

"Are you sure?" Will asked, breaking her train of thought.

"Yes, I'm sure." She didn't want the police involved. Richard hadn't done anything. Not yet. "I'm so sorry about that. I had no idea... I mean he didn't... I'm sorry."

"It's not your fault. Take a little break. I'll handle the clients."

Lucy nodded, still feeling a bit shocked. Richard had yelled at her before. Hundreds of times, maybe even thousands, but she'd honestly thought for a second that he might try to hurt her. Not that she'd been worried. Angry her wanted him to try, but seeing that look in his eyes had shaken her.

They'd been married for thirty years. Why did he care if she worked out or got a new job? Why was he mad? He wasn't just mad, he was livid. Lucy was mad too, but Richard's eyes... They'd been just a bit on the edge of crazed.

She shook her head in disgust. Talk about hypocritical. If anyone was crazy it was her. She actually killed people. Richard was just pissed things weren't going his way. But still. You didn't live with someone for thirty years without knowing them to at least some degree, and Richard was not acting normal.

By the time Lucy left work for the day she'd made a decision. She'd picked him. He was the horse she'd chosen.

But frankly he was going to be a dead horse if she kept trying to ride him. *Your analogy's getting a bit weird.* I know. *What's your point anyway?* I need to divorce Richard. To save his life.

She drove to the gym, parked, and sat in her car, staring out the window. She didn't have the slightest idea how to go about divorcing someone, so she Googled "how do you divorce someone". Lots of websites pulled up. Some offering "do it yourself" divorces. Lucy frowned. That didn't sound like a great idea. She didn't imagine Richard would take it peaceably, and she'd rather have a lawyer between him and her.

Someone rapped on her window, and she jumped, dropping her phone on the floorboard.

"Sorry," Henry said, flashing his wide grin. "Didn't mean to scare you."

"It's okay," Lucy mumbled, stepping out of her car and just staring at him. He was several feet away, but he seemed to take up all the space. His personality, his size, his guns.

"You okay?"

"Huh? Yeah... um..."

"You going in?"

"Um... yeah. Just gotta find my phone. I dropped it."

"Sorry about that. Let me find it for you."

Lucy started to protest, but the words died on her lips as he bent over to search for her phone. He wasn't big like a wrestler big or one of those guys whose arms were bigger than their waist. Henry was just the right size. Tall, broad-shouldered, rippling arms, tight thighs.

"I think I've got it," he said, reaching a bit further.

Lucy angled her head to get a better view. And a seriously fine, tight ass. She was hot all over. Damn, he was good looking. And nice and cheerful and funny. All things Richard wasn't.

"Here you go," he suddenly said.

Lucy startled. She had been so caught up watching the way his muscles flexed she hadn't even realized he'd stood up.

He was smiling at her in that way he did that said he knew she was checking him out and he didn't mind a bit. She felt her face turn red.

"I was... um... I mean... Thanks."

She reached for the phone, pausing when she realized she'd have to touch his hand to take it. She gingerly took the phone, swallowing a gasp when his fingers brushed against hers. Little shocks ran across her hand, and she stepped backward, struggling to breathe properly.

"I would hire a lawyer," he said.

"What?"

"Sorry, I just happened to see your phone. My sister tried to handle her divorce without a lawyer, and it turned into a mess."

"Oh... I mean..." Lucy wished she could crawl into a hole and hide. How humiliating. He must think she was an idiot.

"I don't," she started to say. "I mean, we've been married thirty years, but... I mean..." She stopped herself, but then she accidently blurted the truth. "He's an ass. If I don't divorce him I swear I'm going to bludgeon him to death with an iron or a rolling pin or... or... or..."

"A wooden spoon?" Henry suggested.

Lucy frowned. "Kinda lightweight don't you think?"

He burst out laughing. "I couldn't say. I've never bludgeoned anyone to death."

Lucy stopped herself from saying "It's harder than you think" and just smiled at him.

"I'm sorry," she said. "I didn't mean to unload on you. He came by my new job today and tore into me, and I just realized that I can't stay married to him. I just can't."

"Anytime you wanna unload," Henry said cheerfully, "I'll listen."

"Um... thanks?"

"Now you better get in there. Angela's a real tyrant when her clients don't show up on time."

Lucy laughed. "Angela's no such thing!"

"You've never been late before. This one time..." Henry went on as they walked towards the door, and Lucy giggled as he told a vastly exaggerated story about Angela making a client do a thousand jumping jacks for showing up late.

When she was done working with Angela, Henry helped Lucy with her stance, and she punched at his hands for an hour, listening to his comments and advice.

When she finally left the gym, Lucy just sat in her car trying to decide what to do. She couldn't go home to Richard. She couldn't handle him right now. The anger was still there, just waiting to get out. There was absolutely no way she would be able to hold herself back if he started yelling at her again.

You have to do it. I can't. *You have to.* Damn it, I can't!! *If you don't want to kill Richard it's your only option. There's a jab saw in the glove box.* A what? *A jab saw. Just trust me.*

Lucy closed her eyes. Angry her was planning again, and she hated it. She didn't even know what a jab saw was. She leaned over and opened the glove box. An orange handled serrated knife popped out and tumbled to the floor. The blade looked like a shark's mouth.

How did you do that? *What?* Put that in the damn glove box? *I just did.* But how? How could I not notice? *It's not like you're always paying attention. When you walked past the tool box I just grabbed it.*

Lucy almost wished she hadn't asked. It seemed like she should notice her own damn hand picking up something like a jab saw and putting it in the glove box. But here it was, and she hadn't. She shuddered.

So what do you want me to do? *Kill someone.* Who?! *Anyone. I don't care.* I do! I can't just go around killing anyone. If I could do that I'd just kill Richard. *Right, I forgot. Semantics.*

Lucy growled. She wished she could kill angry her. Now that would be satisfying. *Hey! Not nice!* Be quiet. I have to think.

Angry her was right. Killing helped her control the anger. Killing helped her control the heat, the urge, the mind-consuming desire to destroy. So logically, she needed to kill in order not to kill. *What?* You know what I mean. *I'm not sure I do.* So what do we do? *Oh, so it's "we" now, huh?* Oh for crying out loud. Angry her snickered, then said, *I honestly don't know.*

Well hell. *We could go to a bar.* What good does that do us? *I don't know. If we get lucky someone might try to rape us.* Lucy swallowed a nervous laugh. This was insane. When she was sitting here trying to plan it out, it didn't seem to her like she could actually kill someone.

But she had, and she knew if she found the right person she could do it again. She was absolutely confident that nothing could stop her. Which was stupid. What if they had a gun? Or a knife? Or mace? *Oh, we should get some mace.* No! *Why not?* I don't know. Messy. *Always with the messes.* And what if I got it on me and then rubbed my eyes? *Okay, that would suck.* Yeah.

Lucy tapped her fingers on the steering wheel. She hated this. She wanted a plan, and she wanted a plan now. *What if you go to a seedy hotel then call someone bad like a drug dealer or something?* What I just look them up in the damn phone book? *Good point.*

So what do we do then? *Hit up the south side?* What?! Are you insane?! Only criminals and crazy people go to the south side. Oh... I get it.

Angry her chuckled softly before saying, *You just park, take the jab saw, and go for a walk. Bound to be someone around who will want to kill us or rape us or mug us or whatever.*

Lucy closed her eyes with a sigh. What she was contemplating was insane. She was a fifty-one-year-old woman with an angry side and a jab saw. She should absolutely NOT go to the south side. Ever.

But on the other hand, if she didn't go to the south side, there was a very real chance she would kill Richard tonight. And that was not good. Not only was Richard not bad or evil, if you will, she was also pretty sure that when someone was murdered the first person they looked at was the spouse. It was going to be hard to cover that up. She'd just started living, and she really, really, really didn't want to end up in prison.

13

Richard waited impatiently for Lucille to get home from her stupid gym. He shouldn't have showed up at her new job like that. It had looked bad. He'd just been ticked when Addie had told him where she was working.

It was no better than bussing tables at McDonalds. Maybe it was even worse. Now she looked like a booze hound.

He snarled and paced the bedroom. Maybe that was good. He'd told Addie she was drinking more, so maybe it was good if she looked like a booze hound.

He had to get himself under control. He needed to just let her spiral down the drain. He needed to stop trying to get her back in line. It wasn't easy though. He'd been running her life for thirty years now. It was hard to let go.

"I can do this," Lucy whispered. "I can drive to the south side. Park. Take the jab saw with me. And intentionally kill someone if they try to hurt me."

It sounded really simple when she phrased it like that.

My Better Half

Really simple. But Lucy knew nothing was ever as simple as it seemed.

She put her car in drive and pulled out of the parking lot. It was almost dark, but not quite yet. A bit of sweat rolled down her back. She couldn't believe she was driving into the south side. She must be out of her damn mind. She WAS out of her damn mind. She talked to herself and herself talked back.

She kept driving, and suddenly she crossed an invisible line and everything changed. The lawns were dried up dirt patches. Most of the cars parked on the street looked like they'd run into a wall, several times. Windows were broken, some covered in plastic and duct tape, some gaping open, jagged glass still in place.

There weren't any kids playing in the dead yards. No yells of joy, no whoops of laughter, no toys left out for tomorrow. No one was out walking their dog. No one was out walking at all.

A bicycle lay on its side, wheels torn off, chain hanging uselessly. The sidewalk was overrun with tall, scraggly weeds. Trash lay flaccid against broken fence pickets. The whole place felt dead, and Lucy hated it.

It had once been a very nice neighborhood. Bright and cheerful. Full of love, laughter, and family. But then the factories had closed, and the older residents had died. Property values had gone down. And a bunch of other crap had happened. Now the neighborhood belonged to the really poor, drug dealers, and lower order criminals. No upper level criminals would be caught dead in such a neighborhood.

I hope you know what you're doing, Lucy thought anxiously. The anger wasn't pumping now; it was hiding behind fear. She'd never been so frightened in all her life. Not when giving birth to her children, not when that man had grabbed her boob, not when Ralphy had breathed in her face. She didn't belong here, and she knew it.

Pull over. Here? Lucy slowed, pulled over to the curb, and stopped. There was a liquor store in front of her. Broken neon sign advertising that it was open. There were no circumstances in which Lucy would ever step foot in a store like that.

The windows were covered in grime and old posters of half-naked women. The glass in one window was cracked, letting just a bit of yellow light pour out on the uneven sidewalk. Most of the surrounding buildings were boarded up and empty, but one or two still showed signs of life.

Lucy's hand shook slightly as she reached for her door handle. It seemed ten times as dark here as it did on the north side. And there was a heaviness to the air. A sadness and grief, a hopelessness.

She wished just one of the old streetlamps was still shining, casting its light onto the sidewalk. But they were all dark. A shudder ran down her spine. I don't want to be here, she thought. *Go home then. Kill Richard.* Oh hell.

Lucy picked up the jab saw and opened her door. It was early night yet so there were a few people out walking. Some were going home, some were buying beer, some were stopping at the dusty ma and pop shop on the corner. Most of them walked with their heads down and their hands in their pockets. It was like a different world. A sad, depressed, colorless world.

Lucy put the jab saw in her purse and started walking. Stupidest plan ever, she thought. *I agree.* It's your damn plan! *Still; it isn't very good.* She wanted to run back to the car, but she couldn't. She had to do this. She tightened her grip on her purse and wandered down a side street.

How are we going to tell if someone is bad? *I think we'll be able to tell.* But how? *Just trust me on this.*

Most of the windows in the buildings were dark, and she wondered if anyone lived in them. She wondered why this part of the city was so forgotten, so rundown. The empty doorways looked like empty eyes, following her. The whole place gave her the creeps.

"Little past your bedtime, ain't it?" chided a voice from the shadows near her.

Lucy gasped, jerking sideways, hand searching madly for the jab saw.

"Don't think you belong here, Cinderella," the man added, stepping from a darkened doorway. "You should run on back home."

"I... I..." Lucy stuttered. The darkness made him seem menacing, but his voice was calm and almost mellow.

"You wanna turn around and go on home," he admonished.

"I can't," Lucy mumbled.

He chuckled softly. "Can't? I think you can."

Lucy hissed desperately. She needed this. Badly. She needed it to function, and she honestly didn't know where else to go.

"I can't. I'll just keep walking."

"Listen, lady," he said, voice turning harder. "You need to get the hell outta here. Now."

"I need something first."

He snorted, and his voice turned mocking. "You need a fix."

"In a way," Lucy agreed. She walked forward several steps, intent on going around him, but he stepped in front of her.

"You're gonna get hurt."

She smiled slightly. "I don't think so."

"Damn it, lady. I'm trying to help you."

"I know. Thank you. But I have to... Well, I have to keep going."

She pushed past him, hoping he didn't try to stop her, and kept walking. He let her go, and as far as she could tell he didn't follow her.

Her heart pounded, filling her with dread. She wished he'd been the one. If only he'd tried to hurt her she could already be done with this.

You could've killed him anyway. It's all the same down here. It is not all the same! He was a... a nice guy. *Maybe.* He tried to save us. *I guess. Still, if you'd killed him we'd be out of here already.* I know. Now shut up!

The light seemed to fade even more the further she walked. Her legs were shaking; her hands were shaking. She felt sick. She really hoped someone tried to kill her soon. She didn't have the stomach to keep going much longer.

A horrible yowl sounded behind her, and Lucy spun around, heart thumping, purse clutched to her chest. The yowl sounded again, right beside her. Lucy screamed, then slapped her hand over her mouth. Something clattered onto the street, and two cats streaked across the road, hissing and squalling like mad.

"Just a dumb cat," Lucy muttered, trying to still her panicked heart. She wasn't made for this. She hadn't pulled out her jab saw; she hadn't gotten into a fighting stance; she'd held her purse like a shield and froze.

"We need to get out of here," she sighed. "Now."

"Too late," someone hissed.

Lucy's scream didn't make it past her tongue. One sweaty

hand clapped over her mouth and nose, the other grabbed her arm, pulling her back against a body and holding her tightly.

"You ain't going nowhere," a gravelly voice whispered in her ear. "I've got a taste for woman tonight."

A gag worked up Lucy's throat. He stank. He stank like alcohol and old sweat. She pulled at his hand, but he was holding her so tightly she could barely breathe let alone move.

He jerked her roughly into him, then started dragging her off the street towards one of the buildings. Panic flared, and she stopped trying to move his arm and shoved her hand into her purse, feeling for the saw. She tried dragging her heels to slow him down, but he was too strong for her.

She shouldn't have done this. She was going to die in a filthy building, raped, murdered, who knows what. She didn't want it to end like this. She didn't want to die like this. She had barely even lived.

She couldn't see where he was dragging her, but she could guess they were almost there. The street wasn't that wide. She had to break free, but she couldn't find the damn jab saw.

He was mumbling to himself. "The boys'll be here soon; suppose they'll want me to share. I guess that's alright as long as I get mine first."

Lucy tried to scream again, but she couldn't, not past his disgusting hand. She kicked her legs, but he just gripped her tighter, hurting her arm and her face.

What the hell're you doing? angry her snapped. *Make mincemeat outta this ass!* I can't reach the saw! *So?* How do you expect me to kill him? *Figure it out! Stop being such a damn pushover.* I'm not a pushover! *Are too!* Shut the hell up! I'm fighting for my life here, and you're calling me names! *Bullshit! You aren't fighting anything!*

For a second Lucy hung limp, just allowing herself to be dragged. Angry her was right. She wasn't fighting. What the hell was she doing? She didn't need the saw to fight. She just needed to fight.

She opened her mouth wide and bit down fiercely on the grimy hand clamped over her mouth.

"Bitch!" he growled, pulling her tighter but releasing her face. She slammed her head back and heard his nose crack.

The cold fear, the terror, the helplessness left, burning in the heat of her anger. "Nobody calls me 'bitch'," she hissed, finally ripping her saw free and thrusting it into his arm.

"Shit! You crazy little whore!" he yelled, letting go of her. "Just wanted a little fun! What the hell's wrong with you?"

"Nothing," she replied with a shrug. "Just want a little fun."

She saw the glimmer in his hand just as she jumped at him. She shifted, aiming the saw at his hand instead of his face. She felt the saw hit, felt his wrist rip under the weight of its teeth, heard his cry of pain, heard his knife clatter to the ground.

She pushed into him and jabbed the saw at his face. He dodged, lurching to the side, then started running the other way. She leaped forward, grabbing the back of his shirt and yanking him backwards. He tripped and tumbled to the ground.

She didn't give him a chance to get up. She kicked him twice in the ribs, then straddled him, holding one of his arms against the ground and stabbing him in the cheek with the saw.

He screamed in pain and terror, and she smiled, remembering the terror she'd felt, the fear, the pure dread. She ripped the saw across his face, watching as it tore through his skin.

His free arm tore at her arm and face, scratching her neck.

She jabbed the saw deep into his shoulder, ripping it back out and stabbing again, ignoring his pleas for mercy.

Once his arm stopped moving, she went back to his face. She wanted him to hurt. She wanted him to pay. She wanted him dead.

She shoved the saw between his teeth, watching as blood spurted out his mouth, turning his yellow teeth red. She ripped the saw back out and stabbed it through his eyes, ripping them wide open.

By the time the anger faded enough for her to stop herself his face was gone. The jab saw had torn it to pieces. His cheeks were flayed open, his eyes were dark, bloody holes, and his teeth were broken.

He looked like a wild animal had torn his face apart, but the wild animal was her. She had done that. She didn't mind that she had killed him, but killing him the way she had was just sick.

Her face and hands were wet with his blood. She could feel it cooling on her skin. She swallowed a gag and rolled off his body. She pushed to her feet, flinching as the saw moved in her hand.

She opened her fingers. It was hard to tell through all the blood, but she thought she might have cut her fingers. She opened and closed them, and pain shot up her arm. Her hand must have slipped down the blade. She cringed, imagining his blood mixing with her own. What if he had a terrible disease?

Too late now. Thanks. *Why are you just standing around? Get the hell out of here!*

Lucy shoved the saw in her purse. She should have brought a Ziploc. She should have brought some wet wipes. *GET THE HELL OUT OF HERE!* Lucy jumped. Angry her sounded... angrier than normal. *Move! Come on!*

Lucy looked both ways, trying to remember which way she'd come. Left? she thought. *Hell if I know. Just go!*

Lucy started walking to the left, but froze, heart stuttering. Voices were coming her way. Several voices. Men. Probably "the boys". She searched for a place to hide, but there was nothing.

There was only one thing she could do. Run. She crouched and blundered along the wall away from the voices. She ran as fast as she could, trying to be quiet, regretting now that she hadn't done any cardio. She tried not to breathe hard, tried not to gasp, just ran, hoping she didn't trip or knock into anything.

She heard the voices get louder and angry. She heard someone yell, "Is this a setup?" Someone else yelled "Who the hell killed Leo?" Then the heavy night air exploded with gunshots. She fell to the ground, covering her head and waiting for death.

But the voices didn't come closer. There was another gunshot, an angry shout, and several other angry yells. But they weren't yelling at her. They didn't know she was here.

She scrambled to her feet and started running again. She could see faded yellow light up ahead; she had to be close.

Suddenly she burst out onto the sidewalk near the liquor store. She gasped in relief; she was home free now. She limped towards her car, legs trembling from her exertion, and fumbled for her keys, pulling them out and frantically pressing the button. Her car beeped, and the headlights flashed.

That's when she saw the windshield was gone. Shattered. Broken into a million pieces all over the hood. She ran forward, terror making her sick. If they'd slashed her tires she was screwed.

She laughed in relief when she saw the tires were fine. Whoever it was had broken every window and destroyed the paint job, but the tires still had air. It was almost too silly to be true, but she didn't question it, just jumped behind the wheel, turned the key, and peeled off down the street.

Her heart wouldn't stop hammering. That was so stupid! So damn stupid. We were lucky to get out of there alive! *But we did.* Shut up! I don't want to hear any more of your ideas.

Okay... Okay what? *'Cause I mean the car's a problem.* What the hell do you mean the car's a problem? *Richard'll wonder what happened to it.* Damn it!

Lucy sped through the south side, knowing she wouldn't feel safe until she was back in familiar terrain. I'm never going to the south side again! *I wouldn't say never.* NEVER! *Okay; don't get your panties in a bunch.*

Lucy drove until she was just blocks away from her house, then parked and leaned her head against the steering wheel. "I'm alive," she whispered. She was alive, and she'd done what she'd set out to do. She'd gone into the south side and killed someone bad.

A giddy feeling washed over her. She'd actually done it! Then she remembered her car, and the feeling faded. Fine; so what about the car? *Ditch it near the railroad tracks and report it stolen.* Really? *Really.* But then we'll have to walk. *You got a better idea?*

Lucy didn't, but somehow she knew listening to angry her was bound to get her killed.

14

This is stupid, Lucy fumed as she drove towards the railroad tracks. *Feel better though, don't you?* Lucy didn't respond. She didn't want to respond. She felt so much better it was insane. She felt like she could face Richard and laugh at his idiocy. She felt like she could listen to him complain and yell for hours and not even twitch an eyebrow. She needed to divorce him before she ran out of people to kill.

She pulled off the road and stared at her steering wheel. It was covered in blood. It was a good thing she always kept a box of wipes in the car for cleaning up messes.

She scrubbed her hands thoroughly, hating the feel of the blood on her hands. She cleaned the steering wheel, the shifter, the door handle, every surface she thought she might have touched. She cleaned and cleaned until it almost sparkled. *Looks a little too clean. You should mess it up a bit.* Shut up. I don't have time for this crap. I still have to walk home you know. *Um...*

What? What now?! Lucy was starting to feel a little bit

angry again, and that pissed her off. *You should probably go somewhere and call the cops.* Oh. Yeah. I guess you're right.

Lucy glanced down at her shirt. It was torn, and there was blood on it. I don't think that's a good idea. I'll say I parked it in the driveway. *Why would you do that?* I don't know. I wanted to go in the front door. *Okay; whatever.* Look I can't call the police looking like this! Just deal with it.

She wiped off the car surfaces one more time, shoved all the used wipes in her purse, then used a wipe to start the car, and carefully drove it into the ditch. She couldn't believe she was here. Doing this. The car settled with a jerk, and she took her keys, left the door open, and walked off.

It was dark but not like the dark in the south side. There were plenty of street lights and car lights brightening her way. She needed a different method. Going to the south side had been stupid. *Hey it worked, didn't it?* Barely.

Lucy shuddered, remembering all too well how she'd felt completely helpless when he started dragging her. He'd been so much stronger than her, so much bigger. If she hadn't managed to fight back... Bile rolled in her stomach. She was so glad she had won. She was glad he was dead.

Her phone rang, and she sighed. "Addie, it's well after midnight, why are you calling me?"

"Dad said you were still out."

"And?"

"And I wanted to know if you had a chance to look over any of those websites and articles I sent you."

"No." She didn't bother telling Addie she'd get to it. That would be a bald-faced lie, and she just wasn't in the mood.

"Mom... Why won't you at least look at them?"

Lucy enunciated very clearly. "Because I'm not broke, and I don't need fixing."

"Mom, I didn't mean... I mean..." Lucy didn't respond, just waited for Addie to dig herself out of her hole. She coughed awkwardly, then said, "How's your new job? Is it causing you trouble?"

Lucy sighed. "How so?"

"Well, 'cause you know, all the wine."

"And?"

"Well, Dad said that you've been drinking more."

Lucy's good feelings were swiftly fading. Maybe she should just kill Richard and get it over with. *All right!* No. I'm not really. *Oh come on. You said! You got my hopes up.* Shut up.

A car passed Lucy, and she cringed. Please don't let them stop, she thought desperately. She looked like she'd... well, murdered someone. She breathed a sigh of relief when the car kept speeding down the road. She was only a block from home now. Just a little further.

"Mom?"

"What?"

"Are you okay?"

"Yeah, I was just thinking. And I want to say that your father isn't..." She paused. She knew Addie well enough to know that if she called Richard a liar Addie would get defensive. "Anyway, I do like wine, but I haven't been drinking more. I'm fine. Absolutely fine. Please stop worrying about me. Now it's late. I'd like to go to bed."

"Are you home?"

"Almost."

"Where did you go?"

Teddy was definitely her favorite child. He never called, he never berated or worried or treated her like a child. She saw him once or twice a year. He hugged her, said she was looking good, and left her alone. She should send him a thank you note.

"I went out, Addie. I'm a grown woman. I can do that."

"I just..."

"Love you; goodnight," Lucy interrupted and hung up.

I don't understand why everyone can't just leave me alone. *'Cause they want you to kill them.* No; I don't think that's the reason. Lucy trudged up the driveway and tried the front door. It was unlocked.

She frowned. It had been locked this morning. She'd checked after Nate left. Who had unlocked it?

She slipped inside, locked it behind her, and tiptoed past Richard, who was snoring in the recliner. She quickly started a load of laundry, put the jab saw and the used wipes in the dishwasher, started it, and then threw her purse into the washing machine.

She took a shower, taking her time, reliving the evening. She couldn't believe she'd gone into the south side and walked back out alive. She should be dead, should be, but wasn't. It felt good. Knowing she could handle herself. Knowing she'd been frightened, but in the end he'd been the one begging for mercy. It made her feel strong.

She'd panicked a bit afterwards when all those guys had come her way, but in her defense they'd had guns. *You didn't know that at the time.* So?! They were "the boys"! And it's not like I could take out a whole bunch of guys with a damn jab saw. *I guess.*

If we have to keep doing this we gotta be more prepared, Lucy thought as she dried her hair. *I grabbed the jab saw didn't I?* No; I don't mean like that. We need to be prepared to handle the mess. *Oh... What do you mean?* Lucy rolled her eyes. We need a kill bag with Ziplocs and wipes and new clothes.

Oh... Wow, you're good, angry her said, tone full of awe. Lucy blushed. I just know how to clean up a mess. And anyway mace isn't a bad idea either. *I told you.* Oh shut up.

Lucy slipped on her pajamas and snuck downstairs to get a glass of wine.

"Lucille!" Richard roared. "Is that you?"

"Who the hell else would it be?" Lucy snapped, irritated that Richard had woken up.

"Where the hell have you been?!" Richard yelled.

"Out."

"Out where?"

"I went to the gym."

"The gym?" Richard snarled.

"Yes, the gym. Then I drove around town, then I came home."

"Really?" He managed to infuse the word with so much sarcasm Lucy flinched.

"Really."

His face had turned purple again, and Lucy began to wonder if he might actually have an apoplexy. "How dare you cheat on me!" he accused angrily.

Lucy started laughing. She couldn't help it. "I'm not cheating on you!" she exclaimed. "And how dare you even accuse me! You've been cheating on me since day one!"

"It's different!" he snapped.

"Why? Because you're a MAN?!" Lucy giggled helplessly. She knew she should be mad, but he was ridiculous, with his purple face and his anger.

"Damn it, Lucille! What the hell's going on with you? The gym, the new job, this!" He gestured at her. "If you're not cheating on me then what?"

"I'm not Lucille!" Lucy said with a laugh. "I'm Lucy, and

My Better Half

I'm figuring Lucy out. That's all. And by the way, I want a divorce."

His face went totally white for a second. "The hell you do," he finally hissed.

"I really do."

"You're gonna regret this."

"I really won't."

He snarled something under his breath, then spun on his heel and stomped up the stairs.

Lucy watched him go with a frown. She was proud of herself. She'd stood up to Richard, and she'd done it spectacularly. And she'd been in total control. She hadn't fantasized about killing him even once. But his face when she'd said she wanted a divorce. It was strange. A little like his eyes earlier. Crazy.

She shrugged dismissively. He just wasn't used to not getting his way. It was Richard to a T really.

"Shit!" Richard hissed as he slammed his bedroom door shut. He'd yelled, he'd guilted, he'd manipulated, he'd pulled the bad wife card, but none of it was getting Lucille back in line. She'd been a well-behaved, quiet wife for thirty years. What the hell had happened?

For a minute he'd thought her little crisis would work in his favor, but now he wasn't so sure. He didn't actually care if she cheated on him, although he found it unlikely that there was a man alive who would want to have sex with her. He shuddered in disgust and paced the bedroom, feeling lost, like he was losing control. He hated that feeling. He needed to get this done.

The insurance policy would expire on her fifty-second birthday, and he needed her to expire before that, especially if she was planning to divorce him. That was a kink he could damn well do without.

He kicked his slipper across the room, watching as it flounced uselessly to the floor. He wished he could kick her. But he couldn't raise a hand. Spouses were always the first ones investigated, but fortunately he had no record of abuse. He had never once hit her, never once had the cops called on him. He was the perfect husband.

He frowned. He really shouldn't have gone to her work today. That might look bad if it came out, but he could always just play the poor, deceived husband who'd just found out she was stealing from him and cheating on him. Honestly, what red-blooded male wouldn't get upset if he found out his wife was cheating on him?

He tried to imagine the police interview. "I tried everything to save our marriage," he'd say. "I offered to go to counseling with her; she refused. I tried to get her to go on an extended vacation with me, but she wouldn't do any of it. She just totally shut me out." He'd have to call Addie and drop a few more hints.

If only that damn idiot had done the job right away like he'd said he would. Then Lucille would've been dead before the fool ended up dismembered in a dumpster.

Lucy woke feeling really good. Fantastic. Happy. Relaxed. Hopeful. Energetic. And really damn cheerful. Things she hadn't felt in a long time, at least not all together at once. She stretched for several minutes, knowing no matter what Richard or anyone else did, that it was going to be a good day.

"Detective Sanders."

"Why am I here, Jones?"

Detective Jones grinned around his toothpick. "I got a body I thought you'd be interested in."

"Enough with the big reveal; get on with it."

"Alright. We got a tip on a drug exchange this morning. Missed it though. Couple guys dead. Gunshot. But one guy's different."

"I'm listening," Sanders drawled.

Jones pulled back a tarp to reveal a disfigured corpse.

"Holy hell," she whispered. "She did it again."

"See what I mean?"

"I do. Thanks for the call."

Sanders knelt beside the body, taking a careful look. His face was destroyed. Eyes gone, huge chunks missing from his cheeks. She used her pen to pull his collar down. The killer hadn't touched his neck, the easiest and most obvious way to kill someone.

She examined the rest of the body. A jagged cut on his wrist. Some blood on his arm. And a weird wound on his hand. She leaned closer.

"Stop contaminating my damn evidence!" Denton snapped behind her.

"I'm not!" Sanders leaned back on her heels. "This look like a bite mark to you?"

"Maybe."

"See if you can get an impression off it."

"Don't tell me how to do my damn job!"

Sanders rolled her eyes. So touchy. "It's her."

"You assume."

"Nah, I know. I can feel it. And this time she was totally irate. Look at him."

"I can see."

Sanders stood and turned slowly, cataloguing everything she saw. This was one of the seediest parts of the south side. It was almost like the killer had come here on purpose. She probably had come here on purpose. She'd come here to kill.

She saw a discarded knife several feet away. "Jones," she barked. "Make sure you bag that knife."

"Sure thing."

"And Denton, let me know as soon as you have an ID."

"Damn it, Sanders."

"Yes, I know; you know how to do your damn job." She chuckled softly and started walking back towards the main street.

She was a police officer. She had a gun, and she knew how to protect herself. She couldn't imagine a woman, even her, just walking down this back road in the middle of the night looking for someone to kill. She couldn't even begin to profile someone like that. They'd almost have to be insane.

She paused, seeing a man standing in a doorway slowly smoking a cigarette. "Hey, you see anything unusual last night?" Sanders asked, flashing her badge.

"You mean besides children going hungry, drugs changing hands, and money and sex exchanged on every corner?"

"Yeah, besides that."

He blew out a long, skinny stream of smoke. "Just a lady."

Sanders' neck hairs tingled. This was it. "A lady, huh?" She forced herself not to change her stance or show how interested she was. "Why's that unusual?"

"Her type don't normally come down here."

"What was her type?"

"Put together, clean, money, little bit frightened."

"Frightened?" That didn't quite fit.

"Yeah. Said she needed something, but her voice trembled a bit. She didn't want to be here."

"Huh. Did she find what she wanted?"

"Figure she did. Didn't stay long. Ran off just after the gun shots."

"You get a good look at her?" Sanders stopped herself from crossing her fingers. She could ID this crazy bitch right now.

"Nah. She had brown hair, was about your size, that's all I can say."

Well shit. "Age?"

"Didn't ask."

"You remember anything else, here's my card."

He took it with a shrug, and Sanders knew he wouldn't be calling her. He'd said all he wanted to say.

She'd ask Jones to canvas the neighborhood and see if anyone saw anything, but in this neighborhood, probably no one would talk if they had.

She drove slowly back across town, thinking. She didn't have much. A blood sample and maybe a dental impression. Enough to nail the murderer if she could ever find her. But other than that, she had a normal-sized brunette, with a serious anger problem, who killed bad guys. It wasn't enough to wipe her ass with.

"Any units near Westwood?" the dispatcher asked.

"Sanders here. I'm about five minutes away."

"Can you write up a report on a stolen car?"

"Sure. I got nothing better to do."

"Thank you, Detective."

The dispatcher rattled off an address, and Sanders turned, heading towards a high-end residential neighborhood. She pulled into a driveway and knocked on the door. A cheerful-looking woman opened it. "Detective Sanders," Sanders said, showing her badge. "You reported a stolen car?"

"Yes, Detective. Thank you for coming by. My name's Lucy. Lucy Stevenson."

Sanders felt her eyebrow twitch. Stevenson. Well, shit. It was gonna be one of those days.

"Come in please," Lucy said. "Coffee?"

"Sure."

"Black?"

"Yep. So about your car?"

"Let's sit," Lucy said, gesturing to a different room. "My husband and son just sat down for breakfast, but we can sit in the living room."

Richard paled when she walked into the room. Sanders raised an eyebrow, shook her head to the side, and followed Lucy.

Sanders didn't allow Richard to talk about his wife. She didn't give a crap about his life, his wife, his kids. But she was a little surprised. If she had thought about it, she would have expected something else. Not this cheerful, energetic woman. She would have expected someone a little downtrodden. A little cowed. A little weak. Lucy didn't seem any of those things.

"Please sit," Lucy said. "So I was out late last night. I went to the gym and just drove around town for a bit."

"Why'd you drive around town?" Sanders asked, just because it seemed a strange thing to mention.

Lucy frowned. "To be honest, I was a little annoyed at Richard, and I didn't want to come home."

Sanders stopped herself from saying that made sense.

"Anyway," Lucy said. "I got home late, and I was hoping he was asleep so I didn't park in the garage like I normally do. I parked in the driveway and came in through the front door."

"Was he asleep?"

Lucy grimaced. "At first. But that doesn't matter, does it?" She laughed lightly. "I looked out this morning, and my car was gone."

That explained why she'd started the story where she had. To explain why the car hadn't been in the garage like normal. Sanders stared at her carefully. "And did you ask your husband if he took the car?"

"What?" Confusion flitted across her pretty face. "No. I mean I get up before he does to make breakfast, and I told him I'd reported it stolen when he got up. He didn't say anything."

"Does anyone else have a key to the car?"

"No."

"Did you leave the keys in the car?"

"No."

"Is anything else gone?"

"No."

"Did you see anything unusual last night?"

"No."

"Alright. I'll put out a BOLO."

"A what?"

"Be on the lookout."

"Oh."

Sanders stared at Lucy for a moment. "How'd you get the scratches on your neck?" She'd haul Richard downtown right now if he was abusing her.

"Scratches?" Lucy paled and lifted her hand to her neck, feeling it, finding the red, swollen scratches. "I didn't know I had scratches."

"Did someone attack you, Mrs. Stevenson?"

"What? No!" Lucy blinked widely for a moment, looking like a puppy about to get kicked. "I was working in the yard some yesterday. I must have gotten scratched on one of the bushes."

"I see. Well, if someone is abusing you, hurting you, you can call me," Sanders said, giving her a card. "I can help you take care of it."

Lucy blushed and took the card with a nod. "Thank you, Detective. I'm fine. No one is abusing me."

"Alright. Someone will call you if we have any developments on your car, Mrs. Stevenson."

"Please call me Lucy," Lucy said. "What do I turn in to the insurance?"

"I'll email you a copy of the report."

Lucy smiled brilliantly. "Thank you, Detective Sanders. I hope you have a wonderful day."

Sanders grunted. She didn't have the energy for so much enthusiasm. She couldn't imagine how such a pleasant woman had stayed married to Richard for thirty years. She almost felt sorry for her.

15

Lucy heaved a sigh of relief when the door closed behind Detective Sanders. She'd been afraid she would give something away. But she hadn't. At least she didn't think she had.

Her heart had nearly stopped working when the detective had asked about the scratches on her neck. Lucy hadn't even realized they were there, but as soon as she mentioned it, Lucy remembered the man fighting against her, clawing at her.

She'd managed to come up with a believable excuse. She hoped. Detective Sanders hadn't pushed her for more information, just given her a card and left.

She'd never dealt with a police officer before. She hadn't been sure if she would somehow be compulsed to just spill her guts and confess everything bad she'd ever done. Mostly just killing those four guys.

But she hadn't. In fact in a way, it had been kind of fun. Like she knew something no one else did. Which she did. She'd never had a secret before. She kind of liked it.

Richard closed the door quietly behind him and followed Emily to her car. "What the hell're you thinking?" he snapped. "Coming here?"

She rolled her eyes and gave him that look she did sometimes that said she thought he was a complete idiot. He hated that look. He wished he could slap it off her face.

"I didn't know this was your house, Richard. And even if I did, I still had to take the call. I'm a detective. It's my job."

Richard cleared his throat nervously. "So she just wanted to report her car?"

Emily's eyebrow raised. "Yes. Was there something else she should've reported?"

"What? No!" Richard shook his head. "I was just wondering."

"Are you sure?"

"Yes! What the hell're you implying?"

Emily shrugged. "She had some pretty nasty scratches on her throat."

Richard's face wrinkled in confusion. "She did?"

"Do you even look at your wife?" Emily asked with a snort.

"No! Not if I can help it! Are we still on for tonight?"

She shrugged easily. "Sure. But not until after ten. I gotta work."

Nate watched through the kitchen window as his dad argued with the detective. He couldn't hear what they were saying, but he could read body language, and he'd seen his dad's face when the detective walked in. He'd gone so pale he looked like a damn ghost.

He didn't always like to admit when his wife was right, but this time she was; his dad was a cheating dick. Nate would bet money his dad was cheating on his mom with the detective.

He should go out there and punch his face in, but he wasn't sure there wasn't something else going on. He still couldn't figure why his dad had gotten so pissed at his mom about the ten grand he'd withdrawn from the bank, and he wasn't sure why the front door was always unlocked when he came over, even though he specifically locked it every time he left and he was the only one who used it.

He watched the detective get in her car with a frown. It seemed really strange that the one detective his dad was sleeping with happened to show up when his mom reported her car stolen. What were the chances? Something was definitely wrong; he just didn't know what.

Lucy thoroughly enjoyed the rest of her morning. Her rental car was snazzy, even if it did have the smallest trunk she'd ever seen. No one annoying bothered her at work. The police called to say they'd located her car and that it looked like a teenage prank. And her day only got better.

She'd progressed so much that Angela started her on a new routine. Lucy could already lift more weights than she'd ever dreamed possible, and it wouldn't be long before she reached her goal.

After finishing up with Angela, Lucy went to meet Henry by the bags. It still shocked her how much he turned her on. Every time she looked at him a little tingle ran down her spine.

She smiled shyly at him, and he grinned widely back. "Shall I do a couple slow spins before we get started?" he joked.

She shook her head, trying not to blush.

"Then let's see what you got," he said.

She got into stance and threw a few punches at the pads.

"You're holding back," Henry said after a moment.

"I'm not."

"You are. You're aiming for my hand and punching my hand."

"Isn't that what I'm supposed to be doing?"

"No," he said, grinning at her. She stopped herself from giggling. His smile made her weak in the knees.

"Aim for my hand but punch through it."

"What?"

"Carry through. Punch through my hand."

"I don't get it."

"Let me show you," he said, putting down the pads and walking over to a punching bag. "This is what you're doing." He punched the bag, and it swung slightly on its chain. "This is what you should do." He punched the bag again, and it swung backwards with a hard jerk.

Lucy gasped as it swung back towards him, but Henry stopped it with a solid strike to the center. It jolted back and forth a few times, then stuttered to a stop.

"Wow," Lucy breathed. "You're awfully strong."

He raised an eyebrow. "You wanna feel it?" he joked, flexing his bicep.

Lucy almost drooled. "Could I?"

He laughed. "Why not?"

She reached out a trembling hand and lightly squeezed his arm. "Wow... it's... I mean..."

He laughed again, and Lucy felt herself blush. She was such an idiot. "Sorry," she stammered. "I just..."

"Lucy, relax."

"I should go." She fumbled with her hand wrappings,

wanting to get away from him before she did something stupid. Or stupider anyway.

"Lucy, stop." He lifted her face with a warm finger. Her eyes met his, and she blushed again. "I like it," he said.

"What?"

"When you touch my arm. I like it. In fact, I give you permission to touch any part of me you like," he added in a low voice.

Lucy's eyes widened, and she blushed all over, feeling hotter than she had in days. "I... I... I gotta go!"

She spun around and practically flew into the locker room.

"You okay?" Angela asked.

"Huh? What? Yeah." Lucy quickly changed, stuffing her workout clothes in the bag.

"You sure? You seem... flustered."

"Yeah, I mean... Henry... and then... well."

Angela grinned. "He likes you."

Lucy froze. No one had ever liked her. Not really. "I gotta go," she stammered, then ran out the door.

She breathed deeply as she drove to her photography class. She was feeling things she just didn't know what to do with. She was coping with the anger, maybe not in the best way but the only way she knew how. But this... lust? She didn't know what to do with that. *You do.* I don't! *Come on. He gave you permission to touch him anywhere. ANYWHERE!* Shut up!

If angry her also became horny her, she wasn't sure she could handle it.

"You okay?" Stacy asked as they set out on their photography walk.

"Yep."

"You sure?"

"No! Okay! Damn it. I'm... God, I'm hot. There's this guy at the gym, and he... he..." She couldn't say it out loud. It was too embarrassing.

"Turns you on?"

"Yes, damn it!"

Stacy laughed loudly, drawing the attention of their instructor. "Sorry, Mr. Lauricella," she said, before whispering to Lucy, "You should go for it!"

"No! I mean, one, he hasn't asked! Two, I'm married!"

"Yeah, but you're gonna divorce Richard, and he's been cheating on you for years. You guys are practically already separated."

Lucy didn't have an argument for that. "But Henry hasn't actually asked." *But he did say you could touch him ANYWHERE.* Shut up.

Stacy shrugged. "You should ask him out."

"Um, no."

"Why not?"

"I don't do that."

"Why not?"

"Um... I don't know." But she did know. Her father had said women should never make the first move. Woman who made the first move were loose. Lucy had never made a move in her life. Well, except last night. But that was a different kind of move altogether.

"Shhh. I gotta focus." Lucy turned her camera towards a couple in the park. They were holding hands and leaning in together close like they were sharing secrets. She'd never shared secrets with Richard. She had never loved Richard. She'd barely liked Richard. How had she let her life get so screwed up?

It'd be easy to blame her parents and their rules and their

guilt, but although they might have pushed her towards a path, Lucy had been the one to follow it.

But it was like she'd been given another chance. The would-be-robber slash rapist had helped her realize she didn't have to be Lucille. She could be Lucy. And Lucy was strong. She could defend herself. She could divorce Richard. She could make new friends. She could make the first move. Someday.

Denton examined the blood reports. He hadn't actually doubted Sanders, so he wasn't surprised to see he had a match. What he didn't understand, what he'd really never understood, was why Sanders cared so much.

Someone was killing bad guys, guys with records, guys Sanders would happily lock behind bars. So why did she want to nail this killer so much? Wouldn't it be better if they just let the killer do their thing?

But Sanders would never see it that way. Most of the police force wouldn't. They were the enforcers of the laws, and the killer was breaking the law. He didn't understand why common good only mattered sometimes. In fact he honestly didn't understand the whole system. He thought maybe it was broken.

He sighed and picked up his phone to call Sanders.

Richard hated these seedy meeting spots. That was really the only thing he'd miss about Lucille. She was an obsessive cleaner. Other than that, he wouldn't miss her at all. After his short grieving period he'd retire, sell the house, and move to a beach in Mexico.

He'd drink tequila and surround himself with beautiful, fiery Mexican women. Naturally, they'd love him. Because he'd be rich. He smiled, imagining the hot sun on his face and the cool water lapping his feet.

"I have always depended on the kindness of strangers," a husky voice said, as a thin figure wrapped in a trench coat sat beside him.

"God, that's a stupid security phrase," Richard snapped, scooting further down the grungy bus bench. The bus had stopped running here years ago, but the benches were still used for all sorts of things.

"Well?" the woman said irritably.

Richard sighed and muttered grumpily, "I don't want realism. I want magic."

She laughed. "A little more enthusiasm wouldn't be amiss."

"This is ridiculous. Can you do the job or not?"

"Yes."

"Soon? I want it done soon. Tonight, tomorrow, soon! The last guy waited too long and ended up dead before he got the job done."

"Alright. Did you bring the money?"

"Half now. Half when it's done. The last guy fucked me."

"Fine."

Richard handed the woman a paper bag filled with five thousand dollars. She glanced inside. "If you shorted me, I'll kill you instead."

"I didn't short you," Richard snapped. He handed her a slip of paper. "I've written down the address to our house. I'll be gone until Monday. She also goes to a gym called Health Club, but I don't know if she goes on the weekend."

"No problem."

She took the money and faded away into the darkness. Richard just hoped she was more efficient than the last killer he'd hired. He was sick of meeting in scuzzy places like this. He needed to go take a shower.

Lucy heaved a sigh of relief when she saw Richard wasn't home. She couldn't wait until she never had to see him again. She'd move into a cute, little loft downtown. She'd go out whenever she wanted, cook whatever she wanted, do whatever she wanted.

She dumped out her shopping bag on the counter. She'd swung by a store on her way home and bought a trendy little backpack and some other stuff for her kill bag. She hooked the mace she'd purchased on an outer hook. Then she arranged her two gallon Ziplocs, bag of wipes, and extra clothes on the inside. When she was done, she hung it on the coatrack next to the door. Next time she killed someone, she'd be ready.

I still think a utility belt would be cooler. Like Batman. Little obvious, don't you think? *Only if you get it in yellow.* Lucy rolled her eyes. It was hard to believe this was who she was now. The lady who walked around with a kill bag in case she ran into anyone she could kill. It was totally ridiculous. Who would have imagined Lucille Stevenson had it in her? Nobody. And that's why nobody would ever suspect her.

She poured herself a glass of wine, snuggled into her chair, and started reading a new romance. The love scenes were so steamy they almost had her sweating, but the worst part was she couldn't help but imagine it was her and Henry. By the time she was half way through she was so wound up she could hardly stand it.

She tossed the book across the room. "I gotta get a handle on this," she growled. *That's easy. Just reach out and squeeze.* Lucy felt her whole body flush. She knew exactly what part of Henry angry her thought she should squeeze, and she wasn't going to do it.

The front door clicked, and Lucy jumped. "Richard?" she called out. There was no response.

"What the hell?" she muttered, jumping to her feet. Surely no one was breaking into her house again. That would be ridiculous. "Who is it?"

"Sorry, Mom," Nate said as he entered the room. "It's just me."

"Damn it, Nate! Don't you knock? You like to give me a heart attack!"

"Sorry," he said with a lopsided grin.

"What're you doing?" Lucy demanded.

"I came to check up on you."

Lucy raised an eyebrow. "Check up on me?"

"Yeah, Dad mentioned he'd be out of town for the weekend, and I wanted to make sure you're okay."

"Out of town? He didn't tell me."

"Are you and Dad okay?"

"What do you mean?" Lucy asked cautiously. She wasn't sure what Richard might have told him. She didn't know if he was feeding Nate all the same lies he was feeding Addie.

"I don't know. I just thought Dad's been kinda weird lately, and you've been different too. Not taking his shit as much."

"So is that a good thing?"

"Well, yeah. I mean I don't guess I ever realized how much he harps on you. I don't know how you stand it."

Lucy laughed. "It isn't easy. I wasn't going to tell you kids yet, but I'm meeting with a lawyer on Monday and filing for divorce."

"Oh." Nate sat on the couch and stared at her. "Does Dad know?"

"I told him I want a divorce."

"He didn't say anything to me."

"Why would he?"

"The other day he was asking me about Mexico. He's never talked about traveling before. I mean... It was weird."

That was weird. Richard hated the idea of travel. He complained every single time he had to "crap on someone else's toilet".

"I think it's just because I'm not giving into him anymore," Lucy said with a shrug.

"Maybe. Did he ever tell you what the ten grand was for?"

"No."

"Did he take out more?"

"What? No; I don't think so."

"You should check."

"Why?"

Nate glanced around awkwardly and shrugged his shoulders. "I dunno. If he knows you're going to leave him he might by trying to siphon off the bank accounts."

Lucy paled. She hadn't even thought of that. "But... I mean... That's OUR money!"

"I dunno, Mom. Maybe I'm wrong. I just... He was so weird about the money... Anyway."

"Why the sudden concern?" Lucy demanded.

Nate's face turned tomato red, and he mumbled something. "What?" Lucy asked.

"Lisa said I've been being an ass."

"Lisa? Why?"

"I told her you've been standing up to Dad and stuff, and she said it was about time, and that if you grew a pair of balls maybe you'd kick me out on my ass too."

Lucy burst out laughing. "Your wife said that to you?"

"Yep."

"And you listened?"

"I guess."

"I've never been so proud of you!"

"Damn, thanks Mom."

Lucy laughed, then said, "I'm fine, Nate. Thanks for checking up on me. I'll look at the accounts. Now go home to your wife. I'll see you on Monday?"

He grinned. "Only if you don't mind?"

"As long as you don't complain and Lisa doesn't care, you're welcome anytime."

"Even after the divorce?"

Lucy paused. She hadn't thought of that. Would she still get up at five every morning once she didn't have to take care of Richard? "How about once a week?"

"That'd be nice," Nate said, giving her an awkward hug. "Um... Love you, Mom."

"You'd think I'm dying!" Lucy laughed, pushing him away. "Get out of here."

He rolled his eyes. "I'm just trying to be nice."

"Stop it! It's creepy!"

Nate laughed. "See you Monday."

After he'd locked the door behind him, Lucy burst out laughing. The look on his face when he'd said Lisa had told him he was an ass. She wished she'd been there for the conversation.

She sobered, thinking of Richard. She quickly logged onto their bank account, gasping when she saw he'd taken out another ten grand. Twenty thousand wasn't too big of a deal, but if he kept doing it, their savings would soon be drained. She'd ask the lawyer what to do about it on Monday.

As he left Nate triple checked the door. It was locked. He'd locked it this morning after breakfast, but it hadn't been locked when he'd gotten here just now. He sat in his car for a while watching the house. A few cars drove down the street, but an old sedan drove past twice. He noticed because the driver had glanced at his parents' house on her first pass. On her second pass she looked at him, and he frowned at her. He waited for an hour, but she didn't drive by again and no one fiddled with the door.

He shook his head. He was acting a little insane. He couldn't begin to think of a reason for anyone to want to hurt his mom. She was so... docile. At least she'd used to be. Unless his dad... but he couldn't even think that way. Maybe they were both going through a mid-life crisis.

He glanced up and down the street one last time then drove home.

"I want to stay with you tonight."

"Richard, you know my rules."

"If you don't let me stay the night I'm not coming back."

Sanders sighed. Richard was getting pushy, and that wouldn't do at all. "Richard, listen..."

"No, you listen," he interrupted. "We're always playing things by your rules, and I'm sick of it! I stay the night, or we're done." His expression was petulant, and his cheeks were an ugly shade of purple.

Sanders sighed. She really didn't have time to break in a new sex partner. "I guess we're done then."

His face turned an even deeper shade, and Sanders watched him in irritation. She would not be happy if he burst a blood vessel and she had to call an ambulance. That was simply a conversation she did not want to have.

She didn't have time for this right now. She had a serial killer to catch, and she didn't need Richard getting in her way.

"Get out of that getup!" she snapped. "And then get out of my house!"

He stared at her, mouth moving, words failing to come out. "You're... you're serious?" He finally stuttered.

"Yes!"

She'd never noticed how crazy his eyes looked when he was mad. She'd never realized what an ugly bastard he was either, but that shade of purple did him absolutely no favors.

Richard tore at the buckles on his wrists. "You're gonna regret this," he fumed.

"I don't see how," Sanders said, voice hard. "You do realize you're dealing with a detective, right? You can't threaten me."

Richard's mouth snapped shut. He ripped the rest of his restraints off, threw them at her feet, dressed, and walked out, slamming the door behind him.

Sanders watched him go with a raised eyebrow. She would have to be more careful picking partners in the future. She hadn't realized how on edge Richard was.

She shrugged it off and opened the file on her desk. She had a nice set of dental impressions, just waiting for a match. And she had one more dead bad guy. Rapist, mugger, drug dealer, pimp.

She wasn't upset he was dead. Dead bad guys never upset her. But she still had a job to do. People went around murdering people, even bad people, and she had to stop them. She left it to the courts to work out the rights and wrongs of it all. That wasn't her job. Her job was to find the bastards and bring them in.

And she was very, very good at her job.

Richard hated women. They were emotional and stupid and a waste of time. No matter what he did, it was impossible to please them. Because they were mercurial. Constantly changing.

That's why he preferred hookers. They didn't demand, didn't argue, didn't put up a fight, didn't cry afterwards. They just did what they were told, and they were happy as long as you paid them.

He tossed Cinnamon her money and watched her saunter out the door. She'd helped take the edge off. But he wouldn't be happy until he was wife-free and out of this town.

16

Lucy woke just before five. She wondered if that was ever a habit she would break as she rolled out of bed and started stretching.

She ate a light breakfast, enjoying her Richard-free home. She flipped through the paper, pausing long enough to read about the multiple homicides on the south side. Four men dead of gunshot wounds; one man dead of severe trauma to the head. They still didn't have anything. Zilch. Nothing.

When are we gonna do it again? We just did it. *Yeah, but...* But what? We just did it, and we need a system. Walking into the south side every time we need a fix is not a plan.

Furthermore, Ralphy got us nine days. It's only been one. *Two.* One. We should be able to go at least two weeks, don't you think? Especially if we don't spend any time with Richard. Angry her sighed. *If you say so.* I do. There can't be that many bad people around town. We'll run out if we go out killing every day.

There had to be a way not to have to kill at all, but she hadn't figured that out yet. She'd tried everything she could think of, and it's not like she could google "how to manage anger so as not to kill anyone".

She cleaned up her breakfast dishes and glanced around. Normally she'd clean on Saturday. Dust, vacuum the couches, balance the checkbook, bleach the whites. But she didn't want to do any of that today.

She wanted to go apartment hunting. Then shopping for... just stuff. Then... She didn't know, but she would figure it out.

She looked at ten different loft apartments, but by eleven she'd found the perfect one and even signed the papers. She couldn't move in for two months, but Lucy figured that was just about right.

It was the perfect home. It was located above a bakery, and it smelled fantastic. Lucy's mouth watered just stepping out on the little balcony which would be perfect for a box of tulips. Best of all she liked the saucy landlord, a little elderly woman named Gertrude.

After saying goodbye to Gertrude, Lucy ordered a soup and salad in an Irish pub, thinking how strange it was she'd never eaten in a bar before. She sipped her Irish coffee happily, watching the other patrons, wishing she had her camera.

Her neck tingled, and she looked behind her. There was a couple laughing over burgers. They weren't watching her, but it felt like someone was. Lucy took a slow scan of the room, searching, but she didn't see anyone looking at her. She shrugged the strange feeling off and finished her whisky laced coffee.

Then she walked down the street going into every shop

that caught her eye. She bought crazy-colored socks in one store, open-toed sandals in another. She bought a small piece of artwork with a silhouette of a bird on a wire. She bought three bags of coffee from a coffee shop that did their own roasting.

She was feeling very happy with herself when she finally walked into a cozy used-book store. "Do you have any romance novels?" she asked the clerk.

The young man pointed down an aisle, and Lucy gasped. "Do you mean... are those ALL romance novels?"

"Yep," he said with a disinterested shrug.

"Oh my goodness." Lucy wandered down the aisle, looking from side to side. There were so many books she didn't know which one to look at first. She finally picked up a book with a large muscly man on the cover. He made her think of Henry.

She was caught up reading the summary when a voice whispered in her ear. "Any good?"

Lucy yelped, dropping the book and turning, face hot with embarrassment. "I don't... I mean... I just picked it up."

Henry chuckled softly, looking totally different in his street clothes, a black t-shirt, blue jeans, and scarred work boots. Lucy stared at him. He was even better looking in regular clothes. It just wasn't fair.

"I've only... I mean... I just started..." Lucy closed her mouth. There was no way out of this without looking like an idiot. She grinned and shrugged. "It looked alright. Maybe a little cliché. Bad boy, good girl. You know."

He picked it up and handed it to her with a mischievous grin. "You should definitely get it then."

"I don't know. I was hoping for something with vampires. I have a friend who said... Well never mind what she said."

"Now I want to know."

Lucy turned red again. "Sorry; confidential. So what're you doing here?"

"I like to keep an eye out for old editions."

"Of romances?"

He laughed. "No; classics. Although I do have an edition of *Pride and Prejudice,* and I suppose that is a romance. Anyway, I just picked up a fifties edition of *The Strange Case of Dr. Jekyll and Mr. Hyde.* Not terribly old or valuable, but I like the binding."

"You collect books?" Lucy asked.

"Just ones I like."

"Huh."

"What?"

"Nothing. I just..."

"Did I ruin my bad boy image?" he asked, eyes twinkling.

"Maybe just a little," Lucy said with a shrug. "But it's okay. I still like you."

"How about coffee then?"

"What?"

"Buy your cliché romance and go to coffee with me."

"But... I'm still married," Lucy whispered.

"I'm not asking you to sleep with me," he said with a wink. "Just coffee."

Lucy felt ridiculous. Of course he just meant coffee. What else would he mean? It's not like coffee was code for sex. It's just... She'd never had any male friends. Her parents had always said men and women couldn't be friends. So she'd thought coffee meant... well, more than coffee.

Henry shrugged and added, "I wouldn't mind if someday it was more than coffee. I like you, Lucy."

Lucy stared at him. "Really?"

"Really."

"Why?" she blurted out.

He chuckled and said, "'Cause you have a sense of humor. You smile a lot. You're nice to Angela. You're cute when you blush. And some other stuff."

Lucy just stared at him, for once unaware of the blush creeping over her face. He was smiling, but his tone was serious. He meant what he was saying.

She was hot everywhere, but it felt good. He liked her. He actually liked her. And he wanted to have coffee with her. And someday he wanted more than coffee.

Lucy grinned. "I'd love to have coffee with you."

Just when it was getting to the good part Richard's phone beeped. He grunted in irritation, fumbled for the pause button, and tapped his phone's screen.

He'd expected Lucille to call him and demand to know where he was or something, but she hadn't said a damn thing. Maybe she was already dead. He wondered how the lady he'd hired would do it. Suffocation? Strangulation? Drowning? He didn't really care as long as it got done.

There weren't any messages on his phone, but he was sure he'd heard a beep. Maybe it was the killer, texting to say it was done. He pulled out the pre-paid phone he'd bought and saw he had a photo text.

"That lying bitch!" He couldn't believe it. It was a photo of Lucille, his lying, stupid wife, sitting at a table, making moon eyes at some big, dumb shit. How dare she? Like he wasn't enough for her!

"Just get the job done!" he texted back angrily, fighting the urge to heave the phone across the room. He wished he could kill Lucille himself. He'd slap her around a few times, then maybe run her over with his car. Or strangle her. He'd like to see her stupid doe eyes grow wide with fear and confusion.

Lucy smiled widely as she pulled into the garage. She'd had a wonderful day. Probably the best day she'd ever had. She'd bought what she wanted, eaten what she wanted, spent time with who she wanted.

She'd end the day the way she wanted too. Drinking wine, soaking in her tub, and reading her silly romance novel. She blushed, thinking of Henry.

Henry was a wonderful man. He was handsome, strong, sweet, and funny. He didn't make her feel stupid or weak or less. He made her feel confident, even if she was a blubbering idiot around him. He made her want to say what she thought. She liked him. A lot.

I like him too. I like his ass. I like his... You don't get a say! Lucy snapped. *Why not?* We've been over this. You're... naughty.

Angry her laughed. *I think you should call me "naughty me" instead of "angry me".* Lucy raised an eyebrow. That actually made sense. Angry her wasn't always angry. Sometimes she was horny. Sometimes she was silly. Sometimes she just wanted to touch something she shouldn't like the Tiffany lamp they'd seen in a fancy boutique. But no matter what she was, she was always naughty. Naughty her didn't give a damn about the rules.

I can't believe you didn't invite him home. Lucy felt her body turn hot. Part of her would've loved to invite Henry home. She would've loved to invite him to touch her. Anywhere, everywhere. She wanted him to touch her. Every time his hand brushed hers, she shuddered. But she wasn't ready yet. She was still discovering Lucy and what Lucy liked, and she didn't want to muddle it up with sex.

She sighed happily, twirling around as she walked to the bathroom. It couldn't have been a more perfect day. Richard was gone. She'd found an apartment. She'd bought all sorts of silly stuff, and she'd spent a wonderful afternoon with Henry.

She started the tub filling and went into the kitchen to get a glass of wine. She frowned and glanced out the window. She hadn't been able to shake the feeling she was being watched. Which was stupid. Why would anyone watch her?

She closed the blinds, put her wine and book beside the tub, and stripped. She started to get in the tub but decided she needed music and candles. She pulled Enya up on her phone, lit five candles, and dimmed the light. "Perfect," she said with a sigh.

She heard the tile creak just before a pair of hands grabbed her from behind and pushed her towards the tub.

"What the hell?" Lucy stammered, feet slipping beneath her.

Suddenly her face was right above the water. Lucy struggled frantically, holding the side of the tub, but with each second her face moved closer to the steamy, rose-scented water.

"Damn it!" she hissed as her hands slipped on the slick metal. "I will not die this way!" *FIGHT!* I am! *You're not!* She hated it when naughty her was right, but she didn't know how to fight. If she stopped holding the tub she'd get forced under the water.

Terror was so thick in her that she was having trouble thinking. The only thing she could do was hold the tub and try not to get pushed under. But the water was just in front of her now. If she stuck out her tongue she could lick it.

She braced her arms and breathed deeply, trying to calm herself. She had to break free and there was only one way to do that. She took a deep breath and let go of the tub. The second her fingers left the metal her head splashed under the hot water. Lucy closed her eyes, held her breath, and struggled not to panic.

She gathered all her strength and swung her arm behind her, bashing her attacker in the head with the shampoo bottle she'd grabbed on the way down.

The iron grip loosened, and Lucy jerked free, ripping herself from the water and stumbling away from the tub. She blinked to clear the water from her eyes, then ducked as her attacker rushed her.

"What the hell do you want?!" Lucy screamed.

The woman didn't respond as she bore down on Lucy, grabbing her hair and dragging her back towards the tub.

"Fuck this!" Lucy snapped, shoving her fear aside and letting anger replace it. She shoved the woman away, screaming as hair tore from her scalp. Lucy jumped forward, grabbing one of the lit candles and throwing it in the woman's face. Hot wax flew everywhere.

The woman let out a startled grunt, but the candle didn't slow her down. She grabbed Lucy again, this time by the throat.

Lucy ignored the woman's squeezing hands and grabbed another candle, shoving it into the woman's eye. The woman shrieked, hands leaving Lucy's throat to rip at the wax searing her face.

"This is my house!" Lucy snarled, grabbing her wine glass and ramming it into the woman's face. The glass shattered, tearing skin as it went. The attacker scrambled backwards, one eye sealed shut, face cut and bleeding.

She stumbled towards the door of the bathroom, but Lucy couldn't let her get away, she couldn't let her run. She grabbed the woman's arm and pulled her back, stabbing the woman's other eye with the broken stem of her glass.

The woman shrieked and flailed wildly, trying to hold Lucy off. Lucy pushed past her grasping hands, grabbed hold of her short hair and pulled her towards the tub.

Lucy snatched the soap bar off the rim and bashed it into her attacker's head. Wet blood smeared everywhere making the soap slippery, and Lucy dropped it.

"How dare you?!" Lucy growled, lifting the woman's head up and smashing it into the tub rim. "This is MY house!" She bashed it again and again. Her hands were slick with blood, but she just twisted her fingers into the hair tighter.

"THIS IS MY BATHROOM! MY TUB!" She was so angry. So angry that someone had come into her home and tried to kill her again.

Lucy raised the woman's head again, ramming it into the tub rim with such force the side of the woman's face caved in. Her hands immediately stopped grasping, and she dropped limply to the floor.

Lucy stood over her, lungs heaving. God, she was mad! She wanted to grab a piece of glass and bash it into the woman's face, but she was already dead. Maybe.

Lucy knelt down to feel for her pulse. There wasn't one. She was definitely dead. Lucy glanced at the woman's face and grimaced. And if she wasn't dead, she'd want to be dead. Wax had burned and cooled all over the dead woman's face. Both eyes were ruined, her cheeks were full of jagged punctures, and the entire right side of her head was crushed flat.

Lucy sighed and sat on the bloody tub rim. There was

blood splatter all over the bathroom. Even her skin was coated in blood. Her hands and feet hurt like hell, and she imagined underneath the blood there were lacerations from the glass. But she was alive. And that crazy, bitch, whoever she was, was dead.

What were the chances? She'd been attacked in her home not just once but twice in less than two months. That was unreal. It didn't make sense at all.

Someone wants you dead. That's ridiculous. *Seriously. You're out of your mind. Your mind.* Shut up! Lucy stood, flinching as a piece of glass cut into her foot.

"Always with the damn messes," she muttered. She ripped the shard of glass out of her foot, slipped some dirty socks on and limped upstairs to get clean. She took a shower, cleaned up her feet, wrapped them, got dressed, and went to get the dust pan. She was glad Richard was gone. At least she didn't have to hurry.

"Glass first, then search the body, then cut it into damn pieces," she griped as she swept up the glass.

You should be happy. Why? *We didn't have to go looking. One came to us.* Lucy snorted. I would be happy if it had come to us outside, where I didn't have to clean up the mess. *Gripe, gripe, gripe.* Now you sound like Richard. *You take that back!* No.

Lucy swept up the floor, then searched the body. She only found a phone and some keys. Nothing else. She tried to open the phone, but she couldn't get past the phone lock, so she wiped it down and put it back in the woman's pocket. She put the keys in her own pocket, then she stared at the body for a minute.

"Oh hell," she muttered. "I probably ruined the damn saw." Naughty her laughed. Shut the hell up!

Lucy walked slowly to the garage, ruing the day she hadn't just let that man kill her, and pulled down the red saw box.

She plugged the saw in, crossed her fingers, and pulled the trigger. It jerked to life. "Yes!" Lucy yelled, jumping up and down. "Yes!"

Naughty her laughed again but Lucy ignored her and grabbed the extension cord and a handful of black trash bags as she headed back to the bathroom.

She was amazed at how calm she was. It was like she'd done it a hundred times instead of once.

She started with the arms again. They came off easier than she'd expected, and she wasn't even winded. Working out had really paid off. She shoved the arms in one bag together and went to work on the first leg.

Her arm jerked as the saw grabbed the woman's jeans and lurched forward. Lucy cut the power, but the material was wrapped up in the blade. She unplugged the saw and pulled at the fabric, but it wouldn't budge. She finally got some scissors, cut the fabric away, cut the pant legs open, then started sawing again.

When she was finally done she only had three bags, because she'd tossed the head in with the arms and she'd put the legs together. She carefully cleaned all the blood off the floor and tub, wiping down the cabinets and walls. She washed the bar of soap and candles off, threw them in the trash, and drained the pinkish, lukewarm tub water.

Then she rebagged the body parts, cleaned the floor again, and carried the bags out to the garage. She stared at her trunk in disgust. When she bought a new car she needed to make sure it had a big trunk. The trunk on the rental was barely big enough for groceries, let alone a body.

She shoved the bags in the backseat and went back inside. She put the saw, extension cord, and scissors in the dishwasher and started it. She dumped all the towels and cleaning cloths in the washer and started it. She double checked the bathroom, blowing out the remaining candles and turning off the music.

On her way out to the car she grabbed her kill bag, just in case. She got in her car, started the engine, and backed out into the driveway. It had taken her a while to clean everything up, so it was already after eleven and she didn't have to worry about a bunch of people seeing her.

She paused at the bottom of the driveway. She didn't know which way to go. They'd found the body she'd dumped in the dumpster. She'd used the same method so it probably wouldn't be good if they found this body too, but what else could she do with it?

She couldn't get into the reservoir without paying, and she still thought the bags would float. A different dumpster would have the same problem. And she refused to dump them out in the wild for some kid to find. She sighed and started to drive towards the grocery store. Maybe this time no one would find them.

She dumped them in the same dumpster, amazed how much easier it was than last time. Granted the woman was a lot smaller and lighter, but Lucy didn't struggle at all. She'd have to give Angela a bonus.

When all three bags were dumped, she drove back home and looked carefully up and down the street. The woman's key ring didn't have a fob, so she must have driven an older car. There. Three houses away.

Lucy parked her car in the garage, grabbed a pair of gloves, and headed towards the dark car parked along the curb. She glanced around to make sure no one was out, but it was after midnight, and most everyone on her block was in bed already.

She slipped the key in the lock, opened the door, and sat down inside. It stank like floral perfume and stale cigarettes. Lucy rolled down the window and tried to breathe shallowly.

She opened the glove box, but there was nothing there. She looked under the seats and searched every inch of the car, but there was nothing. Not even a scrap of paper or piece of trash. It was totally clean.

Lucy sighed and rolled the window back up. She thought about moving the car, but figured she may as well just leave it where it was. There were twelve other houses on the block, and not a single thing to connect the car to Lucy.

Back inside she poured herself a new glass of wine and flopped into her chair. *So who's trying to kill you?* I can't... I mean... It's gotta just be a crazy coincidence. *Yeah?* Seriously. Why would anyone want me dead? Up until a month ago I was Lucille Stevenson. Most people probably don't even remember me.

Naughty her tried to say something, but Lucy shushed her. I don't want to talk about it. She drained her wine, dropped her head back, and drifted off to sleep.

17

Detective Sanders could not believe he hadn't learned his lesson. Finding a dismembered head in a trash bag should have cured him of dumpster diving forever, yet here they were. Same dumpster, same diver, same method of disposal.

"Only three bags this time, Detective."

"I can count," Sanders growled. "Are all the body parts there?"

"I don't know."

"Open 'em up."

"But..."

"Do it!"

The uniform grimaced, but did as he was told. All the body parts were there. She'd economized this time, but it was definitely her. Same neat little knots tying the bags closed. Same jagged cut marks. Same totally destroyed face.

So why were three bodies left where they were killed and two dropped into the dumpster? And why the same damn dumpster? Surely the killer knew they had found the first body.

Sanders carefully pulled the bag back from the victim's torso. She'd been surprised to see a woman. She'd assumed the killer was targeting men before. Bad men, but men.

She heard a beep near the body and rolled the torso up with her foot. There was a phone in the victim's back pocket. She pulled on a glove and fished the phone out. Locked. Sanders stared at the pin pad and typed in "1234". The phone opened.

"Amateur," Sanders muttered.

"Sanders!" Denton yelled, striding up to the trash bags.

"I know. I haven't. I'm done." Sanders pushed past Denton and walked back to her car, hoping the phone would give her a clue. Any clue, just something to help her nail the killer.

The last thing she needed today was to go to the chief and tell him they had a serial killer loose in the city. She'd rather meet a nice man, settle down, and have two point five kids. Sanders shuddered and opened the text message screen.

A number, no contact. "Is it done?"

"Is what done?" Sanders muttered, scrolling up. "Oh shit."

Richard waited for an hour, but his hired killer didn't respond. He finally called Lucille, holding his breath, hoping she didn't answer, fighting not to curse when she did.

"Richard."

"Lucille."

"You okay?"

"Yes. You?" he asked stupidly.

She was quiet for a moment, then she said, "What do you need?"

"Nothing. I just wanted to check in with you."

"Really?"

"Yes, goddamn it! I'll... um... see you tomorrow."

"Okay."

He hung up the phone with a growl. What the hell? How was it possible that he could not hire a competent killer? Maybe his luck hadn't changed. Maybe his luck would never change.

"Get your ass back in here!" Richard yelled at Cinnamon. "I'm not done with you yet!"

It was Richard. No. *Yes.* No! *Why can't you see it?* Why? He has absolutely no reason to kill me or want me dead! *You told him you wanted a divorce!* So? The most I'll get is half the house. *You're being naive.* You just want an excuse to kill Richard, and it's not going to happen.

Her phone rang again. Nate.

"Hey, Nate."

"Hey, Mom. How you doing?"

Seriously? "Fine; why?"

"Just wanted to check up on you."

Lucy laughed. "That must be going around."

"What?"

"I just got off the phone with your dad, and he said the same thing."

"Seriously?"

"Seriously. I don't think he's ever called to check on me."

"That's weird."

"Everything's fine, Nate. Relax. Enjoy your Sunday, and tell Lisa hi."

Lucy paced through her house, feeling totally at loose ends. She didn't want to clean, and she honestly had nothing else to do. She hadn't realized how much of her life she'd used cleaning. It was kind of pathetic.

She finally decided to go to the gym. When she left the

house she saw the woman's car was still parked up the street. She wondered how long it would be before someone called it in.

She glanced in her rearview as she drove, feeling once again as though someone was watching her. "This is ridiculous," she muttered, scanning the cars surrounding her but seeing nothing unusual. "The stress must be getting to me."

Naughty her snorted. *Or someone's following you.* Why? *Why do you need a reason?* Why would someone do something without a reason? Everything I do, I do for a reason. Naughty her didn't respond.

Lucy parked, grabbed her bag, and jogged into the gym. She'd never gone when Angela wasn't there, but she figured she'd just run through their routine and then maybe punch at a bag for a while. It was certainly better than cleaning.

Detective Sanders watched Lucy Stevenson trot into the gym with a frown. It couldn't be her. She was so... damn cheerful. And bouncy. She simply could not imagine Lucy Stevenson completely disfiguring someone's face in an absolute rage. Of course, she had been married to Richard for thirty years, and that could drive anyone insane.

She pulled out her phone and called Denton. "Find anything yet?"

"There's a second blood, and it matches the others. Definitely the same killer."

"Tell me something I didn't already know!"

"You assumed. Now you have actual proof."

"Damn it, Denton! Did you find anything useful?!"

"No."

"Shit." This was all going to blow up in her face. She just knew it.

Richard watched Detective Sanders watch Lucille with a frown. Why was Emily watching Lucille? He didn't think she'd suddenly decided to get jealous. She'd never been the type.

He ground his teeth in frustration. If Emily was following Lucille it was going to make it that much harder for his little assassin to kill Lucille. But his assassin hadn't returned any of his texts so maybe she'd skipped town with his money.

Everything was going to hell, and he was running out of time.

Denton traced Silvia's face through the glass. He wished he could touch her real face just one more time. He hated the cool feel of the glass; her skin had always been warm and soft. He missed her. He wished Sanders would put half as much energy into putting Eddie Harris behind bars as she was putting into this vigilante.

The newest victim had been a killer for hire. She'd been picked up multiple times, but they could never make anything stick because she was so good at her job. Just like Eddie. Everyone knew she'd done it; they just couldn't prove it.

It always came back to the evidence.

I liked killing a woman. What? *It was kinda cool. We should do it again.* Lucy rolled her eyes. It's Monday morning; it's literally been less than forty-eight hours since we killed her. *So?* So?! So we don't need to kill again so soon. We don't even need to talk about killing! What's wrong with you? *What's wrong with you? 'Cause you know I'm YOU.* Just shut up, Lucy sighed.

She'd heard Richard come home late last night, and she wasn't looking forward to seeing him this morning. Saturday and Sunday had been so lovely, even if she had been attacked by a crazy killer lady.

Richard grunted when he sat at the table and saw the toast and jam. "Would it have killed you to make some scrambled eggs or something?" he grumbled.

"No."

"Then why the hell didn't you?"

"Didn't feel like it," Lucy replied with a shrug. Richard was always so much easier to handle after a kill. It's like she took all the anger in her life and just shoved it into that quick little moment of killing someone. It made things much more pleasant.

Nate filled his coffee cup and watched Richard silently.

"How's the gym?" Richard growled.

"Fine."

"Have you met anyone new?"

Lucy stared at him for a moment. His lips were tight around the edges, and he seemed sharper, more bitter than usual.

"A few people," she said cautiously, unnerved by what seemed like an attempt at a causal conversation.

"Any men?"

Lucy sighed. "Richard, I told you. I'm not cheating on you."

Nate choked on his coffee. "Damn it, Dad! What the hell? Mom would never cheat on you!"

"Really?" Richard snarled. "Not even if she met someone tall and dark and musclebound?"

Sounds like Henry to me. But that would mean... *He's been following us!* Lucy paled. If Richard had been watching her that would mean... But if he'd seen her do anything surely he would have called the police.

"Dad! What the hell's gotten into you?" Nate snapped.

"Why don't you ask your mother?!"

Lucy wasn't entirely sure what he meant. He hadn't hinted at murder just adultery. She smiled at Nate and said, "Your father's just grumpy this morning. Don't mind him. Anyway, I have an appointment with a lawyer, and I don't want to be late."

Nate finished his breakfast and left before his mom came back downstairs. He couldn't believe his dad. The way he was acting was insane. Accusing his mom of having an affair. And the way she'd just sat there, so reasonable, like his dad hadn't done anything wrong.

And the damn door had been unlocked again. And that freaking car from Friday was still sitting on their street. He wasn't overreacting. There was something going on, and he didn't like it.

As Lucy drove across town, she wondered at Richard's strange attitude. He'd supposedly been out of town, but had he really been here watching her the whole time? And if so, why? *Let's kill him.* NO! Damn it! Stop bringing it up! *Whatever.*

The meeting with the lawyer took an hour and a half. Lucy filled out all the necessary paperwork, specifying that she wanted half of everything, but she wasn't asking for anything more. When she was done, she felt twenty pounds lighter and twenty years younger.

She drove to work, served wine to several honeymooning couples, fielded a few phone calls, chatted with the delivery men, and bought a bottle of wine so she could celebrate later with Stacy.

"Sanders here."

"It's Denton. I got a hit on your hitter."

"What?"

"Blues picked up a car this morning, fake plates and registration. We found a fingerprint, and it matches the hitter."

Sanders heart thudded. "Where did they pick it up?"

"On Vine."

Shit.

"A Nate Stevenson called it in, said he'd seen it Friday going up and down his parents' street. Said he thought it was suspicious it was still parked there."

Sanders banged her head on her desk. Shit, shit, shit.

"You okay Sanders?"

"Yep. Fine."

"K. That's all I got."

That was enough. She'd wanted evidence; she'd wanted connections; she'd wanted suspects. Well, now she had them.

After work Lucy went through her routine with Angela.

"You've really improved," Angela praised as Lucy cooled down.

"You're an amazing trainer. The other day I did something I struggled at before I came to you, and it was a breeze!"

"I'm glad. There's a new Yoga class opening up next week. If it works out you should sign up. I think you'd like it. But in the meantime, I think Henry's waiting for you."

Lucy blushed all over.

"Geez; you guys are pathetic," Angela laughed. "You blush every time you look at him. And he looks at you like he'd like to... Well you get the idea."

Lucy wished the floor would open up and swallow her. "I can't... I mean... I really like him," she whispered. "But I'm still figuring out who I want to be, you know?"

"I get you. Just don't wait too long. Somebody else might snatch him up."

Lucy felt a burst of red, hot anger at the idea of someone besides her snatching Henry up.

"You ready?" Henry asked with a wide smile.

Lucy glared at him. He better not even think about letting anyone else snatch him up.

"You okay?"

Lucy almost growled. *Get a grip, woman! What?! No one's snatching anyone! At least not yet. In fact, you should just suck it up and do the snatching 'cause you know you want to.* Lucy frowned. It had to be a bad sign that naughty her was being the reasonable one right now.

"Lucy?"

Lucy shook her head slightly and smiled at Henry. "Sorry; I was off in la la land."

"Is it nice there?"

"Could use an umbrella."

"I hear that." He tucked a lock of Lucy's hair behind her ear, leaving a trail of heat on her skin. "Shall we?"

"Um... yeah." *Snatch it, girl!* Shut up!

Richard stopped half a block away from the gym and hissed in irritation. He couldn't watch Lucille if Emily was watching her, which she was. And it was going to be a little more difficult to do what he'd planned if he couldn't watch her. Everything was falling down around his ears, just like always, but this time he wasn't going to let it.

"I'll see you tomorrow," Lucy said, waving goodbye to Henry and stepping into her car. She put the keys in the ignition but paused, looking around the parking lot. She still felt like she was being watched, but she didn't see anyone.

The idea of Richard sitting out there somewhere watching her made her feel ill. He'd never been the crazy jealous type, but she'd also never given him a reason to be jealous. She wished she'd thought to divorce him sooner. She didn't want to live with him for another two months.

She glanced around one more time. She didn't see Richard. She didn't see anyone that looked like they were following her. She must be getting paranoid. *Someone is trying to kill us; you should be paranoid.*

Lucy didn't respond. She wanted to argue. She wanted to say it was just a coincidence, that no one would try to kill her, but she couldn't quite get her mouth to form the words. She couldn't quite say them because she didn't quite believe them.

She believed in chance, but two random killers in the same house within two months? On nights Richard just happened to be gone? It wasn't happenstance. It wasn't. She just didn't know what it was.

18

Richard stared in disgust at his reheated soup. This is what he got. After thirty years of slaving away to make sure Lucille had everything she needed and wanted, he got reheated soup. Vegetable soup with hunks of carrot at that.

He'd picked her because she was docile, because he knew he'd be able to carry on however he wanted and she wouldn't do a damn thing. And she hadn't. But it was boring being married to a woman like that. He hated coming home to her vapid face and cold body parts. He hated touching her. He hated sharing his toothpaste with her.

He couldn't wait to be rid of her. Couldn't wait. Really couldn't wait. He needed her gone now. Before the divorce went through. Before her birthday. Before Emily figured out whatever she was trying to figure out.

He flipped open the paper. At least he didn't have to deal with her insipid conversation. "How was your day, dear?" "Did you do anything interesting?" "Where did you go for lunch?"

He couldn't count the number of times he'd wanted to stuff Lucille's mouth full of socks. Or newspaper. Rocks. Anything that would shut her up.

He scanned the headlines, choking on a carrot when he saw a headline reading "Second Body Found in Grocery Store Dumpster. Serial Killer on the Loose?"

He forgot about his soup and read the article, eyebrow twitching as he did. He reread the line "Detective Sanders, lead detective on the case, offered no comment".

He read the victim's name and stared at her mugshot, feeling sick to his stomach. She hadn't taken his money and skipped town. She'd ended up dead in a dumpster. Just like the last one he'd hired.

Was it possible... Could... No... He shook his head in disbelief. Not Lucille. She was too dumb. Too cow-eyed. Too stupid to even wipe her own ass without permission.

He frowned. At least she had used to be.

"Here's to divorce!" Stacy said, downing another cup of wine.

Lucy laughed. They were sitting on Stacy's back porch, surrounded by solar lights and sweet smelling passionflowers. Stacy's husband was inside making them tiny cucumber sandwiches.

"My divorce," Lucy said, tipping her own glass back.

"God, yes! I'd never divorce Frank. Not only is he very handy to have around in case of emergencies, but I also really like his ass. Don't tell him," Stacy whispered "He thinks I keep him around for his brain."

"I heard that," Frank chuckled. "Here's your sandwiches, ladies. Don't drink too much or I'll have to lock myself in the bathroom tonight." He winked at Lucy. "She's a handsy drunk."

Lucy burst out laughing. "I'm sure that's very hard for you."

"You have no idea."

"You have a wonderful husband," Lucy said after Frank had gone back inside.

"I do," Stacy said with a sigh. "So what about your guy?"

"What about him?"

"You gonna ask him out?"

"I dunno."

"Why not?"

"I just... I hate the idea of just going from Richard to another guy. Like I need a man."

Stacy smiled. "It's not like that, Lucy. You don't NEED a man, but you can certainly enjoy having one in your life."

She's a smart lady. Hush. "You don't think it's... I dunno... weak?"

"Weak?" Stacy ate a sandwich, then said, "Hell no! Could I live without Frank? Sure. But would I have as much fun? No. A man, a partner, a friend, should always add to your life, not take away or come up neutral."

"Wow; you're smart when you're drunk."

Stacy sniffed. "I'm smart ALL the time. Just um... don't forget to protect yourself."

"Huh?"

"You know, um... well, you know. Birth control."

"Oh." Lucy blushed all over, feeling just like she was having the birds and bees talk with her mom years and years ago. "I um... well..." Lucy paused, thinking. She hadn't actually had a monthly issue lately. She'd been so wrapped up in the anger and then everything else that she hadn't exactly noticed.

"Damn," she whispered. "I'm old."

"What? You're not old!"

"I think I've just hit the change."

"Really? Hey, that's good! Now you don't have to worry about it!"

Lucy rolled her eyes. She didn't mind not having a monthly issue, but it meant her youth, her vitality, her motherhood was gone. It meant a new chapter, a new phase, and a new body.

She supposed in a way it was fitting that everything should happen at once. The change, the divorce... *Henry.* No. *Why not?* I don't know, damn it!

She'd only ever been with one man, and she'd hated it. Just because Henry made her feel things she'd never felt didn't mean she'd like having sex with him. What happened if she had sex with him and hated it? *You say, 'yuck, I hated that; thanks anyway'.* Lucy couldn't help it. She laughed out loud.

"What's funny?" Stacy asked.

"Nothing, I just... nothing." Lucy chuckled. Naughty her had a point. It's not like she was buying the horse. She just wanted to take him for a test drive.

"We should get together for your birthday next week," Stacy said, eating three sandwiches at once. "You can invite Mr. Muscles."

"No!" Lucy gasped.

"Why not?"

"That's tacky. Or something. Isn't it? I can't hang out on my birthday with Henry and leave my husband at home."

"Soon to be ex. And why not?"

Lucy didn't know. She just knew both her parents were rolling over in their graves. She was divorcing her horse and thinking of taking a test ride on a different horse. They would be horrified. Fortunately, they were dead. So they couldn't yell at her or guilt her or make her feel like she was a bad person.

"So?" Stacy asked.

"We'll see."

After they finished both bottles of wine a sober Frank drove Lucy home. "I'll pick you up in the morning so you can get your car," he said as Lucy climbed out.

"Okay," Lucy agreed, feeling lightheaded and happy. "Go home and enjoy your handsy wife."

Lucy meandered inside. She'd never gotten buzzed before. It was fun. She didn't think she was drunk. She could still walk in a straight line, and she was pretty sure she could say the alphabet backwards if she tried.

"A, B, Z, D, E, F, Ghee, H, I, L, M, N, O, P, P, P, P, P... *I don't think you're getting that quite right.* Am too. Where was I? *At P, P, P, P, P, P...* Right.

Lucy wandered upstairs, fell into bed, and drifted off to sleep.

Richard watched Lucille's chest rise and fall as she slept and wondered what it would feel like to hold a pillow over her head until she stopped breathing. He wanted to do it, but he needed to wait.

That was a much too obvious way to kill her. He needed to kill her in a way that looked like an accident. Or like someone else had done it. Or like it was self-inflicted. He was pretty sure he had Addie freaked out enough that she'd buy suicide. And if Addie bought it, the police would too. Especially if Lucille had done what he thought she'd done.

In which case, the guilt had just been too much for her to bear. She hadn't been able to live with it anymore.

He liked that. It made him look like a saint. And he'd already double checked the life insurance policy. Suicide was covered.

This was the part of the job Sanders normally loved. When she'd finally caught the scent and was closing in for the kill. But this time was different. This time she was going to get caught up in the crossfire, and she didn't like it a bit.

She'd conducted three interviews today, and she was beginning to piece together a time line. The day after the first victim had died, Lucy Stevenson had joined a gym, which didn't seem like much, but for a woman like Lucy Stevenson it was a major change in behavior.

The day after the second victim died Lucy Stevenson signed up to Facebook. Not necessarily strange, but still.

Not long after that, she'd walked out on her job of fifteen years. Dr. Banks had been a mouthy son of a bitch, so Sanders wasn't really surprised, except Lucy had already put up with him for fifteen years. Seemed a little out a place, especially given the fact that she'd landed a job the very next day as a wine tour guide or some such shit. Which was only one day after an angel had killed Ralphy.

And then, Lucy Stevenson's car had been "stolen" the morning after that man had been killed on the south side. There had been no glass in the Stevenson's driveway, no glass in the ditch, and no evidence that the car's wiring had been messed with.

To top it off, the dead hitter's car had been found on the Stevenson's street just a day after the hitter's body had been discovered in a dumpster.

Sanders rubbed her head in frustration. She was making wild accusations just like Denton always said she did. She had absolutely no proof. And since she'd snitched the hitter's phone from the crime scene she hadn't entered it into evidence so she had absolutely no way to officially tie Richard in. And she was sure he was tied in.

For the first time since she'd started going, Lucy skipped the gym, but only because it was the only time her doctor could fit her in.

She'd finally looked at Addie's websites this morning and the information she'd found there made her feel sick. Maybe she WAS broken. She was displaying most of the symptoms of perimenopause which meant maybe she really hadn't been herself.

"So Lucille, why are you here today?" Dr. Stephens asked when he entered the exam room.

Lucy tried not to fold into herself. She hated Dr. Stephens. He always made her feel like a child.

"Well, I think... um... I think I'm going through the change."

"And why do you think that?"

Lucy ground her teeth. It wasn't so much the question, but HOW he asked the question. "I haven't had a period recently."

"Are you pregnant?"

Lucy almost laughed. "No."

"Did you take a test?"

"No."

"Then how do you know you're not pregnant?"

Lucy's hand twitched. She closed her eyes and breathed deeply. I will not strangle him, she thought. I will not. *Why not? He's an ass.* Because we'd get caught. I mean, because he's not bad. *Right. Semantics.*

"Because, Dr. Stephens, I haven't had sex in well over a year, so I cannot possibly be pregnant."

"Oh. I see." He stared at her for a moment like she was a curiosity he'd like to examine before asking, "Have you experienced hot flashes?"

"Yes," Lucy ground out. She was experiencing one right now.

"Mood swings?"

"Yes."

"Insomnia?"

"No."

"Irritability?"

"Yes." A lot. Right now. Aimed at him and his condescending voice.

"Depression?"

"No."

"Lack of control over your emotions, like crying or weeping?"

He made it sound like such a weakness. "No," she hissed.

"Sounds like perimenopause all right. I'll write you a script for some estrogen and progesterone. Should take the edge off. But it's important to remember that you control your emotions, not the other way around."

We have to kill him. Lucy clenched her hands tightly in her lap. Can't. *Can. Use the knee thingy.* The reflex hammer? *Yeah!* No. *Okay, the ear thingy then.* Shut up.

"Thank you, Dr. Stephens," Lucy said, silently begging him to leave the room before she accidentally killed him.

As she left his office, she breathed deeply trying to control her urge to do him severe bodily harm. She knew she couldn't kill everyone who pissed her off. It's just that so many people made her mad. Was it because of the hormones? *Don't be ridiculous!* I'm not! What if Addie was right this whole time? *She's not. We're not broken. We don't need fixed!*

Lucy didn't respond. She was afraid naughty her wasn't right this time. Talking to yourself and having yourself refer to yourself as "we" pretty much screamed "broken".

She picked up her medication and went home. Richard was there. Waiting for her.

"Where have you been?" he snapped.

"The doctor's. Why do you care?"

"I have every right to know where my wife is!"

"Okay," Lucy replied, fists clenched at her side. "Where were you this weekend?"

"Out of town," Richard growled.

"Where? Why?"

"None of your damn business!"

"Likewise," Lucy snarled. *Kill him. Just a little.* There is no such thing as killing someone just a little, Lucy thought as she stomped into the kitchen to take her new pills. *Sure there is. Just stab him in the eye a bit. Just one eye.* Lucy laughed. You're deranged. *No, you are.* Shut up.

Richard glared at her as she went upstairs, but Lucy ignored him. She wouldn't be stuck with him much longer. Even if the divorce hadn't gone through yet, she was moving out in just two months, and she couldn't wait.

Richard had to stop procrastinating. He needed to kill her today or tomorrow, the next day at the latest. But he wasn't sure how to do it. It's not like she'd take a handful of pills willingly. And he couldn't exactly force her to drink a bottle of laced wine.

Maybe suicide wasn't the answer. Maybe a mugging. But he didn't have a gun, so he couldn't just shoot her. He didn't want to deal with gushing blood so a knife was out. He'd have to strangle her. That was the only clean way to do it. But he couldn't use his hands. He didn't want to leave any trace. He needed a garrote. A tie was too soft. A wire too thin.

He punched the wall in frustration. If Emily was following Lucille it would be impossible to kill her outside of the house. And strangling her inside the house was too obvious. He had to figure it out. He was a man. He was smarter than both of them put together.

He'd make sure Emily was occupied, then he'd lure Lucille out of the house and strangle her near the gym. Then when he was questioned he'd confess that she'd been cheating on him with someone from the gym. He grinned. It was the perfect plan. The only question was would he do it tonight?

19

Lucy woke feeling rather cheerful. Only two more months, and she'd be free of Richard forever. More or less.

She made oatmeal for breakfast because she enjoyed the look on Richard's face whenever he saw it on the table. She even laughed when he said it was like eating "pureed shit". Nothing was going to bother her today. Absolutely nothing.

A man trying to order a case of wine asked her if she was stupid when she couldn't understand what he'd said. Her finger twitched, but she didn't fantasize about killing him. Just apologized for the misunderstanding and asked him to please repeat himself.

As she was driving to the gym a young idiot in a fancy yellow car ran a red light causing Lucy to slam on her brakes. She missed him with just inches to spare.

She thought about yelling out her window or honking, but she didn't. She didn't chase him down, didn't wonder what would happen if she rammed her car into the back of his.

Addie called, but she ignored it. She wasn't ready to admit

that Addie may have been right about a few things. It freaked her out to think that all her anger could have come from something as ridiculous as hormones. If Richard knew he'd never let her live it down.

She'd just take the medication for a few days and see what happened. Maybe it would help. Maybe it wouldn't. If it did, she'd find a way to tell Addie she was right.

She walked into the gym, waving at the receptionist, and wandered back to meet Angela. As they went through the routine Angela added more weight than ever. Lucy frowned at the extra weights in concern. She didn't want to get enormous or anything.

"You don't think my arms are getting too big, do you?" she asked Angela anxiously.

"What?"

"Too big. I mean, I still want to look feminine and dainty."

Angela raised an eyebrow. "What?"

"I don't want to get all muscly," Lucy said, turning in front of the mirror.

"Since when?"

Lucy frowned. She didn't know. It hadn't bothered her before. She'd been excited when she'd lost weight and when she'd chucked that lady's body parts into the dumpster without nearly dying. But she didn't want to lose her femininity. Her mom had always said there wasn't a man alive who wanted a muscular woman.

Lucy grimaced. What did she care what her mom said? Or what a man wanted? She wanted to be strong. Capable. Independent.

"You're right," Lucy muttered. "I don't know what I was thinking."

When she was finished with Angela, Lucy met Henry by the punching bags.

"You ready to hit me?" Henry asked with a wide grin. Then he winked, "Or would you rather hit ON me?"

Lucy's face didn't turn bright red like normal. She didn't stammer either, but only because she couldn't think of a single thing to say. She shouldn't be flirting with Henry. She shouldn't lead him on. That's what she was doing. Leading him on. Encouraging him. That was the worst kind of thing for a woman to do. That's what got women in trouble.

"I have to go," Lucy mumbled, suddenly feeling very confused and overwhelmed.

"Wait, Lucy; are you okay?"

"I'm fine," she lied.

He touched her arm. "Are you sure?"

She stared at his hand in confusion. She felt absolutely nothing. No tingles, no heat, just his hand on her arm. "Yes," she said quickly. "I just have to go."

She practically ran out to her car, jumped inside, and locked the doors. What was wrong with her? Why was she suddenly so unsure? Why were her parents and Richard telling her what to do again? And why was she listening?

She waited for naughty her to offer an opinion, but she didn't. She didn't say a thing. Lucy frowned, suddenly realizing she hadn't heard naughty her all day. Naughty her hadn't said a word when that man had called Lucy stupid. She hadn't suggested beating that idiot driver to death with his own fuzzy dice. She hadn't mentioned any of Henry's wonderful unmentionables.

What was going on? Where was naughty her? Where was Lucy's confidence, her spunk? Where the hell was Lucy?

Lucy drove home in a panic. She couldn't lose everything

she'd worked so hard for. She couldn't. She'd finally been a person, an individual. She'd finally been free of all the crap that had weighed her down her entire life, that had kept her docile and meek.

But she could feel her freedom slipping away. She could feel the worry and the training slipping back in, confusing her thoughts, making her question her clothes, her hair, her job, everything, and she hated it.

She parked her car, ran into the house, and opened a wine bottle. She didn't bother with a glass. Richard would chastise her if he saw. He'd say she was being uncivilized, but she didn't want a glass. She wanted to make sure she drank the whole bottle, because she was terrified she'd do something stupid, like apologize to Richard or cancel the divorce. And the only way to stop herself was to get drunk, fall asleep, and hope she felt more herself in the morning.

"God," Lucy mumbled, trying to open her eyes. Her head hurt like hell. The empty wine bottle rolled off the bed and clanked on the floor. She grimaced. No wonder her head hurt. She'd drunk the whole bottle.

She tried to shake the cobwebs from her thinking, but that only made the pain worse. "Ohhh," she moaned, clutching her head. "I wish I hadn't done that."

Why did you do it? Hell... I don't know; I can't remember. *Dumb.* Lucy's head popped up. "Hey! Angry me, naughty me, you!" *Yeah?* You're here! *Yeah?* But you weren't! You were gone. You left me. That's why I did it! *What?*

Thinking hurt, but Lucy did it anyway. Yesterday. You weren't there. And I got... I dunno... weak. I was weak and scared and... Oh hell! I was Lucille again! *Yuck.* Where were you?! Lucy demanded, feeling a tad betrayed. *You still don't get this, do you?* Get what? *I am you. You are me. We are.* Lucy frowned. She wasn't sure she did get it. *I'm just you without all the crap.* What crap? *All the crap you put on yourself. The restrictions, the rules, the do this's, the don't do that's. See?*

My head hurts too much to think about this right now. Lucy looked for her phone so she could check the time, but she didn't see it. She must have left it someplace weird when she got home last night.

She stumbled downstairs, surprised to see it was already eight o'clock. At least Richard was gone. She didn't think she could deal with him right now.

She filled a glass with water and downed it. "Damn, I forgot to take my pills last night," she mumbled, picking up one of the bottles and shaking out a pill.

"Oh my god!" *What?* Lucy stared at the pill bottle in shock. Richard was actually right. Addie was right. Lucy couldn't believe it. She'd been irritable. She'd had uncontrollable bouts of anger along with unbearable heat or hot flashes. "Oh my god," she whispered.

All this time, all this time she'd been agonizing over it, wondering why, asking what had happened, why she was suddenly so angry, and it really was just as simple as her hormones being out of whack.

It's menopause! *What?* Menopause. It's making me angry. It's making me kill people. She laughed a little hysterically. It's just hormones, emotions, lack of control. *What? Oh, I get it. You think the pills made you "normal" again. Toss 'em in the trash!* Are you kidding me? I've been killing people just to keep everything under control. Which I can do with a stupid little pill! *Yeah, but that stupid little pill will make you Lucille again.*

Yeah. It would. She would stop killing people. She would stop being so angry it hurt. She'd stop blushing every time she saw Henry. She'd stop thinking about him naked. She'd stop going to the gym and taking photographs of random people. She wouldn't get drunk with Stacy or move into the apartment over the bakery. She would stay married to Richard. Forever. Lucy would die. But other people would live.

Who cares? They were all BAD people! BAD! Who gives a shit if they're dead?! I do! I killed them! Did you see them? Did you see their faces? She was a monster. She was a monster, and she'd done monstrous things and taking these little pills would fix her, make her well, make her normal.

Throw the pills in the trash! naughty her demanded. NO! *Do it!* SHUT UP!

Lucy dropped the pills in her mouth and choked them down before naughty her could talk her out of it. *You're gonna regret that.* I won't. I know I won't. *Like hell! You're seriously going to let Richard abuse you for another thirty years?!* Lucy hoped she died first. She didn't want to be with Richard another minute, let alone thirty more years.

THROW THE DAMN PILLS IN THE TRASH!!!!

No. I can't. What kind of person would I be if I did? *A smart person.* But naughty hers voice was already fading, becoming less and less.

Lucy slipped to the floor and sobbed. She didn't want to be Lucille. She didn't want to be Mrs. Stevenson. She wanted to be Lucy. She wanted to be brave and bold and a little bit crazy. But how could she? How could she?

After a few minutes she wiped the tears from her cheeks and stood. She had to go to work. She couldn't be late. She imagined naughty her would laugh and say "Who cares if you're late?" But Lucille cared. She cared very much because it was part of who she was, part of who her parents had trained her to be.

She managed to make it through her day smiling and pretending to be cheerful, but in truth she felt wretched. She wanted naughty her back. But she couldn't; the guilt she felt, the fear, the terror, the absolute shame, it was too much. It was just like Dr. Stephens had said. She needed to be in control of her emotions, not the other way around.

She couldn't let something as ridiculous as hormonal imbalances lead her around by the nose. It was a choice. Her father had always said it was a choice. And it was. She had to choose life. Not her life, but others. How could she take that away from them? Even if they were bad.

She didn't go to the gym after work, but she didn't go home either. She couldn't stand seeing Richard yet. Couldn't stand the idea of facing him without naughty her, without Lucy.

Detective Sanders stared at the files in front of her. It was all right there. Like pieces of a puzzle fitting together to make a scene. And what an ugly scene it was.

There was a knock on her door, and she stood. She just needed to make sure. Just needed to confirm one tiny thing. And then she'd nail them both.

"Richard," she said, opening the door wide and letting him in. "Thanks for stopping by."

"Change your mind, did you?" he smirked.

"Actually I have a question. Take a seat."

His eyebrows drew together, but he sat, crossed his legs, and waited for her to talk. She'd never realized how cold his eyes were. She couldn't believe how stupid she had been.

"It's about your wife."

"What about her?"

"You said you wanted to be with me. Were you planning to leave her?"

"Why do you care?"

She aimed for a casual shrug. "I just wondered."

"Lucille's been acting strange lately. I've considered leaving her, but I decided to stay with her. For our children." He smiled, and if she hadn't known him as well as she did, she might have thought his whole spiel was genuine.

"What do you mean by 'acting strange'?"

"She's been drinking more, she quit her job, she's been staying out late, running around, doing god knows what."

"Interesting. Were you aware there was a hitter's car parked outside your house?"

"Hitter?"

His voice stayed even, but she heard the tension in that one word. "You know," she said. "A hitter, professional killer."

"What is it exactly you're fishing for?" Richard asked, lips tilted slightly up.

She hid a grimace. Somehow he knew she knew. She could see it in his eyes. Time to change tactics.

"Here's what I think," she said, propping her hip on her desk and taking an aggressive stance. "I think you were getting a little tired of your wife. Thirty years is a long time to be married to someone you don't actually like."

"So?"

"So I think you took out a hit on her."

Richard's eyebrow rose. "Is that what you think?"

"It is. But see I think for some reason she snapped, killed the hitter, then freaked out, and dumped the body."

"Lucille?" Richard snorted. "Killing someone? Ridiculous!"

"Maybe." She shrugged, keeping a close eye on him, watching his every move. "But I think she did. And then I think she got a taste for it. I think she killed three more men, because she wanted to."

His eyes widened briefly, and she felt a surge of satisfaction. So he hadn't known about the others. "Then when the first hitter failed, I think you took out another hit on her. And she killed that one too."

He chuckled softly. "Do you have any evidence to support this ridiculous claim?"

She didn't, but she'd figure that part out later. She had him. She knew she had him, but she still didn't have the why. And she needed the why. It was going to look pretty bad if she started running around demanding search warrants and throwing accusations if she didn't know the why. Normally she wouldn't care, but she was certain Richard wouldn't keep his mouth shut about their previous relationship, so she needed to be absolutely certain she could nail him to the wall.

"Why not just divorce her?"

"Because," Richard said with a slow smirk, "if I divorce her, you stupid, dumb bitch, I can't collect on the two million dollar life insurance policy."

She saw his hand move and reached for her gun, but it was already too late. The taser hit her with enough force to knock her backwards off her desk.

"You should have left it alone," Richard snarled as he kneeled over her and lifted her head, slamming it into the floor.

Should have told Denton, she thought as blackness took her.

"Goddamn it!" Richard snapped. This was a complication he didn't need. He'd have to change his plan slightly, but he could do that. He was adaptable.

He pulled a pair of latex gloves from his pocket and put them on, then he stalked to Emily's bedroom and opened the closet where she kept her bondage paraphernalia. He grabbed the leather cuffs and ball gag, rolled her over, cuffed her hands, and shoved the gag in her mouth.

In a way he kind of preferred this. She had rejected him. After all he'd given her and done for her she'd looked him in the face and refused him. It seemed fitting that she would die along with his cold, ugly, whore wife.

He quickly searched her house, looking for any evidence that he'd ever been there. He found nothing. He went through the files on her desk and found the photo of Lucille and her playboy. He crumpled it and shoved it in his pocket. He'd burn it later.

He glanced through the rest of the files. There was nothing else to connect him to the murders, so he left them where they were and turned to deal with Emily.

She was awake now, watching him with furious eyes. She'd thought he was stupid, but he wasn't. He was smarter than her. She'd soon see that.

He took her phone off her desk, used her thumb to unlock it, then deleted his phone number and all his texts and call logs.

Once he was sure there was nothing else to connect him to her, he grabbed a rug and rolled her up in it, then tossed her over his shoulder and carried her out the door. He locked the door with her spare key, then dropped her in the trunk of his car, opening the rug around her face so she wouldn't suffocate. That wouldn't do him any good at all. Then he stepped into his car. He had a lot of work to do.

20

Lucy drove for hours. She knew it was pointless, but she wasn't sure what to do. She didn't want to go home. She didn't want to go back to being Lucille. She wanted to be Lucy. She wanted to live Lucy's life.

She wanted the apartment above the bakery. She wanted the gym. She wanted Henry. But she wasn't sure she could have any of that. Not without naughty her.

It was after midnight when she finally headed home. Surely Richard would be asleep. Surely she could just sneak in and go to bed and not deal with him until the morning.

But he was awake and waiting for her. "It's about damn time you got home!" he snapped, shoving a gun in her face.

"Richard," Lucy stuttered. "What're you doing? Why do you have a gun?"

"You stupid bitch! Have you still not figured it out?"

"Figured what out?" His eyes were totally mad, and Lucy felt a frisson of fear run down her spine. He was going to kill her. Richard, her husband of thirty years, was going to kill her.

"Get in the living room," he ordered. "Now!"

Lucy stumbled past him, jerking when she felt the cold of the metal against her back. Everything slowed down. She could hear Richard's harsh breathing behind her. She could feel the breeze coming in one of the open windows. She heard one of the floorboards creak beneath her foot.

She should have told her children she loved them. She should have taken what Henry offered. She should have skinny dipped in the moonlight. She should have never let naughty her go. She was going to die, and it was all because of a stupid little pill.

Richard shoved her into the living room. Lucy stumbled forward, gasping when she saw Henry sprawled on the floor, tied up with an orange ratchet strap, mouth full of rags.

She started towards him, but froze when Richard yelled "Stop! Don't go anywhere near him!"

Lucy stared helplessly at Henry. His eyes were livid, and he was straining against the strap, struggling to free himself. "I'm so sorry," she mouthed. His eyes softened for a second, and he winked at her.

"What the hell're you doing?" Lucy asked, turning to face Richard, wishing she'd killed him one of the thousand times she'd wanted to.

"Freeing myself."

"Of what?"

"You, this place, my life. Oh and her." He pointed behind him, and Lucy saw a woman stuffed beside the couch, bound and gagged, face drawn, eyes absolutely furious.

"Detective Sanders?" Lucille whispered. "Why her?"

Richard sighed. "Are you seriously going to make me explain everything?"

Lucy wished her heart wasn't pounding so hard. If it

would only stop maybe she could think. She needed to think. Richard was a fat, old man. Surely she could take him. But he had a gun. And she was scared.

"You and your playboy hatched an elaborate plan to kill me to collect my life insurance policy," Richard said, gesturing towards Henry.

"What life insurance policy?" Lucy asked in confusion.

"The two million dollar policy we took out right before Teddy was born."

"Shit," Lucy whispered. "It really was you! You hired them to kill me. That's why you took out the money."

"Brilliant, Lucille! It only took you dying to figure it out."

He hated her. He always had. And she hated him. How had it taken her so long to see him for what he was? An abusive, cheating, bag of shit. He deserved to die, and she was going to be the one to kill him.

"But why Detective Sanders?" she asked, trying to buy some time to think.

"Why? Mostly because she figured it out. Also I've been sleeping with her for months, and she feels like a loose end. Don't you think?"

Lucy looked between Richard and the detective in confusion. He'd been cheating on her with the detective? The same detective who'd come about her stolen car? What were the chances?

"I'm actually a little surprised you had it in you," Richard said thoughtfully. "Who would have thought beneath that frigid exterior beat the heart of a cold-blooded murderer?"

Lucy flinched at his words then snarled. She didn't care what he thought. He was insane. And furthermore, they'd all been self-defense, just like this would be.

She wanted to rush him, but she was scared he'd shoot

Henry. She'd never forgive herself if she got Henry killed. She slid an inch closer, hoping he wouldn't notice.

"Here's what happened," Richard said. "You and your playboy met at the house with plans to kill me. Meanwhile Detective Sanders realized that you're a serial killer team and showed up to arrest you. A struggle ensued, and you shot Detective Sanders with her own gun."

He laughed madly, then swung around towards Detective Sanders, pulling the gun's trigger. Lucy screamed, rushing forward, but it was too late.

Blood burst from the detective's chest, and Richard pivoted back around and thrust the gun to Lucy's head. She froze, feeling the heat of the barrel against her forehead. If he pulled the trigger now she was dead. Both she and Henry were dead.

"I forgot something," Richard said with a snort. "Silly me. Detective Sanders managed to kill your boy toy before you killed her." He started to shift the gun towards Henry.

Everything slowed again as Lucy watched Richard's arm move. She knew she had only a second. She slipped her hands in her pockets, searching for a weapon, and wrapped her fingers around a cool, slim tube. The mace.

She ripped the cylinder from her pocket and jumped towards him, spraying his face. He screamed in pain and pulled the trigger. The gun exploded next to Lucy's ear, deafening her.

She slammed her whole body into Richard, knocking him off balance. They fell to the floor together, and Lucy grabbed his arm, smashing it into the floor, trying to knock the gun from his hand.

"What the hell did you do?" Richard screamed, dropping the gun, knocking her off his chest, and clawing at his face.

"You stupid bitch! I'll kill you!" He was gasping now, tears gushing from his swollen eyes.

"Nobody calls me 'bitch'," Lucy growled.

"I'll call you whatever the hell I want," Richard wheezed, suddenly rolling to his knees and lunging towards her.

Lucy struggled to stand, but Richard was already too close. She punched at his face but missed, and his hands grasped her neck and started squeezing. He pushed her to the floor, holding her there, squeezing her throat and banging her head into the polished floorboards.

"I'm gonna fucking kill you!" he screamed.

Lucy clawed at his hands, but they were immovable, like iron. Her chest was burning; she couldn't breathe. He was killing her.

She stopped fighting him and felt frantically on both sides, searching for the mace, anything. Her fingers brushed the cool metal of the gun handle, and she grabbed it. Her vision began to fade, but she brought the gun up, pointed it at his ugly face and pulled the trigger.

For a second she was deaf and blind. She still couldn't breathe. She was still dying. Then Richard's hands fell from her throat, her lungs opened, and air flowed into them.

She took a greedy gulp of air, blinking to try to clear the blood from her eyes. His body suddenly collapsed on top of her, and she gasped, struggling to roll him off.

His dead weight finally slipped to the floor, and Lucy breathed deeply, wiping the blood from her eyes, and scrambling across the floor towards Henry.

"Henry! Are you okay?" she rasped. He winked, and Lucy was flooded with relief. She didn't see any blood on him. He was okay. He was okay. She tore out his gag. "I'm so sorry," she sobbed. "I'm so sorry."

"I'm okay, Lucy. It's okay."

"God, it's not okay! My husband tried to kill you!" Lucy fumbled with the strap. "And I don't know how to open this."

"Breathe."

"I am breathing, damn it! I just don't know how to open this damn thing!" She was shaking all over. She was freezing. She was covered in Richard's blood. He had tried to kill her, and he had almost succeeded. Her neck throbbed from where his hands had strangled her.

"Just pull up on the inner clip," Henry said softly.

"Okay." Lucy grasped the clip and pulled. There was a snap, and suddenly Henry was free. He wrapped his warm arms around her and held her tightly.

"God, I'm so sorry, Henry!" Lucy sobbed, burying her face in his chest.

"Lucy."

"What?"

"Shut the hell up."

Lucy laughed through her tears, feeling the band around her heart loosen. She felt his chest rumble as he laughed too. "You're okay," he said. "I'm okay. It's okay."

Lucy closed her eyes, wondering if she was asleep and this was really just a nightmare brought on by too much wine. Richard couldn't have really tried to kill her, could he? But he had. And he was dead.

She was alive. Henry was alive. Everything really was okay. Her heart stuttered. She hadn't actually checked Richard to make sure he was dead. She pushed away from Henry just as she heard a rasp of fabric behind her.

She shoved Henry down and jumped to her feet. Richard was standing behind her, gun in hand, one side of his face gaping open, blood oozing from his torn flesh, covering his face, neck, and chest.

She watched in horror as his finger moved on the trigger. She should have checked. Why hadn't she checked?

Blue glass exploded on Richard's face, knocking him backwards. His hand dropped slightly, and Lucy jumped forward, slamming into Richard and pushing him to the floor. She snatched a shard of glass from the rug and stabbed it into his neck.

The glass broke in her hand, and she grabbed another one, stabbing him again. His hands tore at her face, but she ignored them, ripped the glass out of his neck, and drove it in again.

She remembered all the times he'd lied to her, treated her with disdain, yelled at her. She remembered the hurt and the pain and all the hidden fear.

She wasn't scared now. She was angry, and she was going to make sure Richard never hurt her again. She slammed the glass shard into his neck over and over and over, watching his partially ruined eye widen with terror, watching what was left of his face tighten in pain, and finally watching the life fade from his eye.

He was dead. She was certain he was dead, but she wasn't done. She was going stab him again and again and again. She wanted to destroy him. She wanted him to pay.

She ripped the shard out, but a warm, firm hand gripped her wrist, holding her back. "He's dead," Henry said. "That's enough."

She fought against him for a moment. It wasn't enough. It would never be enough. But he was right; Richard was dead. He couldn't be punished anymore.

She dropped the glass shard, and Henry released her. She

stared at Richard's disfigured face for a moment. He looked nothing like her husband, nothing like the man she'd built a life with for thirty years.

"Come on," Henry urged, pulled her gently away.

"Wait," she said. She'd thought he was dead once before; she wouldn't make that mistake again. She checked his neck for a pulse. He was dead. This time he was really dead.

"Sorry about the vase," Henry said, drawing Lucy into his arms.

She started laughing. "I hated that vase; Richard's mom gave it to us." She hugged him tightly, so relieved he was okay. "Oh my god, Detective Sanders!"

Lucy ran across the room, but even before she reached her, she knew Detective Sanders was dead. Her shirt was soaked in blood; her eyes were wide and glassy. Lucy checked her pulse anyway, feeling sick at her stomach.

"I'm gonna call the police," Henry said.

Lucy nodded. She was totally screwed.

21

I cannot believe we finally got to kill Richard! I am so psyched right now! Lucy sighed. She was so not in the mood for this right now. Shut up! she snapped. *No! Look at him! Richard is dead, and we killed him!* Shut up. Seriously. Just shut up. This is not the time. We're about to get nailed for so much shit.

Lucy closed her eyes. She could not believe any of this. It was just so unreal! I should... I mean... She sighed. Thanks for the mace. *Yeah, I just thought it might come in handy.* Yeah. Lucy shifted her foot awkwardly. She didn't really know what else to say.

NOW THROW THOSE FUCKING PILLS IN THE TRASH!!! naughty her screamed. I already did, Lucy replied. Earlier today. *You did? For me? But... You said...* I know. *So why?* Lucy hissed in irritation. I shouldn't have to explain it! You're me! *But could you?* Oh fine. You're worth it. I'll hunt down every bad guy in town if I have to.

Lucy scrubbed her hands over her face. She'd been all

through this earlier today. She didn't really want to go over it again. Not right now.

I don't... I mean... Damn it, I need you! I honestly don't feel alive when you're not with me. *Aww, I love you too.* Shut up, damn it! I know where the pills are; I can get them back. *You love me; admit it.* Nope.

"The cops are on their way," Henry said, sitting beside Lucy on the floor. "You okay?" he asked, wrapping his arm around her shoulder.

For a moment she didn't answer, she just allowed herself to feel him, to feel his warmth, his kindness, his comfort.

"Yeah," she finally said. "I mean, no. I mean... He tried to kill you!" She still could not believe her husband was a murderer.

"And you. More than once by the sound of it."

Lucy laughed hollowly. She couldn't believe this was happening to her. She'd just started living. She'd just broken free. She had just begun.

"I'm gonna go to prison," she said, fighting back hot tears.

"Nah."

"No, really. I... I... I mean... This isn't my first time," she whispered. She couldn't believe she'd said that, but she wanted him to know, needed him to know.

She felt him shrug as he said, "The trick is not to admit to anything."

"What?!"

"Don't admit to anything. I mean obviously you have to admit to killing ol' dick face here, but outside of that, don't admit to anything."

She pulled away and stared at him. "You're seriously not upset by the fact I've killed before this?!"

"Did they have it coming?"

Lucy thought for a second. "They were all bad guys."

"Then I could give a shit."

A slow smile spread across her face, and she whispered, "I really like you."

"I like you too."

"Even after all this?"

"Even after all this." He leaned close, until his nose touched hers. "I'd kiss you, but your face is covered in blood."

Lucy jerked back. "Oh my god! I need to clean all this up!" She started to stand, but Henry pulled her back down.

"Crime scene. Leave it alone."

"Oh, right. How did... I mean... How did you end up here?"

"You texted me. Said you needed help moving something."

"But I didn't!" Lucy protested. "Oh, my damn phone," she hissed, remembering she hadn't been able to find it before she left for work. "Richard must have taken it."

"Yeah. Anyway, your text said to come on in when I got here. So I walked in, and he tasered me. A couple times actually. When I came to I was all tied up."

"I honestly didn't know he had it in him," Lucy said. "I never thought... I mean..."

"Police!" a voice called out.

"We're in here!" Henry called back.

Soon the room was swarming with police. Lucy and Henry were separated, an EMT cleaned and bandaged her hands and face, and then Lucy was drilled with question after question by an angry looking detective in a bad suit.

"Did you know Detective Sanders?" he snapped.

"No," Lucy said. "I mean yes; I met her because she wrote up a report on my stolen car."

"Your car was stolen? When?"

"I don't know... Um, a week ago? I honestly can't remember."

"How could you not remember?"

Nuts to this. Punch him in the face! NO! We're in enough trouble as it is!

"I just don't remember the day," Lucy stammered. "It was last week sometime, I think."

"Were you aware your husband was having an affair with Detective Sanders?"

"No. I mean, not until he told me right before, I mean, right before he killed her."

"But were you aware he was having an affair?"

"Yes."

"MOM!" a voice bellowed.

"Nate!" Lucy stood, but the detective shook his head.

"You stay right here. I'll talk to your son."

Lucy sat and waited impatiently. She didn't want some stranger telling Nate his father was dead. But she also didn't want to tell Nate she'd killed him. She wasn't sure he'd understand. She wasn't sure what he'd do or say. How would she tell any of them? How could she possibly explain it? How could she tell them what Richard had done? And how was it any different than what she had done?

Well for one, Detective Sanders wasn't BAD. Semantics, remember? Lucy fought a grin. What's your point? *And for two, you never wanted to kill Richard. You were going to divorce him like a normal human being. The two million dollar life insurance policy never occurred to you, and if it had, you still wouldn't have killed him.*

True. *And furthermore,* naughty her went on. *He HIRED someone to kill you. Twice.* We can't tell anyone that though.

No; but it does make a difference. He was a dick. You're not. See? Lucy rolled her eyes. That was just naughty hers opinion; it wasn't very likely anyone else would see it that way.

The detective was back. He sat across from her and said, "When did you file for divorce?"

"Monday."

"Did your husband know?"

"Yes."

"Did he physically abuse you?"

"No."

"Did he mentally abuse you?"

Lucy paused. Lucille would never have said yes. But Lucy could look back over the years and say that yes, yes he had. Just like her father had. She cleared her throat awkwardly. "Um... yes."

He nodded and wrote something on his pad, then asked, "Did you know he was into S and M?"

Lucy stared at him for a second in complete confusion. "What?"

"S and M. Sadomasochism."

She blinked. "Richard?"

"Yes."

"But... how... I mean..."

"When they searched Detective Sanders' apartment they found quite a supply of bondage paraphernalia, not to mention a handful of photographs of your husband in... uh..." He turned red, but finally said, "various positions."

Lucy blinked. "Richard?"

"Yes."

"The dead man in the next room?"

"Yes."

"S and M?"

"Yes." He was starting to sound irritated, but Lucy just didn't believe it.

"Really?"

"So you didn't know?"

"No!"

"Your son mentioned your husband took money out of your joint savings without your knowledge."

"Yes."

"How much?"

"Twenty thousand."

"Do you have any idea what he did with it?"

"No," Lucy lied. She knew exactly what he'd done with it, but she couldn't possibly tell him.

"Can you explain to me one more time what happened after you got home tonight?"

Lucy sighed. She just wanted this night to be over with. If they were going to arrest her, she wanted them to do it already. If they weren't, she wanted to go to bed and sleep for a week. "I got home late," she started.

"Why?"

It took another hour for her to walk the detective through everything that had happened. When she was finally done, he snapped his pad closed and said, "You're not under arrest, Mrs. Stevenson. From where I'm sitting it looks like self-defense, but don't leave town. We'll give you a call when the house is clear."

"You're not going to arrest me?" Lucy asked in stunned disbelief.

"No. Should I?"

"What?! No! I mean, if I hadn't killed him he would've killed Henry."

"Just a reminder, you can't enter these premises again until we give you the all clear."

Lucy nodded numbly. Richard was dead, and she wasn't going to jail. An officer escorted her upstairs to grab some clothes then back down and out the front door. She walked out onto the sidewalk in a haze. Everything had happened so fast her head was still spinning.

Nate and Henry were waiting for her outside. "Mom!" Nate exclaimed, running up and hugging her. "Are you okay? Did they let you go?" He touched her neck gently. "You're all bandaged up! Are you okay? Are you hurt?"

She smiled, trying to put him at ease. His eyes were red, and his face pale. "I'm fine. Just a few cuts. Yes, they let me go. I'm okay. Are you okay?"

"No! Dad, I mean, damn, Mom. I don't even know what to say."

Lucy shrugged. "Me either. I'm sorry."

"For what?"

"This, everything."

"Damn it, Mom! I should have... I mean, I knew something was going on. I should have said something. I never thought... I mean... Damn."

"It's not your fault," she said earnestly. "I didn't have a clue. If you had said something I probably would have laughed at you. I mean, Richard, he didn't..." She sighed. She'd never understand it. Clearly she'd never known him, and she was glad she hadn't.

"What're you gonna do?" Nate asked. "Come stay with Lisa and me. Please?"

She shook her head. "No. I'll be fine. I'll just stay in a hotel for a couple nights. Surely they'll be done with the house soon. Go home, Nate."

"But, Mom..."

"No; please go home. Get some rest; talk to your wife. That's what I need you to do, okay?"

Nate stared at her. She could tell he didn't want to leave her, and it warmed her heart. She wouldn't have ever thought he'd take her side, but she was glad he had.

"I love you, Mom," he whispered as he hugged her tightly. "Please be careful. Call me if you need anything."

"I'm fine. I will. Go."

She watched him leave with a sigh. "He turned out to be a good kid after all."

Henry chuckled. "You weren't sure?"

"Nah. A month ago I thought he was a selfish ass."

Henry laughed. "So what now?"

"I don't know."

He took her hands in his and pulled her closer. "You could stay with me," he suggested.

Lucy closed her eyes, enjoying his warmth, and the way it made her feel. "Not tonight," she finally said. "Ask me again tomorrow."

She felt him grin. "Okay. So where do you want to go?"

"A hotel. I need a bath!" She shuddered. She hated having Richard's blood all over her. She wanted it off. "I feel absolutely disgusting, but at least they let me grab some clean clothes."

"Alright. I'll drive you."

They drove for a while in silence. But Lucy finally said, "You seem really okay."

"I am."

"Really? I mean you were tasered, trussed up like a goose, you watched someone die, then you almost died, and then you watched someone else die. It seems like you should be... I don't know... kinda freaked out."

"I've always been of the opinion that you just deal with stuff as it comes. I, you, we handled it. Crisis over. We're good."

"Seriously?"

"Seriously."

"And if I told you I've killed five other people?"

"Okay."

"In the last two months."

"Okay."

Lucy stared at him with narrowed eyes. "Why on earth would you be okay with that?"

"You said they were bad guys. I believe you."

"You're... I don't know, but you're freaking me out."

He laughed. "Would you feel better if I asked questions or yelled 'why' or 'what the hell'?"

"Yes."

"Okay. Why? Are you insane? How do you know they were bad?"

He parked the car in the hotel parking lot and stared at her. She felt a little unnerved by his eyes. They were calm and serious, without a hint of their normal twinkle.

"They all tried to hurt me first," she said. For some reason it was really important to her that he understand. She couldn't quite believe that he really didn't care.

"I don't think I'm insane," she said carefully. "Although I do talk to myself and myself talks back. And they tried to hurt me first."

"Okay."

"Really?"

"Really. The thing is I've watched you. You're sweet; you're nice; you're kind. You hold the door for little old ladies, you ask people how their day is or how they're feeling.

When Otis passed out the other day at the gym, you dropped everything and ran to help him. You almost got killed trying to save me. You're not a bad person. You're not a murderer. You're not your husband."

Lucy felt her chest loosen.

"I like you, Lucy," he went on. "And I don't care who you've killed or why. Just as long as you keep being you I'll still like you."

Lucy stared at him. His eyes were serious, and she knew he was telling the truth. She couldn't believe it, but he was. He knew what she'd done, and he didn't care. He liked her. Lucy. Not Lucille, Lucy.

"I still have blood on my face, don't I?" she whispered.

"Yep. Why?"

"I just really wanted to kiss you."

"Screw it," he said, pulling her towards him and touching her lips with his own. It was a light kiss, sweet and gentle, but it sent shivers up and down Lucy's spine.

After a second he leaned back and winked at her. "There's more where that came from."

Lucy laughed. "I can't wait." She traced his face with a finger. "I'm glad you're okay."

"Me too."

"I'll see you later?"

"How about this evening? We'll work on your punches and then go out for supper?"

"Perfect."

Lucy stepped out of the car and waved at him. It was already late in the morning, and she was exhausted. All she wanted was a hot bath, a glass of wine, and a soft bed.

She walked into the lobby and up to the receptionist desk. "I'd like a room please," she said with a smile. "With a tub.

The biggest tub you have." The clerk stared at her, face slack with horror. Lucy glanced down. "Sorry," Lucy said. "Yes; I'm covered in blood. I've just left my house. My husband tried to kill me. I killed him instead. The police let me go. Self-defense. Can I have a room?"

The clerk nodded jerkily and started typing. "Room 202," he finally stuttered. "Jacuzzi tub."

"Perfect." Lucy took the key card and walked to the elevator. She wondered if she'd collapse in shock at some point. She wondered if she'd feel guilty or bad once everything set in.

You won't. Lucy didn't respond. She knew naughty her was right. She knew she wouldn't. And not because her emotions were all screwed up. Not because she was going through the change, and she couldn't control herself. Not because she'd decided to keep Lucy alive no matter the cost.

None of that. She knew she wouldn't feel bad because Richard had deserved to die. After all her efforts to keep him alive he'd tried to kill her. He'd killed Detective Sanders. He'd almost killed Henry. Richard was dead, and she was glad. And she didn't feel the least bit bad about it. Killing him or feeling glad.

She had proved them all wrong. Addie, Richard, Dr. Stephens, her mom, and her father. Emotions hadn't made her weak. Emotions hadn't made her less. They'd made her more; they'd made her strong. Without angry her, without naughty her, she'd be dead, murdered in her own kitchen, and her husband would be sipping margaritas on a Mexican beach somewhere.

She was never letting naughty her go. Not ever. She was angry and hot and horny, and she was glad she was all those things. And if she had to kill someone every once in a while to keep it in check, so be it.

She couldn't wait to begin her life as Lucy. She couldn't wait to be whoever she might be. Because she was finally free. Richard was dead, and she was free.

Epilogue

Samuel Denton studied the blood results with a raised eyebrow. He could honestly say he hadn't seen that coming. Sanders must have figured it out, but Sanders was up to her eyeballs in crap. He'd warned her years ago, but she never listened. At least she'd been smart enough to tell him where her photographs were kept. Without them it might have been a little harder to prove Richard Stevenson had orchestrated the whole thing.

Sanders was a good detective. Or had been. She knew how to connect the dots; she could cross her eyes just right and see the hidden picture. Even though she'd pissed him off, he would miss her. But she was gone, and frankly he didn't give a shit if some repressed, middle-class housewife went around shanking a few bad guys.

Sanders wouldn't have seen it that way. Sanders would've wanted to drag her in by the hair and throw the whole damn book at her. Denton fed the blood results into his shredder and dropped the blood samples into the biohazard disposal.

After all, it was contaminated evidence. It certainly couldn't be used in a court of law.

Final Epilogue

"Are you sure you have to go?" Henry asked, stretching languidly beneath Lucy's slick, satin sheets.

"I do," Lucy said, kissing him on his chin and pushing his hands away from her naked hips.

"Just another minute."

"That's what you said an hour ago."

"But I think I can bench press you. Don't you want to see?"

Lucy giggled. "Save it 'til I get back."

She pushed him back onto the bed and went to get dressed. It was dark outside, but her windows were open and she could still smell the fresh scent of donuts and chocolate icing coming up from the bakery below.

"I talked to Nate today," she said as she pulled a long-sleeved, black turtleneck over her head. "He and Lisa just got back from Paris, and they're going to stay in town for a while."

She hadn't wanted anything to do with Richard's two million dollar life insurance policy, so she'd split it between

Teddy, Nate, and Addie. Addie still wasn't talking to her; she blamed Lucy for everything that had happened, and there was nothing Lucy could say to change her mind. She just hoped Addie found her own naughty her someday.

"Good," Henry said. "Did they bring us back something?"

"He said they did," she said, throwing a shoe at Henry's head. "It's all about the schwag with you."

"No," he said, winking. "It's all about the SHAG."

Lucy laughed and let him pull her back into bed. Several minutes later, she pushed him away and rolled out again. "Seriously. I have to go."

"Who's Denton got for you this time?"

"Some guy named Eddie Harris; he's a gun for hire."

"I think I read something about him a couple years ago. He was arrested, but I think he was released. Contaminated evidence or something. Anyway, be careful."

"Always."

Lucy grabbed her kill bag and opened the door. "Love you," she said, blowing him a kiss. "See you in a while."

As soon as the door closed behind Lucy, naughty her spoke up. *How're we gonna do it this time? I was thinking strangulation.* Lucy sighed. You know I don't like to plan ahead. *Yeah, but we've never strangled anyone. It'd be fun!*

We'll see. I'd rather play it by ear. What if he has a humungous neck? *Good point. So how 'bout a cattle prod?* What? We don't even have a cattle prod! *We could get one.* Shut up. *Come on; we should branch out.* I said, SHUT UP!

Lucy climbed into her car and pulled out the address and photograph Denton had given her. She couldn't wait. She was ready for a kill, and Eddie Harris was one very bad guy. A tingle of anticipation ran down her spine. She hoped he put up a fight.

Ready for another great Psychological Thriller? Check out

WE ALL FALL DOWN

1

Tabitha Smith closed the cabin door carefully behind her. She would have slammed it, but she was near Mr. Keller's office and she didn't want him to know she wasn't finished yet.

Every year, it was the same. Year after year after year. She'd asked to leave. She'd begged, but her husband had just looked at her, eyes full of sadness and despair, and said, "Where would we go, Tabitha? Where? And with what money?"

He was right. They didn't have enough money to leave. Not really. And there wasn't anyone who could help them. Not anymore.

"Damn Mr. Keller and his damn camp to hell," she muttered as she headed towards the next cabin.

Snow crunched softly under her feet, and the light of the full moon bounced from one snow drift to another, lighting her way to cabin number one, the last cabin she needed to clean today.

All the guests had departed yesterday, and the snow was packed so hard, it was slick in spots. There were two employees whose job it was to shovel the walks, but Mr. Keller was too cheap to buy decent shovels or any type of ice remover, and so the walks were always snowy and icy, even if they had been "cleared".

Tabitha stepped carefully around the slick areas; after fifteen years of walking from cabin to cabin, she knew every path and icy spot by heart.

Cabin one's porch creaked when she stepped onto it. It always creaked. The only porch that didn't creak was cabin number six. It had always bothered her that number six's didn't creak. It didn't seem natural. Not when all the other ones did.

She opened the front door and frowned into the darkness. Guests never closed the curtains when they left, and the full moon was shining, so it should be fairly bright inside, but it wasn't.

Tabitha set down her cleaning tote and reached inside the door for the light switch. She heard a strange swish noise right before a terrible, hot pain shot up her arm. She jerked her hand back with a scream, stumbling backwards, away from the dark entrance.

The light of the full moon illuminated the porch; and through her pain and panic, Tabitha could clearly see that half of her fingers were gone. Something was inside the cabin. Something sharp and deadly.

She clutched her bloody fingers to her chest, trying to stop the bleeding, gasping when a black shadow moved into the doorway. A screech tore from her throat and terror spiraled through her chest as she turned to run. The porch creaked under her feet as she dashed back out onto the icy pathway. Snow crunched under the soles of her boots. Her breath came out in gasps of frosty cold.

She couldn't hear anything over her screams. She couldn't hear the steady pounding of the feet behind her. She couldn't hear the axe slicing through the frozen air.

She jerked to a halt as the axe buried itself deeply into her spine. One final gasp of terror passed through her lips, then she dropped to the frozen ground with a whimper, eyes blinking slowly as she watched the blood ooze sluggishly from her finger stumps.

Black shoes stopped in front of her, and she tried to look up, but she couldn't move. Numbness had taken over her. The searing pain was gone. The terror was gone. She didn't even feel it when the axe was jerked from her back and blood burst onto the sidewalk around her.

A strange sense of peace filled her as her lungs shuddered one final time and her heart gave one last feeble pump. Finally, was her last thought. I can finally leave.

The townies of Copper Cliff firmly believe that talking to yourself means you're crazy, loopy, not right in the head. But if that were truly the case, Abby Brooks would have been certifiably insane since she was ten years old. Because, as everyone knew, she talked to herself, a lot. What they didn't know, is that someone else talked back.

Remind me again why you're doing this? Because I have to. *You should just leave.* Abby snorted. And go where?

Anywhere. Right. And what will I put down on my application? Thirty-four-year-old loser seeking job. Skills: cleaning toilets, measuring wood, and repainting old siding. *What about running a cash register?* Sure. I can also run a cash register from circa nineteen-sixty. *You make it sound so bad.* It is. It really is.

In truth, Abby knew she wasn't a loser. She had some viable skills, viable to Copper Cliff anyway, and she liked who she was as a person; but every time she imagined leaving, she couldn't think of anything she could possibly offer the outside world. There were surely smarter and more skilled people out there already. There wouldn't be room for her. She couldn't help but recall something her dad had said once about a small fish in the ocean. *I don't think that's right.* You get the point though. I don't belong out there. I'm a Brooks. Brooks live and die in Copper Cliff.

Well, at least it's work, the voice said reasonably. Are you kidding me?! I'd rather walk through town naked than work at Antler Ridge Camp! I'm like the first townie in thirty years to work at the camp. I... Abby shook her head in disgust as she turned up the long road that led to the camp.

"I don't understand it," she whispered. She didn't want to work at Antler Ridge Camp. Townies never, EVER worked at the camp. It just wasn't done. The owner, Mr. Keller, had his own staff. They took care of repairs and maintenance. They didn't need Abby. *Must not be a normal repair.* I hope it's just a light bulb or something stupid so I can just get the hell out. *Right, like your dad would send you all the way out here to change a lightbulb.* You could've let me pretend. *Sorry.*

For some reason, Abby's father had insisted she handle this project from start to finish. Normally he talked to the clients first and got all of the details, then passed the job on to

Abby, but not this time. "You'll be running the business someday," he'd said cheerfully. "You need to learn to deal with the clients and all that good jazz." In reality, it was a waste of her time. She didn't handle the contracts or the billing so she was going to have to run everything by her dad anyway.

She just wished it wasn't the camp. Any other job would have been fine. She wouldn't even mind retrofitting all the forest services' onsite toilet facilities. *Really?* Really!

There were a ton of reasons why Abby didn't want to work at the camp, or set foot anywhere near the camp for that matter. One, it was common knowledge that the camp workers were weird and socially awkward. The camp in general was weird. Groups came from all over the country to attend it for a week or two at a time. Mr. Keller said it was a church camp, but no one really knew what went on up there. They could be holding séances or orgies or Kool-Aid sessions or virgin sacrifices or non-virgin sacrifices. Who knew?

You're being ridiculous. It's a family camp. There're parks and slides, pools, an ice-skating rink, a tubing hill, and horseback riding. It's supposed to be fun. Like a vacation. No, it's not fun. It's a terrible place, Abby argued. Her inner voice was wrong this time. Antler Ridge Camp was not fun.

The snowy road blurred, and Abby tried to regain her focus. She didn't want to get sucked into memories, but her mind got away from her and wandered off, sifting through her memories until it found the one it was looking for. The one Abby tried unsuccessfully to keep locked tightly away.

Antler Ridge Camp. Summer. Abby had gone up with her cousin Jen and some other townie kids for a day of townie fun. Mr. Keller had planned it as a way to improve relations between the campees and the townies. It hadn't worked.

Laughter tinkled through her mind. "You're it!" a girl laughed, tagging Abby's shoulder. Everything was green, and flowers poked randomly through the grass, looking like scattered, broken ornaments.

"I'll get you!" Abby yelled, chasing after a blond-headed boy.

Abby shook her head, forcing the memory away, and focused on the road right in front of her. She didn't want to see it. She didn't need to remember. She remembered well enough.

The laughter and summer heat fought its way forward again, but she pushed it back into the darkness of her mind, trying to bury it beneath a thousand other memories. Happy ones.

The road curved, and Antler Ridge Mountain suddenly came into view. It towered above the other peaks, making them seem small in comparison.

Antler Ridge Mountain was the only mountain Abby refused to step foot on. She'd hiked all the other peaks surrounding the valley, glorying in the view from their summits, but she'd never gone near Antler Ridge. She just couldn't make herself.

Part of her wanted to conquer it, just like she'd conquered all the others, but to get to the hiking trail she would have had to drive right through the camp, and she didn't want to do that.

A red cabin roof suddenly poked through the trees, like a bloody cut marring the forest landscape, and she took a sharp, terrified breath. Disgust curled in her belly. She was pathetic, and she knew it. It was stupid to fear a place, but she couldn't help it. She hated it here.

Mr. Keller grinned charmingly as he opened his door to

admit Abby into his office. His grey hair was slicked back tightly, and his mustache was oiled to the point of greasiness.

"Mr. Keller," Abby greeted him, trying to use the cheerful Brooks' tone her family was known for. "How are you today?"

"I'm doing just wonderful, Ms. Brooks," he replied as he shook her hand vigorously. "I'm so happy your father could spare you for our little project."

Abby swallowed a snort. Spare; as if her dad wouldn't squeeze every cent he could out of Keller.

"What exactly is your project, Mr. Keller? Dad didn't give me any details."

"Sit down, Ms. Brooks, and I'll tell you all about it."

"Call me Abby." She sat carefully in the worn plastic folding chair that faced Keller's desk and waited for him to explain why she was there.

"Would you like a soda?" he asked, opening a mini-fridge to display a number of off-brand soda pops.

"No, thank you." She wished he'd just get on with it. She'd only dealt with him a few times at the store, but she knew he had a tendency to beat around the bush. Indefinitely.

"Lovely weather today," he said as he sat across from her.

"Yep," she agreed.

"Do you enjoy winter sports, Ms. Brooks?"

"Abby, and no, I don't."

"You don't?" His eyebrow tweaked in surprise. "Copper Cliff is a strange town to live in if you don't like winter."

Abby's eyelid twitched. She wasn't good at this part of things: the back and forth, the small talk, the blah, blah, blah. She liked to get right to things. Grab the bull by his horns. Dive right in. She didn't want to dance around the mulberry bush all freaking day getting to the point.

"I didn't say I don't like winter," she said as evenly as possible. "I just don't like winter sports. Now about the job?"

"Hum. What about ice skating?"

"Nope."

"Tubing?"

"No."

"Skiing?"

Abby ground her teeth, forced a smile, and said, "No. I like snowshoeing. Could you please tell me about the job?"

"Yes, of course. Have you been up to Antler Ridge Camp before?"

She stared at him in disbelief. How could he not remember? *It has been over twenty-four years. I still remember! Like it was yesterday! You were standing right there. He wasn't.* He should remember. Everyone should remember.

"Once," she finally bit off.

"It creates a lasting impression, doesn't it?" he said proudly.

"Yep." A permanent, scarring, life-defining impression.

He stood and walked to one of the walls, gesturing towards a large, framed site map. "Antler Ridge Camp!" he exclaimed. "Built on land claimed by my great-great-grandfather in 1878."

Abby sighed and tried to get comfortable in her chair.

"His original cabin is right here," he said, pointing to a portion of the map. "He built it with nothing more than his own two hands!" Abby rolled her eyes. "It's the center of the camp," he went on. "Right smack in the middle of the Ranch."

Abby's ears began to buzz at his mention of the Ranch, but she forced the buzzing away and tried to listen to what he was saying, no matter how unimportant it was.

"It's a museum now," he said proudly. "Showcasing the history of the Keller family and the Antler Ridge Camp."

"Fascinating," Abby said, nearly vibrating with frustration. "But about the job?"

"Yes, of course. You can see that we have forty-three cabins and three lodges available for guests' use. In addition, there are twenty-five cabins for workers and their families. We also have five recreational buildings." He pointed to the map again. "This one is an open gym for basketball, indoor soccer, and volleyball. This one—"

"I'm familiar with the layout and scope of your camp, Mr. Keller," Abby interrupted. "About the job?"

"The last several years have been tough," Mr. Keller said, face drooping in sad dismay.

Abby bit her tongue. She wasn't good at sitting still, and she just knew she'd be here all day if he didn't get to the point soon. She wanted to force him to get on with it, but she knew better, so she smiled and tried to pretend interest.

"Of course, as a resident of Copper Cliff you've witnessed the slump. The camp suffers, so does the town; am I right?"

He was right, but she'd be damned if she'd admit it. "Does this have to do with the job, sir?"

"I'm getting there. Patience, Ms. Brooks." He grinned widely, flashing overly-white teeth, and she smiled back, trying desperately to channel her gregarious father, or at the very least, her even-tempered Uncle Dwayne.

"As I was saying, hard times. Church camps don't have the same draw they did twenty years ago. People used to want to spend time together, bond, create memories that would last a lifetime."

His voice and the room faded; and for a second, Abby was back on that summer slope chasing the blond-headed boy.

"People don't connect that way anymore though," Mr. Keller said, the bitter edge to his voice cutting through Abby's memory. "Now they send a text or play a video game together." He snorted. "What kind of lifetime memory is that? Do you remember the time we played something or other? Which time?"

He shook his head in disgust. "Do you know what my grandson sent me the other day?" He didn't wait for Abby to respond, but went on. "He calls it a GIF! A GIF. He doesn't call me, won't answer my letters, but he'll send me a GIF! Look at it!"

He fiddled with his phone for a second then held it out to her. She swallowed a giggle, thinking the silly, little yeti waving back and forth was actually pretty cute.

"That's it!" he said irritably. "Not even a text. Just a ridiculous cartoon!" He dropped his phone onto his desk and exclaimed, "Can you imagine if I'd sent something like that to my grandpa?!"

He looked at her expectantly, and she shrugged uncertainly. She wasn't sure what he wanted her to say. He sighed heavily and murmured, "No, things certainly aren't the way they used to be." She nodded, just to keep him moving along.

"People have changed," he said. "And that means we need to change. I've found an investor who's willing to revitalize Antler Ridge Camp's image and help bring out more guests. But for that to happen, we need to get everything up to code."

Finally! Abby thought. "So that's the job?" she said out loud.

"Indeed. I need you to inspect the units, make a repair list, and head a crew to bring it all up to code."

"I'll get started right now," Abby said, beginning to stand.

"I'm sure glad my grandpa isn't here," he said, shaking his head sadly.

Abby grit her teeth and sat back down.

Two hours later, Abby left Keller's office with a set of keys, a map, and a list of the worker families and which cabin each one lived in.

She grabbed a notebook and pen from her truck, glanced at the map, and headed towards cabin number one. It wasn't far from Keller's office, and in her mind it was the most logical place to start.

The camp was split into three portions: the Meadow, where Keller's office was; the Ranch, which she never wanted to see again; and the Foothills. Each portion had a lodge where some of the guests could stay and where all the guests ate their meals, and each portion had a recreational building or two and a handful of cabins.

By her rough math, it would take her nearly three weeks to make a comprehensive repair list, maybe longer depending on the level of disrepair. Keller had said he had a crew standing by, so she'd get through as many cabins as she could today and get the crew started on the updates tomorrow.

See, aren't you glad you came? No! I don't care how awesome this project is; I loathe this place. I'm just glad it's winter. If it was summer... She shuddered just thinking about it.

The walkway was coated in ice, which she thought was a little strange. A place like this should have a guy shoveling and salting the walks regularly so none of the guests slipped. It seemed like a massive oversight on Keller's part. Copper Cliff had a seasonal crew whose sole job was to keep the sidewalks cleared of snow and ice.

She was pretty sure the camp had had guests just last week

because she'd seen some strangers in town at the coffee house. *They could've just been tourists.* Abby snorted. Copper Cliff didn't have regular tourists. It had visitors from the camp.

It's not like Copper Cliff didn't have anything to recommend it. It had a mine tour and two museums, as well as, multiple trailheads and at least three state camping grounds nearby. But it had somehow never made it onto the "official" state tourist map.

Everyone knew that the camp kept the town alive. Her cousin Logan had once said that the camp and town had a symbiotic relationship. Camp fails; the town goes with it. So even though everyone in town hated the camp, the fact of the matter was, they needed it.

Abby's foot slipped, and she steadied herself, glancing down at the sidewalk. Her eyes locked onto a patch of snow, and she stopped walking, studying the snow carefully. That's weird, isn't it? *What? Pink snow? Better than yellow, isn't it?* Yeah, but why's it pink? *Bubblegum flavor?* Abby rolled her eyes. Sometimes her inner voice just wasn't helpful.

She leaned down and gingerly touched the pink snow. It was frozen, so she scraped at it, and pink chips of snow-ice broke apart. Somebody must've dropped something. Kool-Aid or... *Bubblegum ice cream?* You're such an idiot. *I'm in YOUR head.* "Fifteen, thirty, forty-five," Abby chanted, ignoring the snow and reading the "Cabin 1" sign ahead of her.

The porch steps creaked beneath her weight, and she made a note to check underneath and make sure everything was stable. She sorted through the keys, slipped the key for cabin one into the lock, turned it, and opened the door.

It was dark, so she stepped inside and searched the wall for a light switch, flipped it on and turned to face the room.

She froze. The blonde boy's laughter rang through her mind, followed by his screams. Blood. There was so much blood. The screams rushed through her mind like an avalanche, blocking everything else. The smell of fresh, wet blood mixing with the sunny dirt overwhelmed her, making her want to vomit.

Abby closed her eyes, trying to force the memory away. Her inner voice started humming, and Abby focused on the sound, using it to block out the screams. This wasn't a memory. This blood was here, now. It wasn't in her mind. Was it?

She opened her eyes. There was a small pool of blood on the cabin floor, and in the center of it a dead woman. Abby knew the woman was dead because her eyes were wide open and her pupils were huge, almost as large as her irises. Her arms were crossed over her chest, like a mummy in a sarcophagus, and the hand on top was bloody, missing fingers.

Abby's mouth opened to scream, but her mind was searching for the fingers, trying to put the missing pieces back into place. Trying to make the woman whole again. There. Lying on the end table like discarded candle sticks, just beneath the bloody writing on the wall. Two words: "I'm back".

KEEP READING TODAY AT AMAZON.COM

Check out M.M. **Boulder's** full line of books at her Amazon author page:
www.amazon.com/M-M-Boulder/e/B085X3G7NF

Connect online:
www.facebook.com/mmcrumleyauthor
www.mmboulder.com/

Interested in Urban Fantasy? Check out

THE IMMORTAL DOC HOLLIDAY SERIES
BOOK 1: HIDDEN

1

"Wake up, you filthy hedonist!"

Doc Holliday ignored the nagging voice because he was in the middle of a particularly nice dream. He'd just been dealt the winning hand; which he knew because he could always feel it when he was about to win.

The man he was playing against was a hotheaded imbecile who didn't really understand how to play the game, and if Doc was lucky, which he usually was, the hothead wouldn't take losing well, especially since he was young and playing with money he'd stolen from his father. If Doc was very lucky, the hothead would pull a gun.

"Wake up!" the voice snapped. "It's time!"

Doc rolled away from the voice, controlling all his facial expressions as he threw in his chips and called the hand. The hothead was sweating now, chewing his lip anxiously. Doc held back his grin as he laid his cards face-up on the table.

The hothead's face went white. He sputtered for a second before tossing his cards onto the table and demanding, "How'd ya do that? You're cheatin', ain't ya?" His face wasn't pale now; it was bright red.

Doc smiled very slowly, leaning back in his chair as he did. "I don't need to cheat," he drawled. "I've the devil's own luck."

"Gimme a chance to win it back!" the man suddenly pleaded.

"No."

"You gotta!"

"I don't have to do anything. If you can't afford to lose, you shouldn't play. That's just a good rule to live by."

The hothead's hand twitched, moving closer to his gun. Finally, Doc thought, smiling a little wider.

"WAKE UP!!!"

"Damn it!" Doc sputtered, sitting upright. "I was just getting to the good part."

"Two women or three?" Thaddeus asked solicitously, accent making his words crisp.

"No," Doc grumbled. "It wasn't that kind of dream."

"Ah. The old 'I'm going to kill you to get my money back' dream?"

Doc grinned lazily as he stretched. "Something like that. Where's Ana?"

"How should I know? Fortunately, I'm not her keeper. Unfortunately, I appear to be yours."

"I think you have that backwards, Thaddy, old boy." Doc stepped from his bed, picking up his silk robe and slipping his arms through it. "Which reminds me, have I watered you lately?"

"Have I watered you lately?" Thaddeus mocked softly. "Why let me think. It's been approximately five years since you invited Ana to come have a stay. In all that time you've watered me... Wait, it'll come to me. That's right, twice."

Doc chuckled as he ran a finger over one of Thaddeus's shiny green leaves. "Thank god you're so low maintenance."

"Thank god for the maid who waters me regularly! If it wasn't for her I'd be dead. She's quite frightened to come into your bedroom, you know. She believes you're a Tlahuelpuchi."

"Really? Now, how ever could she have gotten that idea?"

"I do get bored," Thaddeus grumped. "And I may have told her a fairytale or two."

"I hope you educated her, instead of feeding her prejudice," Doc said softly. "I once spent a very pleasant summer with a Tlahuelpuchi."

"You're not an infant, are you?"

"That's just a myth," Doc said, stretching his neck. "Any type of blood will do."

"Oh, well, that's certainly less frightening!" Thaddeus snapped.

Doc shrugged and poured himself a glass of whiskey.

"It took me two years to get Rosa to even talk to me," Thaddeus muttered. "She's extremely superstitious." He was quiet for a mere second before he added, "It's not easy living as a plant. Especially when my only source of conversation decides to take a five-year, vampire-induced hiatus."

"My, you are grumpy." Doc poured himself another shot of whiskey, then tipped some into Thaddeus's pot. "Maybe some whiskey'll take the edge off."

"Goddamn it, Doc! You know I can't handle whiskey!"

Doc's eyes widened innocently. "You can't?"

"I don't know why I try. You're not worth it."

"That's what they all say. Are you going to tell me why you ruined my dream?"

"You told me to, you worthless wretch." Thaddeus's crisp words were starting to soften. "It's time. Señora Teodora."

"Oh." Doc blinked, and his plush hotel suite was gone, replaced by a different hotel room. Not as plush, not as clean, and filled with the scent of death.

He was lying in the bed, staring at the cracked ceiling, coated in sticky sweat, sheets soaked from his constant perspiration. He hadn't planned to die this way, not like she had, drowning in her own blood in a filthy bed. He'd planned to go out in a blaze of glory. One card game too many. One card sleight too obvious. But he had the devil's own luck. Except in anything that mattered.

Another cough racked his broken frame, and he welcomed it. Welcomed death. Asked it to come, but it didn't.

"Whiskey," he rasped.

Kate shook her head, sorrow making her eyes huge. "Whiskey isn't good for you. You know that."

"I'm dying. What the hell do I care? Get me some damn whiskey!"

She must have taken pity on him because she stood and left the room, hopefully in search of the best whiskey they had to offer. Not that he'd be paying for it.

He rested his hand on the cool ivory handle of his six-shooter. It would be faster to just eat a bullet, but he rather liked his face and he didn't want to ruin it. No one would attend his funeral if his face was a bowl of mush. He laughed softly, trying not to trigger another coughing fit.

The door opened, but it wasn't Kate; instead a rather old woman entered. She didn't particularly look old. Her face was lined, but not wrinkled, and her hair was thick with only a few streaks of grey. Her eyes were sharp as a hawk's, and he knew her hands were strong enough to squeeze the life from a man's neck, not to mention his other parts.

"Señora Teodora," he wheezed, "come to make sure I die?"

"No." She sat beside him and studied him with the eye of a woman used to death. "You haven't much longer."

"I should expect not," he chuckled, gesturing towards a pile of bloody linens in the corner. "I can't imagine I have much blood left."

"You still do not take life seriously."

"Why would I?"

"I have forgiven you for seducing my granddaughter."

"Really? Is that why you're here? To absolve me of my sins?"

She spat contemptuously to the side, then said, "Do not speak to me like I am one of them. They destroyed my culture, my people, and if they knew what I was they would burn me and think nothing of it."

"Then why are you here, Señora? I'm dying, and I'm afraid I don't have time for games."

"You've never had time for anything but games."

"True enough," he chuckled.

"Do you regret it? Do you wish you'd done something else?"

"You mean marry like my brother did? Have children, then die, leaving them grief stricken and fatherless? I'd rather live my own life over and over and over again." His heart clenched, thinking of Francisco. He hadn't been with him when he died, and he should have been. He didn't have many regrets, but that was one.

"If you lived past today, would you choose a different path?" she asked.

"No."

Doc blinked and looked around his elegant suite with a grin. He was Doc Holliday. There was no other path.

"Why can't you drink brandy?" Thaddeus slurred.

Doc laughed heartily. "Because I'm a whiskey man, Thaddy. Always have been."

"I utterly despise you."

"Shall I lose you in my next game?"

"Only if you lose to a nubile young nudist."

"Male or female?"

Thaddeus made a strange noise which Doc assumed was a growl. Sometimes he wished Thaddeus at least had a face. It wasn't easy reading a plant's moods.

"I'm back," Ana sang cheerfully as she sauntered into the bedroom. "Doc!" she exclaimed. "You're upright!"

"Yes. I'm afraid our staycation has come to an end." He kissed her fondly, grazing his hands over her slim form.

"But we were just starting to have fun," she pouted. "One more night?"

He pushed her away gently, stepping backwards so her fangs couldn't touch his skin. "A night with you, my dear, turns into a hundred."

She smiled widely, fangs glinting for a second before receding into her gums. "I will miss you," she said, licking her lips seductively.

"It's never a goodbye, Ana," he said, yearning to sink into her arms for just another minute or two. He couldn't though. The time had come, and he needed to be clear headed, not drugged into lust and happy dreams by the lovely sedative she injected into his veins every time she was near him.

"Go," he insisted. "Before I give into temptation."

"Call me anytime," she murmured throatily, tracing her fingertips over the tattoo covering his naked chest before turning and leaving the room.

"I'll miss her," Thaddeus muttered drunkenly. "Her hips were perfect."

"Indeed. But we have work to do," Doc said.

"You have work to do. I'm taking a nap."

"Sleep well, old friend," Doc whispered, pouring another bit of whiskey into the clay pot before throwing open his heavy brocade curtains and gazing out at the city beneath him.

He hadn't been outside his suite in five years, but at a glance, not much had changed. Another building or two perhaps, but it still looked like Denver. Modern Denver, not Denver as he'd first seen it. That was an entirely different thing. He couldn't have imagined back then that Denver would ever turn into this sprawling, towering mammoth.

He opened the window, letting the breeze brush over his chest. He hadn't been hiding so much as taking a break. Every now and then he needed a break to remind himself how much life there was left to live. There were more hands of cards to be played. There were more women to be thoroughly bedded.

Hell, there's more whiskey to be drank, he thought as he took a sip and breathed deeply.

If living forever meant he had to take a breather every now and then, it was a small price to pay. Thirty-six years just hadn't been enough. Now that he was heading towards two hundred, he could honestly say he'd lived. If Death came to collect him tomorrow, he might not even fight it. Well, not tomorrow. He had to take care of something first; then he wouldn't fight it. Maybe. He'd just have to see.

Doc chuckled softly, amused at himself, and then indulged in a leisurely shower. After he'd dried, he studied his clothes and carefully picked a white shirt, dark grey vest, and black trousers. As much as he'd enjoyed being naked for the last several years, it felt good to get dressed.

He'd missed his knives. He strapped a small knife around his ankle and one around his thigh that he could access through his pants pocket. After he'd donned his shirt, he buckled his special knife harness across his chest. His vest hid it completely, but he had easy access to both knives, the one under his shoulder blade and the other one in the center of his chest.

He buttoned his vest, enjoying the feel of the buttons between his fingers, rolled up his shirtsleeves, and slipped on his bracelets. He had five for each wrist, and each one was made of horse hair, or something more exotic, and held a stone meant to block psychic or magical attacks.

He hadn't lounged around doing nothing the last hundred and fifty years. He'd acquired knowledge, he'd found friends, lost friends, and collected more than a few enemies. He'd honed his skills; he'd learned new skills; and he'd endeavored to understand the world in which he lived. Both worlds, the regular one and the Hidden one.

But unfortunately, he still wasn't ready. For everything he knew, there were hundred things he didn't. A hundred and fifty years, and he'd only scratched the surface.

For the first time in years, there was a very small part of him that was nervous. Señora Teodora had entrusted him with a task, and he was very much afraid he was going to fail.

KEEP READING TODAY AT AMAZON.COM

How about a Coming-of-Age Urban Fantasy? Check out

THE LEGEND OF
ANDREW RUFUS

1

Worst summer ever, Andrew Rufus thought sullenly as he tossed his baseball towards the ceiling for the fifteen hundredth time. He was bored. So bored that he might actually consider reading one of the books his mom had brought back from the library.

He glanced at the stack of books and shuddered. He didn't give a crap about leprechauns or the secrets of Middle-earth. If only his mom would bend on the no television in his room rule. After all, it's not like he could help the fact that he had a broken leg.

He tossed the ball again, but he wasn't paying attention so it slipped from his glove and rolled onto the floor. "I guess that's that," he muttered.

He counted the neon stars on his ceiling, but he already

knew there were a hundred and six of them. He'd known that since yesterday morning.

"You need anything, baby?" his mom hollered up the stairs.

"How 'bout a TV?" Andrew yelled back.

"Anything you can actually have?"

"No," he grumbled.

"Alright. My online meeting's about to start. I'll check on you when it's done."

"Whatever."

"I heard that!"

"Whatever," Andrew mouthed sulkily.

If he didn't do something soon he was going to scream, so he grabbed a book from the pile at random and read the title. *American Folklore: Pecos Bill and Others*. Gag me, Andrew thought, but it had to be better than a book about how to trap leprechauns. And if it wasn't, he'd hobble to the window and hurl himself to his death.

He flipped to the beginning of the story and started reading. He rolled his eyes after a line or two and stifled a yawn. Boring, he thought as he scanned the page. Exactly how long were these cowboy dudes going to keep riding into the sunset? A car chase would definitely be more exciting.

The sun blinded him for just a minute, and he closed his eyes, rubbing them with the back of his hand. He squinted at the page, trying to see the words clearly, but they kept blurring into a mess of brown. Maybe the pain pills were finally taking affect.

He read another line but abruptly coughed as dust swept down his throat, choking him. He reached blindly for his cup of water. His fingers grazed the smooth glass, then he heard it shatter on the floor. Another cough racked his frame, and he dropped the book and struggled to his feet.

The earth suddenly shifted beneath him, and he flung his arms out to the sides, trying to grab hold of his dresser, but there was nothing there, and he started to fall. "No," he whispered fearfully. He didn't want to fall. What if he hurt his leg?

He flexed his legs in fear, gasping in relief when he didn't hit the floor. But then he lurched forward and backward and forward again. What the hell was going on? Was he having a seizure?

He blinked frantically, trying to clear the dust from his eyes so he could see again. He squinted and realized he actually could see, but all he could see was dust. It didn't make sense. Nothing was making sense.

He glanced down, wondering where the floor was. "Holy crap!" he gasped. There was no floor. There was no floor because he was sitting on a horse. A horse. Not just sitting. Riding. That's why he was lurching back and forth. He grabbed hold of the saddle thingy and held tightly, then stared at his hands in utter dismay. Those weren't his hands, but how could they not be his hands? He released the saddle with one hand and felt his face.

"Oh hell," he whispered. It wasn't his face. He knew it wasn't because it was rough and full of angles. It wasn't his nose or his hand or his body. Those weren't his legs. What the hell kind of medicine were they giving him anyway? This had to be a hallucination. It just had to be.

The horse suddenly leaped into the air, and Andrew jerked in terror, grasping the saddle tightly. The horse landed easily, but Andrew didn't. "Crap!" he hissed as he slid precariously to the side. He flung his arms around the horse's neck, hugging it for dear life and desperately hoping it would stop soon.

Then he heard it. An angry voice, gruff and gravely, yelling, yelling very loudly, INSIDE Andrew's head.

WHAT THE HELL'S GOIN' ON?!

Andrew couldn't help it. He screamed; he screamed at the top of his lungs. But the more he screamed, the more the voice inside his head yelled.

WHAT THE HELL YOU DOIN'?! STOP THAT SISSY CRYIN'! RIGHT NOW!!!

Andrew's mind raced, trying to figure out what was going on, but he simply couldn't think. The voice in his head was too loud. Why was there a voice in his head? Where was his body? Where was he? What was happening?

Who are you?! the voice snapped. *You some kinda witch?*

"Witch? What? No," Andrew stuttered, eyes widening when he heard his own voice. It didn't sound right at all. It was deep and menacing, like the voice inside his head. He stared at his hands again. They moved when he moved them, but they just weren't his hands. The wide, red gash from his fall wasn't there. These hands had thin, white scars across the knuckles; they were callused, sun-browned, and huge.

He squeezed his eyes shut. He must have fallen asleep reading that stupid book, and now he was dreaming. That was it. He was dreaming. All he had to do was wake up. He pinched himself. It hurt, but he didn't wake. He slapped himself. Tears welled in his eyes it stung so badly, but he still didn't wake up.

What the hell you doin'?!

"Trying to wake up," Andrew mumbled, weirded out that he was having a conversation with someone he couldn't see. Like he was talking to himself, but he wasn't. It felt like madness.

Wake up?

"I'm asleep; that's the only explanation."

Asleep? I ain't asleep. GET THE HELL OUTTA MY BODY!! NOW!

"I don't know how."

Try! the voice snapped.

"How? I don't know how I got in here." Andrew was trying to remember if he'd ever had a conversation in a dream before, but the voice just wouldn't shut up.

GET OUT!!!

"I already told you, I can't!"

Do it anyway!

"How?"

Just do!

Andrew rolled his eyes and glanced around. This was surely the most vivid dream he'd ever had. It was so vivid he could feel the heat and taste the dirt. Maybe he should back off the painkillers.

"It's just a dream, you know," Andrew said. "I'm sure I'll wake up soon, and then you'll have your body back." What a dorky thing to say. When he woke up, the dream would be gone.

He relaxed his stranglehold on the horse and sat up straighter in the saddle. He wasn't so scared now that he realized he was in a dream. He was certain he could ride a horse in a dream, and if he fell, he'd just wake up. Besides, the horse wasn't actually moving anymore. Surely he could sit on a horse without falling.

When I get my hands on you, I'm gonna tie you in a knot.

"A knot?" Andrew laughed. "Is that really the best you've got?"

You laughin' at me?

"A little. Be pretty hard to tie someone into a knot. Beat me up, sure. Tie into a knot? I don't know."

Who the hell are you?!

This was bizarre, but his mom hated it when he was rude, so Andrew sighed and said, "Andrew Rufus; and you?"

Pecos Bill.

Andrew burst out laughing. Now he knew it was a dream. He felt stupid for not realizing it right away; everything had just felt so real. The sun was burning down on his back. He could feel sweat beading on his skin; he could feel the roughness of the horse's hair beneath his hands; he could feel the grainy dust in his eyes. He'd never had such an intense dream before. It was so real, so vibrant. It had to be the drugs.

What's so funny? Pecos snapped.

"Nothing, it's just… I really am dreaming."

What the hell you talkin' 'bout?! Ain't no dream! What'd you say your name was? Andrew, Andrew Rufus, Andrew thought, wondering if he needed to speak out loud for Pecos to hear him. *Ain't never heard of you,* Pecos growled back. Course not. You're not real. I'm real. I'm dreaming, so I've heard of you 'cause you're in that dumb book I was reading before I fell asleep. *What?!*

Andrew sighed. Dreams weren't usually so complicated. When he woke up, he was tossing the pills in the trash. Listen, I'm not really here. You're not really here. This is all just a dream. *Ain't no damn dream!* Pecos sputtered. *Get out of my body right this minute…*

Pecos went on and on, but Andrew wasn't listening because he'd just noticed three other riders heading towards him. They were already fairly close, and Andrew could just make out their faces. He was suddenly very glad he was dreaming because he didn't know how to make the horse move again, and if this were real life, he'd be riding the other way. He'd never seen such scary-looking dudes.

They had serious expressions on their faces and guns on their hips. Lots and lots of guns. And knives. They were riding into the sun, so their faces were shining, and a shudder ran down Andrew's spine when his eyes locked onto one of the men.

"Somethin' wrong, Pecos?" the man demanded as they stopped their horses beside Andrew's.

Andrew gulped. "Um... I..." He didn't go on, just stared at the man in horror.

He had a stone-hard face, brilliant, blue eyes, and a scar running from his nose to his ear. His tight blond goatee was broken in the middle by another scar which made him look rather sinister. In addition to his frightening face, he had a ridiculous amount of guns strapped all over him, maybe six or eight, and Andrew was certain he wouldn't have any problem using them.

Andrew tore his eyes away and looked at one of the other men. He instantly regretted it. These dudes were so creepy Andrew wished he could wake up right now. He'd never be mean to his mom again. He'd tell her he loved her, because he did. He'd promise to never climb a tree, ever again. He'd keep both feet on the ground, and he'd swear off painkillers for the rest of his life.

The second man wasn't wearing a hat, and his skin was as dark as the surrounding dirt, maybe darker. His hair was loose, flowing down his back in a shimmery, black wave, and Andrew guessed he was Native American, but he wasn't sure. His dark eyes were unfathomable, unreadable, but the worst part was that, in addition to a bow and a few guns, he was wearing so many knives Andrew didn't even try to count them.

Andrew shuddered, wondering what Pecos must look like

if these were the type of guys he hung out with, and glanced at the third man. He actually looked normal enough except he had the widest and curliest mustache Andrew had ever seen. His eyes were a laughing brown, and his lips were curved in a slight grin. He even seemed to be wearing a normal amount of weapons, but Andrew couldn't be sure.

He'd never been around anyone who carried a gun or a knife before, let alone eight of them. He wasn't sure how he'd imagined these guys because he was positive the book hadn't been all that descriptive.

"Pecos?" the blond man asked again, a thread of annoyance in his tone.

Listen you coward, you body thief, you slimy snake! Pecos yelled. *Get the hell outta my body right this damn minute or I'm gonna truss you up and leave you for the coyotes!* How's that better than a knot? I mean, how're you gonna do it?

Pecos growled, and Andrew glanced between the three men, feeling trapped, like the time Chuck had pulled a prank, but Andrew had been caught holding the spray can.

He opened his mouth to reply to the blond man, but Pecos started yelling again, so loud that Andrew flinched. Shut up so I can think! Andrew snapped. *Shut up?! Shut up?! This is my body! You shut up, damn it!* Right now it's my body! So you shut up! *You ain't no man; you're just a coward!*

I'm not a coward or a man, so there! Andrew thought angrily. His head was starting to ache. There was just too much going on. Could your head even ache in a dream? I'm only thirteen, Andrew added. And I didn't steal your stupid body; why would I even want to? I just kinda ended up here. And it doesn't matter, 'cause THIS IS A DREAM!!!

This was getting weirder and weirder by the second. He'd pay good money for his mom to wake him and tussle his hair.

She could call him "baby" and sit by his bed all day asking him how he was, and he wouldn't even mind.

Pecos was still yelling, but Andrew tried to ignore him because the mustached man was talking.

"You alright, Pecos?"

"Um… yeah, just thinking," Andrew replied awkwardly.

"Thinkin' 'bout what?" the blond man snapped.

Andrew cringed. The blond guy freaked him out. He looked like the kind of guy who shot first and didn't bother to ask questions, ever. "I don't know… Just thinking."

The knife man had been watching Andrew or Pecos, whoever he was, intently, but now he spoke. "You wantin' to change your plan?"

Andrew grabbed at that. "Plan? What plan exactly?"

The blond man frowned deeply, but the knife man smiled slightly and replied, "The one you just made."

Andrew sighed; that had really cleared things up. "Let me think about it," he stalled. Help me out here, Pecos? *Ain't helpin' you, boy! You need to disappear.* I really wish I could, but I can't. I've never tried to wake up in a dream before; I don't know how to do it. *I done told you boy, ain't no dream,* Pecos said in a weary tone. Of course it is, but I still don't wanna get shot to death by your gun-happy friends. They'd like an answer, and I don't have any idea what they're talking about.

Ain't gonna shoot me. No, but they might shoot me, and see, I'm in your body in the middle of… of… Andrew looked around. There was nothing as far as he could see except dirt, rocks, little scrubby plants, and what he assumed were cactus clumps. He wasn't sure because he'd never seen actual cactuses before.

Why are we in a desert? *Ain't a desert, boy. Just a bit of dry land is all. We ridin' to stop the snake.* Andrew accidentally laughed. "Sorry," he said quickly. "Just thought of something funny. Still thinking," he added when the blond man opened his mouth to speak.

Four guys to stop one measly snake? You're kidding me right?! You're supposed to be a western legend! You fight things like tornados and rustlers and blue cows or something, right? *Watch it, boy...* Or what?

Andrew was beginning to enjoy himself. He hadn't had any fun in days; not since that stupid, wild, grey cat had knocked him out of the tree. Sure the cowboy dudes were scary looking; but it was a dream; and as such, nothing really bad could happen. And if it did, he'd just wake up. Like that one dream he'd had where he'd shown up to school naked. He'd woken just as the bell rang and right before everyone could file out into the hallway and laugh at him.

This ain't a dream or a pleasure trip or a damn party! If you don't get outta my body right now folks're gonna die! Andrew rolled his eyes. What did it matter if people died in a dream? It's not like they were real. *THIS IS REAL!!! Can't you feel it?!*

Andrew shook his head, annoyed that Pecos was so serious. It's too bad he hadn't had a baseball dream instead. One with Willie Mays and Derek Jeter and Babe Ruth. Andrew would pitch and see if they could get a hit. Now that would have been fun.

The only thing I can feel is the sun, Andrew complained. Is it always this hot? *That's just it, boy. When's the last time you felt the sun in a dream?* Andrew chose not to think about that. It was weird that he was so hot, that he was sweating, that he could feel the breeze cooling him down, but there was an explanation for that. His pain pills clearly had some terrible side effects. They were probably experimental. He shuddered, wondering what else they were doing to him.

I can't believe this, Pecos sighed. *You've gotta be the densest boy on earth.* Andrew frowned. I'm not dense! If I believed you, a figment of my imagination I might add, THEN I would be dense! *Fine, just keep on ignorin' your senses, and while you do, people'll die. Thanks to you.*

Whatever, let's get back to the plan. You're riding to stop a snake. Is that the whole plan? *Yep.* Andrew rolled his eyes. Great plan, super involved, covers all the fine points. *Boy...* "I'm good," Andrew said out loud. "Um, lead the way somebody." He figured it couldn't hurt to play along until he woke up. It was certainly better than counting the stars on his ceiling. Again.

The blond man glared at him, but knife man nodded, turning his horse and riding away. The other two followed him, and Andrew sat, watching them. Um, how do I make the horse go? *Not THE horse; her name's Dewmint.* Okay, how do I make Dewmint go? Pecos sighed. *Pick up the reins, tap with your heels, nice like.* Reins? *The leather straps,* Pecos ground out. Oh. Andrew picked up the reins and tapped with his heels.

Dewmint started walking, and Andrew gasped, clutching her mane with his hands. *What you doin'?* Trying not to fall off! *Ain't you never ridden before?* I've never even touched a horse before, let alone ridden one! Andrew was suddenly very aware how far away the ground was. Are all horses this tall? *Dewmint ain't that tall, just sixteen hands.* Hands? Pretty sure we measure in feet. *Boy...* Never mind; how do I go faster?

Andrew didn't actually want to go faster, but the others were already far ahead of him, and he figured he should probably catch up. Dream or no dream, he didn't want to get left behind in the desert or really dry landscape as Pecos called it. *Heels.* Oh. Andrew tapped his heels again, and Dewmint sped up.

Andrew closed his eyes in fear. But that was even worse, so he opened them again. This is stupid, he thought. Why am I scared? It's a dream! A super realistic dream, but a dream. *Never seen such an idiot in all my days, and that's sayin' somethin'.* Oh, shut up, Andrew snapped. You don't exist, and even if you did, which you don't, it's not possible to take over someone else's body. It's just not. That kinda crap doesn't even happen in movies. You know why? 'Cause no one would believe it!

Andrew tried to relax as Dewmint moved across the ground. He was still far behind the others, so he nudged her again. She sped up, and Andrew clutched the reins in terror. She was going so fast and everything was so bouncy, he felt like his back was breaking. He clenched his jaw to keep his teeth from clanking together with every step the horse took. *Downright embarrassin'. Of all the body thieves, I get a sissy, city slicker boy.*

Excuse me! I'm not a sissy or a… well, I guess I am a city slicker and a boy, but I'm not a sissy! So you take that back! *Ain't takin' nothin' back. What the hell you doin' here?* I told you already! I'M DREAMING!!! So stop asking!

If Pecos would just shut up, this could be the most epic dream ever. He was riding a horse, something his mom would never let him do; he was outside, instead of stuck in his room with a busted leg and no TV, riding through a landscape he'd never seen before; and he had guns, and they were probably loaded. *Don't you dare touch my guns, boy,* Pecos growled menacingly. Can't stop me, Andrew laughed.

He tried to look around, but it was hard because when he took his eyes off Dewmint's head, he felt like he was falling. But when he managed to look right for a second, he realized there were two more horses running behind him, reins attached to his saddle. He looked forward again and saw the others had extra horses too. Why do you have so many horses? *Ridin' hard.* So? *If you weren't a city slicker you would know!* Whatever.

Andrew glanced over Dewmint's head and saw waves of heat rolling off the dirt into the air. He'd never been able to see so far in all his life. He'd always been surrounded by buildings or trees. It felt so empty. He wondered if the desert really looked like this. He didn't think he'd seen many pictures of the desert, so he wasn't sure what his mind was basing this on. He heard Pecos sigh. *Ain't a dream, boy. It's real; as real as the nose on your, I mean MY, face.* Andrew shook his head. It's not real! It's a dream. But since you're clearly not gonna shut up, tell me more about your plan.

Dewmint was going really fast now, and Andrew was having a horrible time sitting upright. He kept sliding from side to side and having to wiggle back into the middle of the saddle. *Relax your back,* Pecos chided. Andrew tried, but every time Dewmint's hooves hit the ground, he jerked.

No wonder people don't ride horses anymore, he thought as he dragged himself upright. *Whadda you mean people don't ride horses?* Can you hear everything I think? *Mostly.* Well stop! It's annoying. *Whadda you mean?* Where I'm from, or when I'm from I guess, people drive cars and trucks and stuff. *Cars?* Like a… a wagon that doesn't need horses. Andrew shook his head with irritation. Why was he explaining this? It didn't matter if Pecos knew what a car was. He was going to disappear as soon as Andrew woke up.

Andrew pinched himself just to check, but he stayed right where he was.

He frowned, looking around in confusion. Everything was super, super real. The details of the landscape, Dewmint's mane, the heat of the sun, the smell of dust, the thirst in his throat, the ache in his rear, the voice in his head. All of it FELT real. But that would mean... He shook his head emphatically. Why was he even considering it?

So what about this snake you mentioned? Pecos chuckled softly. *You ain't gonna like the snake, boy.*

KEEP READING TODAY AT AMAZON.COM

M.M. Boulder grew up in the woods of Colorado. She spent most of her time outside weaving stories in her mind while she explored.

About her writing, she has this to say:

"I write morally ambiguous characters who are pushed to their limits and take matters into their own hands. My stories sometimes bring the darker impulses we may not feel completely comfortable with into the light. There are lies and death and gore, but there is always justice. Justice that's not afraid to get its hands dirty."

She also writes urban fantasy under the name M.M. Crumley.

Follow M.M. Boulder on Amazon.com to receive notifications of new releases or sign up for her VIP email at www.mmboulder.com

Connect online:
www.facebook.com/mmcrumleyauthor
www.facebook.com/LoneGhostPublishing

Printed in Great Britain
by Amazon